MORONS AND MADMEN

Morons and Madmen

Earl Emerson

A MAC FONTANA MYSTERY

▲

for Troy —

Earl Emerson

WILLIAM MORROW AND COMPANY, INC.
New York

It is the policy of William Morrow and Company, Inc., and its imprints and affiliates, recognizing the importance of preserving what has been written, to print the books we publish on acid-free paper, and we exert our best efforts to that end.

Library of Congress Cataloging-in-Publication Data

Emerson, Earl W.
  Morons and madmen : a Mac Fontana mystery / by Earl Emerson.
      p.   cm.
    ISBN 0-688-09334-5
    I. Title.
  PS355.M39M67   1993
  813'.54—dc20   92-42774
                                                                      CIP

Printed in the United States of America

First Edition

1 2 3 4 5 6 7 8 9 10

BOOK DESIGN BY GIORGETTA BELL MCREE

This novel is dedicated to the gallant men and women of the Seattle Fire Department, but especially to Mary Matthews, Robert Earhart, and Matthew Johnson, who gave everything there was to give.

While most of the procedures and the equipment depicted in the Seattle Fire Department are accurate, the characters and incidents in this book are imaginary. The author has nothing but the highest regard for firefighters—as friends, co-workers, and professionals in a dirty, dangerous, and frequently tedious job—and for the Seattle Fire Department, one of the nation's finest.

For finally, we are as we love. It is love that measures our stature. There is no smaller package in the world than that of a person all wrapped up in himself.

—William Sloane Coffin

MORONS AND MADMEN

One

▲

WHERE YOU WAKE UP IN A PUDDLE OF COLD SWEAT AND YOUR HEART IS PUMPING LIKE A NUCLEAR REACTOR WITH BROKEN SPOKES

*Y*ou think you have the best job on earth until Creed's boot drops out of the sky.

Except for wisps of smoke rising from various articles scattered around in the dirt, you are the only thing disturbing the frigid tableau. No wind. Just the frozen dirt, the mounds of gravel, the scattershot rocks, a tire track here and there. Frozen mud puddles that would make any decent schoolchild late for school.

You are wandering in a no-man's-land.

Your fingers are numb and you fumble through your bunking coat searching for gloves. One of your ears is bleeding, and the liquid on the side of your face is frozen.

You shout for the lieutenant, realizing that you cannot hear your own voice. Your head is ringing like a stone bell, your eyes are bleary, and even as you stagger across the landscape, you have a sense that you have wandered on this bleak moonscape before. Everything is raw dirt except for bits of twisted wreckage.

Tears are glissading onto the collar of your bunking coat

where they freeze, you feeling the smooth, rounded nubs of ice when you move your abraded chin just so.

You are looking for a running man, for you have something grim to settle, but you bumble around without seeing anybody. After some time, you spot a fragment of a helmet, but it does not resemble the helmet of anybody you know.

The destruction stretches as far as you can see in any direction. You find nothing that has not been charred, torn, scarred, or striated by the catastrophe. Your cognitive powers have shrunk, but you know this: You are wandering in a blast area and you are alone because the rest of the world is forbidden to enter. It is a miracle a flea has survived, much less a crying man.

You take a deep breath of the frigid air, hiccupping as you inhale, and the breath chills your whole body.

Then you remember:

You and Robert Creed are up late in the galley, cooking popcorn and watching a Randolph Scott/Virginia Mayo flick on the television. The scanner is on, and you hear Engine 58 taking an alarm to the construction sites down near the new freeway. The captain on Engine 58 is a crusty old hand who never lets anything ruffle him, a man bent on appearing even more composed than he is. Captain Weathers gives a radio report stating they have two trailer fires and to send another engine company for the second trailer. The dispatcher asks if he would not rather have more help, but the captain gruffly replies that he needs only one more engine company.

You and Creed jump into your hip boots and begin bundling up, wrapping mufflers around your necks and pulling on sweatshirts, knowing you are the next closest engine company. You pile more clothing on than Creed does, including a wool face mask, because you are riding the tailboard in the winter wind and Creed will be up front in a heated cab. You are both wearing long johns and have been all week. The weather has been so cold, one company in the city is dispatched to remove a frozen man from a tree after he becomes a neighborhood curiosity.

On your arrival you see enough fire coming from the two double-wide trailers to keep a second alarm busy. The freezing wind chafes your face as you stand up out of your tuck on the tailboard. You cannot hear what Creed and Lieutenant Kaplan are discussing in the cab, but your guess is that Creed sensibly wants to call out for more help and the lieutenant, intimidated by the captain on Engine 58, would rather not. As calmly as he can, for you will listen to the tapes afterward and ascertain this, Lieutenant Kaplan tells the dispatcher you have arrived, that you are laying a preconnect. Sometimes it is more important to look the way others want you to than to do the right thing.

As it happens, every man they do not call to the fire is another man who lives through the night.

The trailers are a hundred yards apart. Captain Weathers has two nozzlemen from Engine 58 directing hose streams into what you think are odd-colored flames. The fire makes a loud popping noise, and orange-red snakes of flame leap forty feet into the sky.

You walk like an overstuffed snowman, clumsy and lumbering, feeling the hard ground jolt your spine through your thick wool socks and rubber boots. It is while stretching the line that you spot a man crouching in a ditch beside one of the road graders.

You know arsonists are often among the bystanders firefighters see when arriving at a scene. And this is unquestionably arson. Two trailers. Separated by hundreds of feet. Both burning with a strange glow you cannot recall seeing anywhere before.

When he realizes he has been spotted in the darkness, the arsonist breaks and flees. You are the youngest and fastest on the crew, and there is no disputing that if someone is to chase this suspect it will be you. Nobody on Engine 58 has seen him, though they have been on the property nearly ten minutes.

He is yours.

Dropping the hose line, you bark to the lieutenant that you think you have spotted a torch, and you sprint past. At the time, you feel certain that you are not endangering anybody by leaving, that running down an arsonist is more important than having two men on a hose line that one man can handle.

In your bulky bunking clothes, your long johns and sweatshirts, you gradually lose ground on the runner in front of you, traveling so far over the rough hills that you can no longer hear the sounds of the two pumps. You take out your flashlight and use it to avoid potholes in the dirt. You see your quarry spill onto his hands and knees because he does not have a light. Twice you see this, but still, he remains in front.

And then the blast comes, like the angry hot breath of a demon god.

You are flying through the air, flapping your arms like a goose with a load of buckshot on board, and for a moment you think there is no way you cannot break your neck when you land. You are numb everywhere and sore as hell, and your arms feel as though they have been jerked out of their sockets, but nothing is broken.

And now you are wandering across this barren landscape, not understanding what is happening. You are carrying something, dragging it around. Finally you hold it up to your face and you recognize the speed laces. You want to gag.

It is one of Creed's boots.

And it is heavy.

You are carrying it around like a kid at the beach with a bucket of shells.

In some ways the dream is identical to the incident, and in other ways it is not anything like the incident. The only reason you are not annihilated by the blast with the six other fire-fighters is that you happened to see the arsonist. You happened to give chase. Dumb luck.

A lot of things could happen. It is only one unlikely sequence of events that spares you.

You weigh that sequence of events for years.

And it frightens you. A piece of luck such as yours is so unfathomable that surely it must have expended all the good fortune due you for the rest of time. It is with this thought that you live your life, as if no more luck can be assigned you.

Finally you awaken armored in a cold, clammy sweat. The sweat is years old. It follows you from residence to residence. From bed to bed. And you are sick to your stomach. So sick your heart is beating under your tongue and tears are staining your pillow.

As sometimes happens in the middle of the night, you get a blinding flash of insight.

For years you have been kidding yourself.

After the explosion you join the Arson Investigation Unit back East, transferring out of combat never to return, telling yourself that it was a smart career move and that making the move did not have anything to do with Creed or the survivor syndrome or Linda's pleading with you to leave the department, or any of those things.

Yet it has to do with all of them.

Years later, after Linda's death, you find this wonderful little hick town to settle in. Of course there is luck. And sometimes you put your toe in it. You have a son. You have peace.

What is beginning to dawn on you is that you did not leave combat for any reason other than that you lost your nerve. You lose your nerve and it makes you quick-tempered and you do not know how to handle it.

You realize that after the experience, you never quite regained your equilibrium, never quite reverted to the young devil-may-care firefighter you liked so much. And you cannot live with yourself as any other kind of firefighter.

Settling onto your wet pillow, you realize that it was only after you got older that you learned to negotiate with your pride.

Two

▲

SURVIVORS
WILL BE
PROSECUTED

*F*ifteen years earlier Creed's boot became just another one of those savage little rewards the fire service presents, typically right about the time you expect it, which somehow makes it infinitely worse.

Fontana had been the sole survivor, and even as it was happening, he could feel himself reluctantly memorizing each hideous moment.

After something as fiendish as what happened to Creed and the others came along, you could do one of two things—you could laugh or you could cry. In the firehouse, laughing was always easier, yet most of the firefighters in Fontana's former department quickly slipped into the grip of a strange hysterical mutism wherein even gallows humor about the incident became unthinkable.

When fire investigators finally entered the blast area, having waited for fear of losing more men in subsequent blasts, they discovered that one fire engine was almost unrecognizable, that the other had been rendered into fragments so small nobody bothered to reassemble them. Except for Creed's boot, which

Fontana recognized by the speed laces, nobody bothered to identify any of the body parts.

Now, years beyond it and thousands of miles away, perched on a granite boulder on the rim of the lonely middle fork of the Snoqualmie River under an overcast sky, Fontana let the gentle autumn breeze play with the fishing line while his German shepherd snoozed on the rocks at his feet.

A mile away his son, Brendan, was nervously enjoying his first week of second grade. Back at the station things had been quiet since last summer, and, if you bothered to ask, Fontana would have defined bliss to be any period of time as uneventful as the last ten minutes.

He whipped the fly rod back and forth, watching the line trace a lazy *S* across the green pool and trying not to watch a woman who was making her way along the rocky shore toward him.

"Chief Fontana?"

She stood with her hands deep in the pockets of her denim coveralls, her shoulders hunched forward as if to fend off the cold, although it was balmy this morning, so much so that her face was slightly flushed from the walk. She wore coveralls, sandals with heavy purple socks that had tiny nubs of material clinging to them and a shapeless white cotton shirt that was probably a man's long-underwear top. Her hair was cropped close. She wasn't an unattractive woman, but she did her best to keep people from thinking otherwise. Her eyes were a clear, pale blue that gave her the look of someone who had recently wept, or was about to, her tan as dark as old leather.

"I'm MacKinley Fontana."

"My name is Diane Cooper. I'm a firefighter in Seattle? I was wondering if I could have a minute of your time?"

Fontana began slowly reeling in the line. He hadn't caught any fish and didn't expect to. Fishing for him was a triumph of solitude, a chance to let his thoughts roam, to let the weather and the landscape purge unwelcome memories. "Sure."

"I was at a fire last March. You probably read something about it. The Ratt? Three firefighters died. We were all on Ladder Three together."

Fontana thought it a curious coincidence, his musing about Creed while she had been parking her car at the trail head and making her way toward him. He wondered if it hadn't been some sort of premonition. He laid his pole down on a ledge and slid off the boulder, stuck his hand out. "Pleased to meet you."

Cooper shook hands reluctantly and weakly, then stepped back. She was a large-framed woman, an inch or two taller than his five-ten, with plenty of meat under her wrinkled and shapeless garments.

"Anyway," she continued, turning almost everything she said into a question, "I spoke to a man in New York about you? Clayton?"

"Kenny?"

"On West End Avenue? He's supposed to be the best, but he's booked for months. He said if he ever died in a fire, you would be the one he'd want coming after the bastards. I'll pay you his daily rates—plus expenses?"

"And which bastards do you want me to go after?"

"Whoever was responsible for those three guys dying."

"I thought your department completed an investigation. I read in the papers the fire was accidental and the deaths were deemed a hazard of the profession."

"I don't happen . . . I don't happen to think they were complete. The reports? I want to hire you as an independent investigator. Write your own report?"

Fontana sighed. At his feet, Satan sat up, yawned. He reached down and stroked the dog's head. "Two things. One, I don't do investigations anymore. Two, I had a bad summer. We lost a couple of guys here in our department. So if I did do investigations, I wouldn't do one now."

Diane Cooper considered what he had said. "This is very important. I was the only survivor of that crew. There's a cloud over my head and it will be there until something is done. I need you to look into this and to write a report for everybody to see?"

"Explain to me what was wrong in the two official versions."

"For one thing, they don't say much about me. Almost nothing?"

"What do you mean by that?"

"I mean they . . . they . . ."

"Don't let you off the hook?"

20

Again, it took her a long time to compose her thoughts. "No, they don't say anything much. When you read them it looks like they're trying to whitewash my part in it. They make it look like, without actually coming out and saying it, like it was my fault? They give the facts and not even all of the facts, and when you look at it that way, it does look like I'm at fault."

In many ways, in voice and body English, she had the look of a woman being swept over a waterfall, asking only for a rope in a soft and questioning alto voice that didn't fit her size.

"A thorough investigation could run into big bucks."

"My aunt died three years ago and left me her house. I've been renting it out. I have a bit saved?"

"We're talking maybe ten or fifteen thousand if I have to hire outside specialists."

"I don't think you understand. I have fourteen thousand in the bank. My career is ruined. Everywhere I go people are talking. There's even been newspaper articles that more or less implied those guys are dead because of me. Work is intolerable. I've had to see a counselor. I can't go on with this hanging over me, Chief Fontana. Even some of the women in the department won't speak to me? And those that do, there's a look in their eyes. I'm afraid, if I don't spend the money and get this cleared up, I'll be slowly forced out of the department, and the department's my life, Chief Fontana. Not only that, but the widows are talking about suing the fire department and naming me too. They're talking about suing and then after that, having criminal charges brought against me."

"What would they charge you with?"

"You know as well as I do, when the world wants to bury you, they can use a shovel or they can use a bulldozer? I'm in up to my hips already."

"And you need me to help clear you?"

"People don't think I murdered those three. Not exactly. Not like I had a plan. They think I'm incompetent. Because I'm a woman in a man's job. And you know this job is not like being a bookkeeper or something. Incompetence in the fire service gets people killed."

"So you think people in the fire department have decided, more or less, that your incompetence killed those three?"

"Absolutely. And this is not a question of having people look at me funny. My doctor's told me to leave the fire service or I'll be dead in five years. Ulcers. High blood pressure. I don't think I've slept more than two hours at a crack in six months. But if I do leave now, under this cloud, I'm telling you, it'll kill me anyway."

With the blush of last summer's funerals in Staircase just beginning to fade, Fontana had no desire to slog through anything like this. Then too there was the impending reorganization of the decimated Staircase Fire Department. Satan was knitting up and could now take a gentle walk twice a day. Brendan was in school. Life had banked down to a whimper. Besides, Fontana hadn't moved out to the boondocks to be chief in a one-horse town so that he could drive into Seattle and spend his days sucking on the next guy's exhaust pipes. This out here was the life. A red-tailed hawk on an updraft. The gurgle of water coursing over rocks in the river. Not a worry in sight.

"Ms. Cooper, I really have had a very difficult year. What I want now is a little peace of mind. Some time to myself."

"What you mean is you've read about this and made up your mind? Like the others."

"No, I meant what I said. I've been around long enough to be dubious about most of what I see in print. Especially when it's about something as complex as fire deaths. People who aren't in the service rarely get it right."

She watched the dog for a few moments. "Okay, you're one of those old-fashioned fire chiefs who think women don't belong in the service. I almost died at the Ratt, Chief Fontana. I took so much smoke I lost most of my memory of that night. In fact, that's part of why I want you to look into this? They put me in a hyperbaric chamber to treat me for carbon-monoxide poisoning. All night? But you know one of the few things I remember? The last words I heard as they were driving me away from the fire scene? The chief in charge of the fire, Chief Wallace, said to somebody, 'Some splittail just went off in an aid car. Probably needs a tampon change.' I don't remember much, but I remember that. I'm telling you I'm taking the rap for those three deaths and it's going to kill me if I can't straighten things out."

22

She was reading him correctly on one count. He wasn't sure he wanted to defend someone who might ultimately turn out to be deficient as a firefighter. Her efforts to hire him could easily be a ploy to demonstrate innocence without actually proving it: He realized that even should he find no new angles, she would still have the opportunity to say she had hired a nationally recognized investigator to clear her name. The tactic alone would do much to absolve guilt.

He said, "What makes you think the official reports are missing anything?"

"They just are. All I want is for you to investigate and write a report. Whatever you find, write. I want the truth out in the open. I'm a good firefighter, Chief Fontana. And I'll tell you something I've never admitted to anyone but my parents? There are women in our department who have no business being there. It hurts me to say this because these people are my friends. We have a woman officer who refuses to go into a fire. And some who are not in shape. I'm being lumped in with some people who don't deserve the job. Chief Fontana, I want you to keep this privileged, but I've considered suicide. You're having a bad summer? Think about mine."

Fifteen years earlier, when Fontana picked up Creed's boot and discovered it was too heavy to be empty, he knew his universe had been altered in a way that, despite all the mental preparation he fancied he had been through, he could never have forecast and would never be able to accommodate fully. Diane Cooper was now living in that modified universe as well, except that she was laboring under the mistaken impression that she could make things right.

They were deep in the rock-strewn riverbed, the west shore-line bounded by the dike twenty-five feet higher, beyond that knots of blackberry bushes under tall birches. The river wended down through a gorge from the south and east, then headed north. The trees upstream were mostly Douglas fir, uniformly around thirty feet tall. The water was the green of old leaves in spots, bluish-tinged in others, and sparkling like shattered crystal in the shallows. From time to time a tail fin rippled the surface in one of the infrequent pools.

"Tell you what," Fontana said. "I'll get back to you."

"It's not what I hoped for, but I guess it'll do?"

23

She left her phone number scrawled on a corner torn from a newspaper. She hadn't attempted to burden him with her version of the events or to elaborate on why she thought the official reports were deficient.

It was only too easy for him to imagine what she was going through as a woman in an all-male fire department, or nearly all-male department. In the fire service women were too new to be trusted. When your life depended upon your partner, the mere fact that the politicians said you could trust your new partner didn't mean you could.

There had been only one woman in the ranks back East where he'd been a captain in the Arson Investigation Unit, and now, out here in the tiny town of Staircase where he'd been chief for little more than a year, he had three women in the volunteers; all four were firefighters he was proud to be associated with. Yet Fontana had met some of Seattle's women firefighters, and, while many looked competent, there were others who looked like death chewing on a cracker.

Three

▲

DEATH BITCH

*T*hree days later the first widow showed up. Same rock. Same fly rod. Same killer dog at his feet.

Again, it was overcast, a low cloud cover some people might have termed a high fog. A metallic chill to the air.

As he fished, Fontana spotted two women making their way toward him along the rocky shore, winging their arms out for balance the way storks might stagger across a bed of nails, a woman of about twenty wearing shorts, a white blouse, and sandals and a woman in her thirties who was about thirty pounds overweight and had dazzling blue eyes and a bloated hourglass figure. He found the younger woman appealing, her athletic legs still brown from summer. She carried a thin valise pregnant with goods.

As the women aligned themselves in front of the boulder, Satan sat up and let out a yodeling yawn. The older woman said, "I'm Ginnie Buchanan."

Fontana glanced at the one in sandals. "Laura Sanderson," she said, blushing.

"Fontana. Mac Fontana."

25

Clambering down off the rock, Fontana shook hands with each of them. The older woman carried a bursting purse and wore a navy skirt that seemed to hamstring her. Her skin was pale and her limbs resembled boiled sausages. "Chief Fontana?"

"You caught me."

"I thought you'd be older. We heard she was out here talking to you, so we had to come out and see for ourselves. We asked you first. My lawyer called? I don't know, about four weeks ago. Reba and me got ourselves a lawyer. Reba's husband died at the Ratt fire too. Our attorney called you up, asking if you'd do some digging for us?"

Fontana glanced at the younger woman. "Me? Oh, my husband didn't die anywhere. I'm not married."

"I remember the call from your attorney. I told him no."

"We heard you were working for the death bitch."

"And who would that be?"

"I probably shouldn't call her that, but she got my husband killed and I just got into the habit. You can't work for her."

"Is that what you came all this way to tell me?"

"There's a rumor she came out here to hire you to prove she didn't kill our husbands."

"Whatever we spoke about is confidential."

"Chief Fontana, you know as well as we do women don't belong in the fire department. Four firefighters go into a fire building and only one comes out. What conclusion would you come to? I mean, it's not like a roof caved in on those men. Their deaths were preventable. You can't work for the death bitch."

Ginnie Buchanan's husband had been buried last March. Six months wasn't enough time to rout the despair and bitterness, but it was enough to gather up the resolve to do something about it. Looking on, Laura Sanderson seemed vaguely, almost innocently amused, chewing the inside of her cheek and gauging Fontana's reactions to Ginnie's hyperbole.

"Four times," said Ginnie Buchanan. "I understand our attorney phoned you four times. You never returned his calls."

"I returned one. I told him I'd had a lousy summer and I wanted to sit around and be bored."

"He left message after message at your fire station out here. If you had a phone, maybe your life would be a whole lot easier. That's ridiculous, not having a phone."

Face flushed in the humidity, Ginnie Buchanan leaned against the granite boulder and braced her rump against the rock, the move collapsing her posture as well as making it clear she did not find anything about Fontana even mildly amusing.

"We've heard gossip, Chief Fontana, that the official reports are full of glitches, maybe even outright lies. But we can't get anybody to confirm it. That's why we need you. You're not only a skilled investigator, but you're a fireman. We had another investigator, but he couldn't figure out what to make of the fire stuff.

"The grapevine has it that the last time something like this happened, Seattle's Fire Department paid out a million two in settlements," said Ginnie. "They settle out of court because they don't want it a matter of public record. Their incompetence. You could be a part of that settlement."

"I told your attorney no."

"Can you listen? Is it going to hurt to listen?"

"Suppose you tell me what you think happened at the fire."

"Clinton was deserted, that's what. Reba's husband."

"And?"

"And the department has been making a big issue out of everybody having a partner, but where was Clinton's partner, Cooper? Nobody even knew Clinton was dead. And when they took her to the hospital she didn't say a word about Clinton or my husband being missing. He was deserted too. Never mentioned any of them being missing. All she had to do was say something and somebody would have gone up there and pulled them out."

Ginnie Buchanan's face had taken on a resigned passivity now that they were actually discussing the central question. "Al hadn't been in that long, but he knew what he was doing. He was a good firefighter. He collected photos of antique fire engines since he was a kid."

She gave Fontana a look that was a second cousin to contempt. "Don't you understand? It's just the two of us against the whole fire department. We don't know who to talk to.

27

What to ask. Do you think it was easy for me to come out here? I actually went out and had drinks first. At nine o'clock in the morning I had drinks.''

Fontana took a breath and fiddled with his fishing line.

"The report said Al broke contact with his partner. Supposedly he got himself locked into this tiny little room in the smoke and just sat down on the floor and died. Now, how do you lock yourself into a ten-by-ten room? They said he took off his firefighting gear and stacked it neatly beside himself. It wasn't even particularly hot in that room. Just smoky.'' Her voice was beginning to flutter. "Does that sound normal?''

"Mrs. Buchanan, there are all kinds of ways to die in a fire, including exactly that one.''

"Three people on one crew die and the fourth person walks right on out?''

"It happens.'' Fontana patted Satan's head and made a polite but dismissive gesture with his eyebrows.

"Isn't that murder? If you cause somebody else's death?''

"It could be a lot of things. It could be manslaughter. It could be an accident. Bad luck.''

"Now, don't you tell me Al died because of bad luck. That woman as good as assassinated him.''

"I can't help you. I'm sorry.''

She wasn't ready to accept the answer, nor was she ready to address it. "Does the dog pee on your rugs?''

"Not so's you'd notice.''

"We had a dog like that once. Seventeen years old. We put him to sleep.''

"Nobody ever had a dog like Satan. And he's only eight.''

"He looks like he's a hundred. Well, we put ours to sleep and then we had all the rugs replaced. I'd put him to sleep. And Chief Fontana, Al was a wonderful man. And they say you're the best around.''

"To tell you the truth, I've about made up my mind to look into this for Ms. Cooper.''

Without another word, Ginnie Buchanan pivoted and trudged stiffly across the rocks. Twenty feet away she broke a heel and said, "Shit,'' loudly.

"Leaving without you,'' Fontana said to the younger woman.

"I've got my own car." Laura Sanderson stood with her hands behind her waist, smiling shyly.

Laura Sanderson was a single notch on the wrong side of pretty, but Fontana sensed an air of self-assurance, this despite her apparent shyness. Self-assurance or narcissism, he couldn't decide which. She was one of those people you weren't likely to notice in a crowd, but once you did, you wouldn't be able to stop noticing. Her posture was runway perfect, bringing her only a few inches shy of Fontana's five ten, and her skin was flawless, lightly tanned. Her indigo eyes were so obviously the product of contact lenses that it was hard to look away. Her raggedly cut shoulder-length hair had been hennaed so that it was close to burgundy when the light glanced off it, the dye job a current fad among young people not content with who they were. A rose tattoo marred one ankle. She was an odd combination of class and schlock. "Mind if I stick around a minute?"

"Be my guest."

It wasn't until he had outstripped forty that Fontana came to understand the virtues males prized in women younger than themselves. Skin without the wrinkles they themselves had come to know intimately. Mouths without the bridgework they had endured. Eyes without the reading spectacles they carried in their own breast pockets. Joy without caution. Psyches unblemished by hurt or failure. Youth with a capital _Y_. Bloodstreams logjammed with energy and hormones.

Her gaze was solid and direct, but her smile was self-conscious and disarmingly contagious. Beyond the smile, a quarter-mile away down the river in the direction Ginnie Buchanan had gone, a man appeared, a man with a pair of field glasses. He trained them on Fontana and the woman and stood as still as any of the trees along the riverbank, still and bold and arrogant, for he could not have failed to see Fontana watching him.

Four

▲

A NOTCH ON
THE WRONG SIDE
OF PRETTY

"**Y**ou really don't own a telephone?" Laura Sanderson asked. "Shouldn't the fire chief have a phone?"

"There's kids in town who've never seen a parking meter. The nursing home takes old-timers on day trips into Seattle so they can ride the elevators. I think with only one stoplight, Staircase is the perfect place not to have a phone."

She smiled indulgently. "I'll say one thing. This has got to be one of the most beautiful spots on earth."

"The real estate agents drag Japanese buyers through on tour buses. They stop old ladies pruning hedges in their yards and make offers on their houses. By the way, how did you folks find me?"

"One of the firefighters at your station gave directions, said you would be working late this week so you were taking the mornings off."

She was staring at Mt. Gadd, due east, a forty-two-hundred-foot edifice that rose steeply from the valley floor, dwarfing Little Gadd, a slab that had slid off a couple of million years ago, and which hovered directly above them. Little Gadd was a tree-clad butte a thousand feet in elevation with gray, mossy cliffs. From Fontana's position a man with a good rifle could have emptied a water barrel on either mountain. He might have pointed out the goats grazing on the upper slopes, but he didn't want her getting rhapsodic. Fontana felt as if this were his secret spot and the more people who knew about it, the more it became tainted.

She said, "I'm writing a book on women in the fire sector. I'm concentrating on Seattle because they continue to be one of the innovators in the country. When this fire at the Ratt Building came up, along with all the allegations and rumors and so forth, it seemed like the perfect centerpiece for my book. The incident typifies in a heated microcosm everything that happens to women in the work force and, in particular, in historically male-dominated professions."

"I'm not sure I understand."

"The single woman survivor is a perfect paradigm of everything that might happen to a woman. I've already done seventy interviews and a lot of groundwork. I thought if you were going to look into this we might pool some of our knowledge? In an informal way, of course." Laura smiled, her indigo contact lenses wet. "I have all the groundwork, and you know about fires and firepeople. We could be a team. If you're going to investigate this, the sooner you finish it up, the sooner I can start my book." She passed the heavy valise to him. "The official fire reports are inside. Lists of names and home addresses. It'll save you a lot of time. Just Xerox them. I'll be around town for a few hours. Maybe I could meet you somewhere later to pick it all up?"

"I wouldn't mind looking at this material you've gathered, but the team idea is not what I had in mind. And I'd rather not owe anybody anything."

"Use whatever you want. I just want you to get this report done so I can read it. No obligations."

"Thanks. The fire station? Three-thirty?"

"It's a date." Judging by her smile, she'd chosen her words carefully.

Their business concluded, neither of them said anything for a few moments.

"You like dogs?" she asked.

"Just this one." Laura regarded him with an ambiguous look that dimpled the corners of her mouth and revealed perfectly aligned teeth.

Satan arched his head appreciatively as she stroked behind his good ear. "I can tell by the way he looks at you for cues that you two get along."

"Hard not to like something that smart. Sometimes in the middle of the night I catch him studying the *Encyclopaedia Britannica*."

"What happened to his side here?"

"Got shot."

"Jesus. Recently?"

"Sort of." Her indigo eyes widened. "By the way. There's a man standing beside a tree down there on the dike watching us. You know him?" Startled, Laura turned and squinted into the distance, unseeing. "By that tall tree. Near the road. On the left."

She leaned forward and squinted harder. "Is that a man?" The figure turned and walked unhurriedly away.

"He's leaving."

"I don't know who it would be." She turned, trying to conceal her dismay. "I bet you think I'm too young for a writer. I've won awards, you know. For two years I've been a contributor to *Rolling Stone. The New York Times* has picked up my stories, and I've sold to *Cosmopolitan*. That's good for twenty-two."

Fontana whipped the fly rod around and flung the hook across the river, let the lure catch on the current and drift. Twenty-two. She looked about that. Or even younger. She had long legs and was prettier than he had thought at first, her complexion smooth enough to have been poured on.

"This whole fire thing confounds me. I think somebody really did something weird at that fire to get those guys hurt," she said.

"Look," said Fontana. "Nobody wants to believe something like the fire at the Ratt wasn't somebody's fault. Anybody's fault. People get notions. If they can keep an investigation going then it's not really over, almost as if their loved ones are not really dead yet. Hope becomes a commodity. Blame becomes a crusade."

"So, how does someone get locked into a ten-by-ten room by himself in the middle of a big fire? That's what happened to Buchanan."

"I saw an experienced fire captain back East get burned to death tangled up in a bicycle. Don fifty, sixty pounds of equipment. Work until you're exhausted in a suit that allows you to sweat but doesn't allow you to cool off, then throw yourself down in a building you've never seen before and turn on the cooker until it's a thousand degrees at the ceiling. Put on a blindfold of smoke so you can't see any further than the tip of your nose. Spin yourself in circles until you can't tell left from right. I've seen exhausted guys sit down and quit two or three feet from an exit."

"But he removed his helmet, gloves, and coat and stacked them neatly beside himself. Almost like a suicide. Or like maybe somebody held a gun on him and made him sit there."

"You don't believe that?"

"At this point, I'd believe almost anything. I really think Ginnie has a point. I don't think anybody really knows what happened at that fire. Why those three guys are dead."

"Carbon-monoxide poisoning? The guy in the room? I've heard of it happening that way. Maybe somewhere in the back of their mind they think they're getting ready for bed. They're getting sleepy and weak and they're delusional. They take their clothes off and lay them out. I've heard of it.

"And as for the widows. When it comes to why a loved one died, you feel better if you can place the blame. Know what I'm saying? That way you don't have to feel it was fate or bad luck or just their time to kick the bucket. Those are helpless feelings. Placing the blame is a feeling of power, if somewhat mitigated power. We pin the blame on some Dugan and somehow we're getting even, and it seems as if things are being settled. They're not, but it seems like they are. We're taking control of a helpless situation. It gives survivors a feeling of resolution."

Laura Sanderson gave him the earnest, not-quite-understanding-it-all look of a disciple. He couldn't tell if she was sincere or was engaging in subtle mockery. "I have a feeling about this. Diane Cooper and some of the others won't talk to me. There's got to be a reason."

Fontana climbed back onto the boulder with his fly rod and said, "Sometimes I think I should found a Dull Man's Club for those of us who appreciate afternoons with nothing to do but pick up your kid after school."

Her voice flattened out as if she were a diabetic just awarded a lifetime supply of gourmet chocolates. "You have a kid?"

When he nodded she managed to sound vaguely disappointed and a trifle curious at the same time. "Does your wife work in town here, then?"

"Linda passed away a couple of years ago."

"I'm sorry." She thought about that for a few moments. "And you don't like thrills? I mean excitement?"

"Not much."

"Funny thing for a fire chief to say."

They looked at each other for a few seconds, and after a moment she turned and hiked across the irregular riverbed until she disappeared at the end of the dike road behind a tall clump of wild lilacs. The man with the binoculars had long since left. Though he hadn't been close enough for a positive identification, Fontana felt he didn't know him. Even from this distance there had been an insolence, a brazenness, as the man watched with the arrogance of a tomcat that had yet to be neutered. It angered Fontana enough that he had considered sending the dog after him, but Satan was still ailing.

An immature osprey soared high along the mountainside to the east, working its way closer until it finally measured the sky overhead.

After a while Fontana climbed down, picked up the valise, and wedged his backside into the rocks next to Satan, hoping the sun would come out and warm things up while he read, but knowing it would not.

Five

▲

UNTIL IT KILLED YOU

According to the National Fire Prevention Association report, on Friday, March 23, of that year Al Buchanan, Clinton Vine, and William Youngblood lost their lives on the fourth floor of a five-story structure on King Street, just a few blocks east of Chinatown.

Buchanan, a Seattle firefighter of thirteen months, was discovered toward the front of the Ratt Building in a small room by himself in a kneeling position, slumped forward, his head almost to his chest. The skin around his nostrils and mouth was blackened with soot. His eyes, which his mother had labeled baby-blue but which his wife claimed held a sprinkle of rust, were partially open. Normally assigned to Engine 32 in West Seattle, he had been working a debit shift on Ladder 3, which meant he was working outside his normal cycle with a crew other than his own.

The officer on Ladder 3 that night had been William Youngblood, a firefighter who had been assigned as acting lieutenant for one shift. Youngblood died on the fourth floor too, in nothing more than a cubbyhole, forty-six feet from the spot where

Buchanan was found. Both men died from the inhalation of products of combustion, carbon-monoxide poisoning, although Youngblood's death was complicated by the fact that he had broken his leg. The fracture could not be reliably explained, and, at first, investigators thought the break might have occurred after death.

Later, the suspicion surfaced that while Buchanan and Youngblood were teamed up, Youngblood had fallen and broken his tibia and fibula, and Buchanan, unable to carry his partner, had ventured out for help, becoming disoriented along the way. It was as good a working theory as any, and now a few in the department subscribed to it. An alternate theory that Buchanan had collapsed from heat exhaustion and that Youngblood had gone for help and had broken his leg along the way had also been posited in the reports.

The third dead firefighter, Clinton Vine, was discovered in the basement at the bottom of an elevator shaft, impaled on a large steel rebounding spring set into the concrete at the base of the shaft, one of three such springs to keep the elevator from bottoming out. The carbon-monoxide level in his bloodstream was significant, but a broken neck, fractured skull, and ruptured major organs were what killed him.

The Ratt fire had taken place in a five-story partially renovated building that once had been an apartment complex but later had been sectioned into offices and artists' studios. The first floor had housed a dentist and three or four city-run youth-employment divisions.

Floors two and three had been partitioned into makeshift audio studios and regularly leased out to bands, who sometimes violated city building-code regulations by "crashing" in the building overnight.

The fourth floor had been a mishmash of partially completed office cubicles and unused, aging apartments.

The top floor, the fifth, was mostly warehouse space, with a row of tiny offices along the west wall.

An elevator shaft extended from the fifth to the first floor with doors opening onto each floor in between. It was into this shaft that Clinton Vine had fallen. The elevator car was no longer in the building and the doors on the other floors had been nailed shut, as had the access doors to the maintenance well in the basement, contributing to confusion during the search; consequently Clinton wasn't located until the other two fallen firefighters had been carried to Harborview by medic units.

Initially, the fire broke out near a space heater in the basement, in a stack of abandoned newspapers. A separate investigation conducted by the Seattle Fire Department's Fire Investigation team deemed the fire accidental.

The first units were dispatched at 1755 hours.

"Smoke from the building, laying a preconnect," had been Engine 6's radio report. However, as soon as the officer and nozzleman kicked in the outer door to the basement, they were driven back up the stairs by a ball of flame, followed by torrents of heavy black smoke. One member of Engine 6's crew suffered minor facial burns during the retreat.

Ladder 3 showed up next, and Acting Lieutenant William Youngblood gave a comprehensive radio report. "Ladder Three. We've got a four-story [he was mistaken—it was five stories] building with heavy smoke from the first floor and basement windows. Uh. The entire, uh, area is laid down with smoke and fog. We're going to make a search of the first and second floors."

Ladder 3's crew eventually broke a window at the southwest corner of the building, used a baby ladder to enter and performed a quick search of the first floor, which was surprisingly free of smoke at that time.

When Ladder 3 got back out to the street, a command post had been set up. Also, Ladder 1's crew had put up their aerial and was attempting to ventilate the structure from the roof. This would have been done by cutting large rectangles in the roof with chain saws.

It was determined shortly after the command post was set up that the fire had extended up through the walls into the upper stories of the building. In the early stages of the fire this extension bypassed the first floor.

At 1803 hours heavy black smoke became visible in the windows of the fourth and fifth floors.

At 1806 hours two additional engine companies were called by Chief Freeze, who was at this time King Street command. At 1808 hours he called a 311 alarm. At 1811 hours Deputy

Chief Wallace arrived on the scene and took over King Street command. Wallace controlled the fire ground until the end of the fire. At 1831 hours Chief Wallace learned there were two trapped civilians on the top story of the building. At 1942 hours radio messages were exchanged regarding two female fire victims in a medic unit. It was the first mention of same in any of the radio traffic.

At 1934 hours firefighter Diane Cooper was discovered wandering at the side of the building, disoriented, incoherent, and semiconscious from smoke inhalation. Forty-five minutes later search crews found Buchanan's and Youngblood's bodies in the smoke on the fourth floor. It wasn't until much later that Clinton Vine's body was discovered in the well of the elevator shaft.

Firefighting, thought Fontana. It was the best job on earth—right up until the moment it killed you.

Six

▲

TURN AROUND
AND SHRIEK

Jick Frick lived next door to the Staircase fire station with his son and eighteen-year-old daughter, Hedy, who was all bad skin stretched over bones like blades and a pair of water-pitcher breasts that belonged on a woman wrestler, an aberration most strangers, male or female, felt an obligation to remark upon once outside her presence. The Fricks' roof was draped in moss, their lawn crisscrossed with wrecked Camaros and dilapidated pickups that had carried FOR SALE signs so long the sun had burned out the penciled prices.

Accessed by a steel ladder on the inside wall, the fire station's fifty-foot hose tower had afforded, from a small ventilation window at the top, a view into Hedy Frick's bedroom that had lured more than one fireman up the steel rungs after dark. Fontana would have put an end to it when he became chief, but before he arrived Bobby Joe Allan leaned out the window one night with a hot cigarette between his lips, sucking it to a fine glow as he watched the Frick house.

Hedy Frick, who only infrequently glanced out her window, detected the small orange ember outside the fire tower, moved closer to the window, staring myopically into the pitch-black night at the tiny glowing dot until, at last, she understood.

It was then that she turned around and shrieked.

Her blinds were never opened again, and for that Bobby Joe never really earned the forgiveness of his brethren.

One firefighter who had never gotten excited over Hedy was Kingsley Pierpont. Kingsley was also the only professional fire-refighter in the Staircase department left alive after last summer.

Kingsley fingered his cropped mustache as he tipped the rolling chair in the chief's office dangerously backward. He was one of the few African-Americans in town and was now the acting lieutenant for the department, the next highest rank above firefighter. "What's up, Chief?"

"Think you could handle things around here for a while?" Fontana said.

Kingsley gave him a dubious look. "How long's a while?"

"Couple of weeks."

"You going on vacation? I've been telling you to do it."

"It's not exactly a vacation."

"This doesn't have anything to do with those two women were up here this morning asking about you?"

"Why?"

"I knew one of the guys who died last spring. Clinton Vine. Clinton was a player, see, before he got religion, but he paid for his mistakes. Paid cash every month. None of his kids wanted for anything if he could help it. Reba never did think the fire department gave Clinton a fair shake. She's hotter'n a one-armed pimp's two-dollar pistol over his death. You know, some folks have to blame everything goes wrong in their lives on the white guy? That's her."

"Maybe if I find some answers, it'll change her mind."

"Real doubtful."

"Mo around?"

"The Porsche was outside last I looked."

Fontana picked up a complete set of bunking clothing and toted it upstairs to the mayor's office.

Seven

▲

MAYOR MO'S
LONG-LOST DOG

"*I* want a raise, Mo.

"What?"

Not yet thirty, Mo Costigan, the part-time mayor of Staircase, spent the remainder of her sixty-hour work week at an accounting firm she had founded in Bellevue. She lived alone in a large house on the posh side of town and was considered a genius by those who didn't know any better. Shorter than average, Mo had a buxom figure, wide hips, and a Napoleonic swagger; had once boasted of coming from middle-European peasant stock, the sort of ancestors, she said, laughing nervously, "who looked normal only with hoes in their hands."

Her hair was brown and wiry, flaring out around her jawline. Fontana knew she was smarter than a whip, but still he was apt to think of her more as someone who drove around with a coffee cup on the roof of her car than as mayor; as someone who wore broken sunglasses because she got them free from her pharmacist father rather than as a successful CPA. Yet she had saved the city almost two hundred thousand dollars when a fraudulent contracting company tried to bilk the council on a sewer job.

"I want a raise, Mo. Our salary scale is upside down. The chief makes less than the lieutenant."

"You know, before you came on board everybody who'd held the job of fire chief also held the job of sheriff, a combined position. Since you no longer want to be sheriff, only chief, we prorated the position. Unfortunately that put you below the pay of lieutenant. I thought we were fair about it. So did the town council. So did you, if I recall."

"Fine. Bobby Joe got himself killed, so now we need a new lieutenant. I'll quit as chief and you can hire me back as lieutenant."

"Don't be silly."

"I'm not joking."

"But you're the chief. The chief is the chief and the lieutenant is the lieutenant. If you were the lieutenant, who would be the chief?"

"Hire a new chief. Pay him lieutenant's pay. Make me the lieutenant and give me chief's pay."

"But you're already the chief."

"Okay. Commission two new lieutenants, a first lieutenant and a second lieutenant. Fire me and I'll be the first lieutenant and I'll make real chief's pay and the second lieutenant will make what lieutenant's pay should be. When we hire new firefighters, we'll call them assistant chiefs. The first lieutenant will be in charge of everybody and the second lieutenant will be in charge of the assistant chiefs. Then we can hire a chief to do the windows."

Mo attempted a laugh, but all she did was bare a few crooked teeth and make a noise like a bloodhound sniffing under a door. "Mac, you're not being reasonable."

"You know as well as I do I could triple my salary by talking to the council. I came to you because I didn't want to embarrass you by going over your head."

Mo touched an index finger to the tip of her chin. "We're up to our elbows in applicants for those new positions, in budget statements, working with the contractors on the ridge project, you name it. We've got to hire three new firefighters.

I was thinking we should hire two women and a minority. What do you think?''

"An awful lot of people applied. Over six hundred. Only two of them were women. You want to hire two new women you're going to need a bigger pool to draw from. What you should do is hire three chiefs and break me to lieutenant.''

"Don't be ridiculous.''

"Couple days ago I heard a rumor *you* were asking for a hike in salary.''

"Huh?''

"Don't play dumb, Mo.''

"Goddamn you, Chief Fontana.'' When she danced with him at the Bedouin Friday nights it was "Mac,'' and sometimes, after a few beers, it was "Sweety,'' but the "Chief Fontana'' came out of the holster at times like this. "I never fail to get a splitting headache talking to you.''

"That's because you try so hard to be devious, Mo. Anyway, I'm going on vacation.''

Mo looked up from the paperwork she had been pretending to study. "Say again?''

"My vacation. I'm taking it now.''

"Well, sure. You're entitled to vacation time. I mean, after last summer and all. A few days.'' Fontana dropped into a chair, propped his feet on the edge of Mo's desk, and scratched Satan's head. Mo wrinkled her nose, for, though she adored most dogs, she detested Satan.

"I'm due two weeks,'' he said, thinking about the discomfort he had felt after spotting the man with the binoculars. "I might need a little more.''

"Chief Fontana, you're the most exasperating person! I'll give you four days. We've got chaos here. I need you to help reorganize the department. I can't do it myself.''

"Yourself? Blessed mother. You're not even supposed to be messing in it, Mo. The council agreed.''

Mo, when provoked, had been described as a tyrannosaur on the rag. Fontana thought the sentiment harsh but couldn't help thinking of it now. He liked tough women, liked Mo a lot, and if she ever figured that out, things between them might become less complicated.

She said, "One would think a relative newcomer and neophyte to the political amphitheater that this valley has become would welcome guidance from somebody who has lived here her whole life."

"Mo, lighten up. By the way, here are your turnouts. The first training session is Saturday."

"You . . . you said you thought I was too squeamish to be a volunteer."

"We can take you along slowly with the aid calls." Fontana handed her a body loop and lay on the floor on his back. Satan gave him a curious look and twitched an ear. "Tie me up."

"What?"

"If you can get me up and carry me to the doorway, you're strong enough for the job. You have to be able to carry your partner to safety. I'll talk you through it. I know those big old thighs of yours can do it."

Mo was on her hands and knees midway through the exercise, had steadied Fontana's limp body carefully on her back with her skirt hiked up her thighs, when Bernard Cornwall entered the office, three or four men in business suits stacked up behind him in the doorway. Bernard said, "Uh, excuse me. I'll come back later."

The oldest and most distinguished member of the council and, discounting Mo, the single most powerful figure in town, Bernard was a man people talked about putting into the race for the state legislature.

"Bernard, don't go," Mo gasped, unable to finish her thought while balancing Fontana's 160 pounds. The combination of trying to talk and packing Fontana on her back caused her to break wind. Bernard snicked the door shut, certain from the insane grin on Fontana's face he had disrupted something quite private and most likely quite depraved.

"Oh, fiddlesticks."

"Very good," said Fontana as she stood unsteadily and lugged him to the door.

"My thighs are not big. You said 'those big old thighs.' You slipped that right past me."

"I like them."

They seemed to have reached a truce, and for a fraction of a second Fontana had a deranged notion that this might be

44

the time to tell her Satan had killed her dog last year, had snapped up the little guy and shaken him dead before Fontana could put a halt to it. At the time, he hadn't had the stomach to fess up, had chucked the carcass into a Dumpster and pretended ignorance when Mo posted LOST DOG placards around town. Fontana had spent almost a year trying to figure out how to tell her, thought about it briefly each time they met, and always came to the conclusion that there had to be a better time.

"What exactly is it that you like about my thighs?" Mo asked, but Fontana was already halfway out the door.

Eight

▲

INDIGO EYES

"**H**e looks like you," Laura Sanderson said after Brendan had gone inside the fire station. "Or does he look like his mother? Do you think?"

"Like Linda."

"How did she die, anyway?"

"Car accident." She let his comment simmer, sensing his reluctance.

Some women picked up an afterglow from skimming through a child's orbit, though Laura was apparently not one of them, possibly because she had so recently wrapped up the skeins of childhood herself. Fontana wasn't much past forty, but he felt prehistoric next to her, couldn't help calculating she had been in diapers the year he came out of the army. Diapers.

"I love this town. Three different strangers said hello to me." Laura was ebullient as she stood gazing up at Mount Washington to the southeast and directly south to Rattlesnake Mountain, where the logging companies had clear-cut patches off the hillsides until Fontana thought they resembled sores on a baboon's rump. "It's stunning. It really is. This whole valley."

"A lot of adultery in this town," Fontana said. "Every winter the loggers get cabin fever and the wife-beating starts up. The library's only got eight books, and four of those are repair manuals for riding lawn mowers. We get ninety-five inches of rain a year."

"For the love of Pete, I'm not planning to move here."

"It floods so bad there aren't any cats in town. Most drown every winter and the others hitchhike to L.A."

Preoccupied with her own thoughts now, Laura folded her thin arms in front of herself while her indigo eyes went blank.

"If it's all right, I might tag along on some of your interviews. You are going to talk to some people about the Ratt? In the Seattle Fire Department I've met every kind of person you could imagine and some you couldn't." The look in his cold blue eyes caused her to hesitate.

"Thanks for the offer, but I won't need help."

Her disappointment was obvious and unnerving. Satan, who had been looking up at them as if following every word of their conversation, limped inside the station through the half-open door and lay down in the hallway, blocking foot traffic, letting Moses, the station cat, nap on top of him. The former owner of Satan was in the penitentiary. The former owner of Moses was dead.

"Let me give you my card," Laura said. "I'm house-sitting in Seattle. That's the number."

"You're not from around here? I didn't think so."

"I'm an army brat. When I get angry you might hear a little dash of Texas, where we lived until I was seven. 'Bout all I remember of Texas is I used to think armadillos were born dead alongside the road."

"When we first moved out here Brendan used to think hawks slept in the sky."

"I've been going around asking about you. You've built yourself quite a little reputation." He sighed. "I meant that in the very best sense. You're like some sort of famous person here or something. Seems like, even though you've only lived in Staircase a while, almost everybody knows you personally. And they like you. Except, I think, there's a contingent with a respect for you that borders on . . . alarm. I guess you killed someone last summer, justifiably I'm told?" Fontana was amazed at how much he resented this conversation. Last summer he had been forced to kill a man, to turn a gun on someone else he had once considered a friend. It made him sick to think about it, much less to have it brought up in the context of making him a famous person. "And that dog. He makes *everyone* nervous."

"The dog's harmless. Look," said Fontana, stepping into the station and motioning for her to follow. "Let me give you back those materials. I've copied everything I'll need."

Unaccountably, she lingered in the doorway; some sort of split personality, one moment brash, the next shy. Somebody was shouting exuberantly in the back of the station, Brendan's joyful laughter a sharp counterpoint to the shouting, like a spoon being rattled inside a glass jar.

After he gave her back the valise, Mac watched her stride down the sidewalk past the Fricks' to where she had parked, busying herself with the materials in the valise, orienting herself toward her car, the path out of town, and the rest of her life. Fontana could see she was a congenitally busy woman, that their interlude together, easygoing as it had seemed, was an anomaly, a temporary pact of abatement she had entered into only because that was what his disposition seemed to call for.

After dinner, when he and Brendan trekked through the trees to make arrangements with their neighbor Mary for babysitting, they found her and her mother in matching pink nightgowns sitting in front of a newscast. The story intrigued Mac. In a rural neighborhood of West Seattle an explosion had destroyed a house. Fire officials, along with the police, had determined the cause to be a stockpile of ammonium nitrate. A helicopter overview of the site showed that the house was obliterated except for pieces of the foundation and a disheveled davenport on a distant neighbor's roof.

Later, after reading to Brendan in bed, Fontana had his hand on the light switch when his son said, "Do you ever think about Mommy?"

Fontana went back and kissed his son's brow once more. "All the time, Brendan."

"Maybe I should write a letter to her. We're writing letters in school. I know she wouldn't get it, but maybe I should write one."

"I think that would be nice."

The radio was playing "To Know Him Is to Love Him" by the Teddy Bears when an alarm came in for a car in the ditch near Exit 38 on Interstate 90. It took an annoying amount of willpower, but Fontana reminded himself that he was officially on vacation and did not respond to the beeper. It was a strange sensation not to be lugging Brendan next door to Mary's couch. He was involved in something other than running a Podunk fire department now. He was going to help a good woman clear her name. At least he hoped she was a good woman. And he hoped what he would be going to do would clear her name because the alternative would be putting the final nail of accusation into Diane Cooper's casket.

The last thing Fontana thought about before falling asleep was the ammonium-nitrate explosion on the news. In 1947 a shipload of ammonium nitrate caught fire at a dock in Texas City, Texas, and all 27 members of the Texas City Fire Department were killed, along with 460 others. Ever since, firefighters have been seeing ammonium nitrate and muttering, "Texas City, Texas."

When Fontana heard it, he muttered, "Bob Creed."

Nine

▲

KEEP YOUR HANDS ON YOUR WALLETS

*T*he night bled a heavy, dripping fog onto the valley.

It was nine by the time Fontana packed a talkative Brendan off to school with a lunch box and a good-bye hug. On the way Brendan recounted how he'd spent part of yesterday afternoon watching a dog named Barney roll around on a dead rat in the road.

Fontana had shaved off his beard while the boy supervised. Afterward he studied himself in the mirror. Blue eyes. Brown-blond hair that was thinning a touch. A mostly unlined face that cracked into a million smile wrinkles at a fit prompt, then took on the angular planes of a bare-knuckles fighter when things got rough. Fontana was a hard man, but, then, he wasn't so hard that old ladies didn't giggle when he joked about kissing them.

With Satan panting in the backseat, Fontana drove the Staircase chief's truck, one side of which bore twenty-seven bullet holes filled with Bondo, into Seattle. Near Issaquah the sky became filled with high, broken clouds. The state patrol was

working I-90 hard, the roadside peppered with red-faced motorists and stiff-backed troopers.

It wasn't until he had gotten into the wrong lane twice,
cooped up by a swarm of tailgating motorists, that Fontana
realized he was being followed. A lone figure in a red Ford
Mustang, the souped-up version. Probably because traffic was
so heavy, the Mustang stayed on his bumper the way a crazed
motorist out for revenge might.

Fontana took the Rainier Avenue exit and then pulled a
right at Charles next to a minimart, drove a block, took another
right, and stopped twenty feet from the corner on a quiet side
street. He opened the door and got out in time to greet the
Mustang. The man in the Mustang now had a ski mask over
his head. He stopped at the intersection and pointed a pistol
at Fontana through his open passenger window.

Mac didn't have time to jump, or dodge or duck or curse,
for the car roared away up the hill in a cloud of exhaust and
screeching rubber. No shots had been fired, but they would
have been had Mac been armed. He was shivering with rage.
The rear license plate had been obliterated with mud. From
the way the driver held himself, Fontana believed he was the
same clown who had been watching him and Laura at the
river yesterday.

Five minutes later Fontana could still feel the anger in his
gut when Reba Vine said, "Come in. Sit down. Thank you for
coming. I didn't think you would really come."

Reba Vine was an African-American, exotic enough that he
thought he might have seen her face in fashion layouts, as
many pounds underweight as the other widow had been over,
a thin giant of a woman, with little party-hat breasts.

It was a comfortable-looking home on Forty-second Avenue
South, east of Rainier Avenue near Andover, the structure
fronted by a rock garden that was in turn bisected by slightly
crooked concrete steps.

"Ginnie called last night and told me you were working for
the death bitch. That's what Ginnie calls her. I called your fire
station this morning hoping you would drop by. I didn't think
you would."

"I *am* working for her."

"Clinton was in eighteen years. He never even got hurt before this. Not at a fire. There's some people get hurt every time the alarm sounds. Clinton jogged three miles every night. Played all-city ball. He had peripheral vision and knew how to watch out for himself."

Reba's knees were cocked at odd angles to her body, bony elbows out, a generic sort of anger oozing out of every pore and joint. She wore a satin robe over a nightdress and looked as if she hadn't been awake more than five minutes. She forked a bony hand through her straightened, coal-black hair. She was startlingly beautiful.

"Please sit down. I've been thinking about this and I want you to know where I stand. Have a seat there. Right there, dear." She directed him to a large leather chair with brass studs on the rim.

A painting of Martin Luther King, Jr., hung on the wall over the fireplace. Four Bibles as well as a large crucifix were displayed in different parts of the house. There were no signs of children, though according to Kingsley, Reba and Clinton had a daughter around eight years old.

"You've got no right to work for that woman," Reba said, pacing. "You should be helping us sue the department, Ginnie Buchanan and me. Mr. Fontana, let me explain some background. After he was in the department about a year, Clinton saved three children from a burning house. You know what he got for it? Two people in his battalion who had never spoken to him began speaking to him. Nobody ever officially said a word to Clinton about him and those kids, even though there was a chief standing right there when he brought them out. That chief is chief of the department now. Harcourt Thurmond. That same year, some white fireman in the North End did some work with the Boy Scouts and got Firefighter of the Year out of it. You ever work under that sort of pressure, Mr. Fontana?

"Clinton didn't want anything but to be one of the guys, to do a job and leave something behind for his child. Clinton never wanted much and he never complained.

"I'm madder than hell, Mr. Fontana. That's what. I'm mad because I'm afraid you're going to be another part of the cover-up. Because Clinton was a black man, they threw his life away. You always hear Seattle's got one of the finest departments in the country, but where do you hear that? Seattle. It's rotten. And the sooner you figure that out, the sooner you can figure out what really happened.

"In the early days, whenever anything around the station came up missing, the first couple of years Clinton was in, they figured he did it. Some captain lost his wristwatch and accused Clinton of stealing it from his locker. In front of everybody. They were going to write charges on him. Later the captain found his watch in his coat pocket, but did he ever go back and apologize?

"Clinton had to fight fire twice as hard as the next man because everything he did was watched. He could never relax."

Fontana said, "Bill Youngblood and your husband knew each other pretty well, right? They worked on the same crew?"

"When I met Clint ten years ago, one of his best friends was Bill Youngblood. Funny, because Clint didn't have any white friends outside of work. Then, awhile back, something came between them. What happened was, white bread got burned trying to get a promotion, so he blamed it on the closest brother. One time you turn the tables on white bread, and he cries like a child."

Fontana said, "If you're asking me to prove Clinton Vine died because the SFD is racist, you're going to have to find yourself another man. I'm not saying that won't be the outcome, but I'm not on a crusade. I'm looking for the facts of what happened on March twenty-third. Three people died that night."

"You know as well as I do," said Reba, "if they changed the rules things would go back to the fifties overnight. I guess you don't remember the good old boys? Your son gets a job. Your sister-in-law gets a job. Anybody gets a job except the brother off the street. Somebody wants to rent a house, we're sorry, it's already been rented. Then the sign stays up three more weeks. The hospital's full tonight, ma'am, you'll have to take your bleeding girl across town."

"I'm not here to debate social consciousness," said Fontana.

"No, I guess you're not. But you just look for a cover-up when you're out there looking. You just look to see if Clinton had been white, that he wouldn't be alive now. You just look."

"I'll keep that in mind, Mrs. Vine." Fontana knew that one

of the men he was planning to speak to this morning, Chief Freeze, had been directly responsible for Clinton Vine's crew during the fire, and possibly responsible for the deaths. From prior experience with the Seattle department, he also knew that Chief Freeze was black.

"You'd better go now," said Reba.

Ten

▲

FREEZE

On Beacon Hill Fontana found a supermarket with a phone booth outside, dropped some coins in, and dialed the firefighter who had gone up the fire escape in back of the Ratt and brought down two civilian women single-handedly.

"Patrick Easterman?"

"Speaking."

"My name is Mac Fontana. I'm fire chief out in Staircase, but I'm investigating the . . ." The connection went blank.

Fontana dialed again, but Easterman's line was busy. Thinking he had dialed so quickly Easterman hadn't had a chance to hang up, he waited a few moments before trying again, yet the line remained busy. Easterman didn't live far, was obviously home, so Mac drove there. It was a brick tri-level overlooking the Puget Sound in West Seattle, a ritzy home for a man on a fireman's salary. He probably worked a second job.

A tiny prune-faced woman with graying hair that had either been brown or red at one time answered the door with a smile and a disjointed look in her eyes as if she were having a hard time focusing. She was probably in her late forties or early fifties, but except for the radiant smile, was aging poorly. After Fontana explained who he was and what he was there for, she said, "Certainly. Certainly. Pat's around somewhere. He was just puttering with his snowmobile engine out in the work shed. You have a seat, Mr. Fontana."

He waited in the living room, watching a ferry traverse the sound on its way to Bremerton and the naval shipyards. West Seattle was its own little community, separated from the rest of the city proper by a bridge and two branches of the Duwamish River. It was a promontory—one long hump of land. After a while Fontana sat on a davenport that looked as if it hadn't been used before and thumbed through a *Better Homes and Gardens*. It took twenty minutes for Mrs. Easterman— passing through the dining room—to discover him once again. "Oh, dear, did Pat go off to do something?"

"I don't know. I haven't seen him."

"Oh, dear. Well, that's strange. I told him you were here. He said he'd be right on up. Well, actually he grunted. But that meant he'd be right on up. Pat's not much of a talker. I wonder if he's forgotten. Let me go see. I'm so sorry for this." She was gone five minutes the second time.

"I'm just so embarrassed," she said, breathing heavily when she returned. "I don't know what ever could have happened to him. His truck is here, but I don't see him anywhere, Mr. Fontana. If you want to wait a little longer, I can go check over to the neighbors. I'm sure that's where he must be."

"Thanks. I can take a hint."

"I'm so sorry for all of this. It just isn't like Pat."

Fontana had a feeling it was, though.

He drove across the Alaskan Way Viaduct and took I-5, the interstate that skewered Seattle on its jaunt from Mexico to Canada. He passed skyscrapers and then Lake Union, spiny with boats, a float plane skimming the surface; beyond that, Queen Anne Hill's apartment houses and a diadem of three TV towers from which some intrepid soul strung Christmas lights every December. He took the Forty-fifth Street exit off the freeway, headed west past the zoo, and down the long hill.

The Ballard area was known for its Scandinavian immigrants, the government boat locks, and the marinas, along with acres of cozy neighborhoods crammed with small side-by-side houses. The Shilshole Marina contained some of the city's most prized seafood restaurants and night spots.

A few minutes before ten o'clock Fontana parked in the back of Station 18 on N.W. Market Street, noting that the chief's van was still in quarters, as was the truck company. The pumper and aid car were out.

After he identified himself, a tall, hook-nosed uniformed woman named O'Leary let him in the back door and ushered him across freshly mopped floors to the chief's office. A chief was in charge of a battalion of seven or eight fire stations along with all the apparatus and men therein, and would automatically be in command of any fire in his district. Seattle's fire department contained seven battalions. Seven battalion chiefs working at any given time.

Flashing a gap-toothed smile that had its own goofy charm, Chief Freeze appeared a trifle bewildered to see him. Because of his stature, Freeze gave the appearance of having been clumsy as a youth. When he stood to shake hands with Fontana, he was almost a foot taller, his palm rough and cavernous and so dark, it made Fontana's hand appear pale. In a starched, white short-sleeved chief's shirt with blue and gold bugles on the collars, Freeze was friendly, nervous, and difficult to understand, for he had an inner-city accent so thick Fontana found himself reviewing everything Freeze said to make certain he had heard it correctly. Fontana knew this speech pattern had to be an incredible deficit in a job in which quick communication was imperative.

Freeze trundled an extra rolling chair across the room and shut the door, the chief's paperwork for the day laid out on the bedspread of a bunk, his tidy desk illuminated by a neon tube lamp.

"I believe you were the first chief at King Street last March?"

Still smiling, Freeze said, "The Ratt Building? I'm not so sure maybe I should have a lawyer standing by advising me."

"Fine with me," said Fontana. "I can come back at your convenience. What I'm doing is investigating the Ratt fire for Diane Cooper. She wants her name cleared."

"I never accused her." Freeze tried to laugh it off, his laugh almost a conspiratorial giggle. He was one of those people who had a difficult time keeping his thoughts off his face, striking

Fontana as someone who was chronically the only one laughing in a room. "Besides, I bring a lawyer in here, you'd think I was trying to hide something."

After they had both considered their positions, Freeze reached down, tugged off one of his enormous black dress boots, and stuck a hand inside his sock, rubbing the ball of his foot.

"Could you tell me what you saw when you arrived at King Street?" Fontana asked. "What you saw and what you did."

"Smoke from the building," said Freeze, laughing. "Engine Six said smoke from the building. That was an understatement like you wouldn't believe. All's I saw was smoke. I was coughing up crud for a week."

"I understand you weren't the overall commander very long."

"I started off as incident commander, then, when Wallace took over as the IC, he had me Division C commander. I dropped in holes twice making my way round to the back of the building. Even with a flashlight you couldn't see nothing for smoke. My knee still giving me a little song on that one." Chief Freeze continued puttering with his sock. "There wasn't no wind that night. I don't know there was any at all. And it colder'n a witch's tit. Pacifically for me, just standing.

"The smoke came out and laid down around on the road in front like a space movie. I guess Sixes found the location okay, but by the time I got there, I had to slow way down just to see where I was. All of a sudden I'm about four feet from the bumper of Ladder Three. They was parked or I probably have killed myself. Sixes tried to take a hose line straight to the basement when they should have laid exposure lines inside at the stairs. Everybody was makin' mistakes."

Engine 6 was the hose company housed in the same station with Ladder 3. The engines, or pumpers, carried hundreds of feet of hose and usually had a water tank of four or five hundred gallons. In Seattle, ladder trucks carried all the rescue equipment, heavy tools, and ladders. The only water a ladder company carried was in two-and-a-half-gallon pump cans. At a building fire, hose companies and ladder companies were both needed, so they had to work in conjunction with each other. In the East and in some other cities on the West Coast, fire departments had special rescue units, but in Seattle the truck companies performed the search-and-rescue operations.

"Anyways, they try to get in the basement door in front 'cause that's where the heaviest smoke was coming from. The whole building was cooking. That was when I called two more engine companies. We never should have put anybody in there."

"Why did you?"

"Ladder Three initiated their search on their own heads! They was inside when I come on the scene. There was peoples standing in front. Maybe they told the acting officer on Ladder Three somebody was trapped. I don't know. Seattle's so aggressive, we go in every fire building. It's gotten more than one firefighter killed."

"Did you know the acting officer on Ladder Three?"

"Everybody knew Youngblood."

"What'd you think of him?"

Freeze answered with an untutored shrug, though his eyes deadened in a way that said he hadn't really liked Youngblood. "He's gone. How you expect me to answer a question like that? He's gone."

"So, then what happened?"

"It was around that time I called a 311 and Wallace got there and took over. We tried to set up a staging area, but the incoming units were all lost in the smoke. Later, firemens told me it was smoky for five and six blocks around there. So smoky it killed a couple cats in the yard next door."

"What made you call the 311?" A 311 was an automatic call for a specific amount of extra units and chiefs, rather than calling for them one at a time.

Freeze gave off a low-amperage smile. "I hate to do a multiple because then all the brass from downtown comes in and starts second-guessing everything you already done. Me and the brass downtown don't get along so hot." He laughed, something he did often, not because things were funny, but to camouflage embarrassment. He was beginning to perspire in the large bald spot on top of his head.

"You know, one thing I never mentioned when they were making out their official reports, the NPA guys and them, I never told them about my radio."

"What about your radio?"

"Sometimes it would cut out on me."

"So Ladder Three might have called down to you and you might have missed it?"

"No, I don't think so. But I had to go around and get another one."

"You were Division C chief after Wallace came in? That put you directly in charge of Ladder Three?"

"Yeah. They brung around a fifty-five-foot ladder and put it up in the alley. Ladder Three. Jostled some wires when they first extended it. I thought they were going to get zapped. Wallace wanted to put an aerial back there but there were a bunch of parked cars in the way."

"Where'd they go with the ladder?"

Freeze's voice rose and his features were suddenly shot through with animation. "The *fifth* floor. Why you people keep on me about which floor? All the way up with a fifty-five is five stories, right? How many feet to a story? Hadda be the fifth. They got it in a window on the fifth floor. That's where I told them to search. That's where our information said people were trapped."

It took Fontana a few moments to decipher everything Freeze had said, to cut through the inner-city dialect. "The eyewitnesses say two of the three dead men were found on the fourth floor. Nobody was found on the fifth."

"I can't help that."

"It seems to me if they had persons trapped, or reports of such, they would have stopped everything and tried to get them down. Wallace had Ladder Three walk all the way around the building with a fifty-five-foot ladder? That had to take a while."

"No, no, no, you don't understand. You simpleminded or something? Ladder Three was already in the back with that ladder when Wallace called me on the radio and told me to have them go to the fifth floor and search." Freeze had grown verbally abusive with the slippery ease of a man who did it frequently and with impunity, one of the unbecoming perks of power.

"Somebody had an aerial up the front?"

"Ladder One, but it was all tied up putting firemens on the

roof. There was a shitload of firemens on the roof cutting holes. You could hear saws through that whole fire. Wrecked a bunch of saws."

"Who went up first?"

Freeze smiled guilelessly. "You're the first person ever ask that. I guess it wasn't Clint, because we was bullshitting. He went last. First? I don't know."

"What was your next contact with Ladder Three?"

"I had a lot going on back there too. You know, I had Ladder Three upstairs doing their search, and then I had two crews back going into the basement. A lot of fire in the basement. I guess my next contact was when I seen Cooper in back of the medic wagon."

"And how long after they went up was that?"

"Couldn'ta been too long. I mean, they were using half-hour bottles. So you figure twenty-five minutes for the bottle plus a few minutes. They had her stripped down to this T-shirt and panties. Her color looked like a gutted fish. All pink and gray. One of the medics make a sign like she was gonna die. That kind of scared me . . ."

"So you sent Ladder Three's crew up the fifty-five to search the building and the next you saw of them was around the front when you saw Cooper in the medic unit?"

"That's right."

"What do you think happened upstairs? To Ladder Three."

"The way I see it they went in, got theirselves turned around, and then ran out of air. Simple as that. And Cooper coming out of it by herself? I never even worked with her before that fire. If I worked with her, maybe I would have my own opinion. Maybe she panicked and ran down the stairs on the inside. I don't know. I just know people are always saying how pretty she was. For a fire-department babe, sure. But she's got blue eyes and big tits. That's all. In a fire station, blue eyes and big hooters. You got that, they'll say you looking pretty."

"Who figured out Ladder Three was in trouble?"

"I guess Chief Wallace did when he said he was sending a crew around to go up to the fifth floor to search for Ladder Three. Before that Chief Reinhold come around to all the division commanders asking about Ladder Three. But he didn't seem too bothered. He just asked if I seen the others from

Ladder Three. I told him they must be around front with Cooper."

"Did he ask you if Ladder Three was still upstairs?"

"I told him they hadn't come by me. As far as I knew they were still up there. Or out front."

"And that's the basic crux of the situation, isn't it? Ladder Three was missing and while they were missing they were upstairs dying, right?"

"Basically."

"But you hadn't been there the whole time, either. In the alley. Had you?"

"Easterman was keeping an eye out. Easterman saved those womens. I took him off Engine Twenty-eight's crew to be my aide, so he was back there the whole time, even if I wasn't. We had that alley covered."

"But if you had it covered, why didn't you notice Ladder Three hadn't come down? Weren't you supposed to be keeping track of them?"

"Hey. I didn't see Cooper come down and she made it safe. I thought they did too."

"Until they came around asking about them, right?"

"Right."

"Why didn't they do it on the radio? Call out for Ladder Three? That would have been quicker than walking around the building asking people, don't you think?"

"Probably didn't want to panic nobody." To Fontana, it seemed a bizarre perspective. In a fire situation the issue of a missing firefighter has to be addressed immediately, for minutes often meant the difference between life and death, yet Seattle had sent a chief around on foot to ask about the missing crew from Ladder 3. The question was, who did Seattle's brass think was going to panic? These were seasoned firefighters. Or they should have been.

"Tell me this, Chief Freeze. When you went around the front of the building and noticed Diane Cooper in the back of the aid car . . . "

"Medic unit. It was a medic."

"Didn't it occur to you something was wrong?"

Freeze shrugged and his face went blank. "You think this hasn't been brought up to me? We were fighting a hell of a basement fire and you know what those are like. Those people fucked up on their own. Ask Cooper why she didn't say something about her crew bein' in trouble. It was *her* crew. Ask her."

When the alerter for the station hit, Freeze jumped out of his chair, zipped up his loose boot, grabbed his white chief's hat, and went out to the watch desk. He got into his white chief's van on the apparatus floor and vanished up N.W. Market in a small carnival of flashing red lights and whooping electronic sirens.

Two other firefighters were in the room, O'Leary and a man named Ryker. "So, you been talking to the big cheese about the Ratt?" Ryker asked.

"Were you there?"

Eleven

▲

FIREFIGHTERS
HIDING IN CLOSETS

"Hell, yes, I was at King Street," said Ryker, his broad torso bowing outward like the taut underside of a loaded hammock. He flattened the wings of his mustache with index finger and thumb as if it were a pet and glowed with the ruddy look of a Scot from a long line of ruddy Scots. "You're that guy working for Cooper, aren't you?"

"Rumors fly pretty fast, don't they?"

"Why doesn't she just *tell* you the truth? She was up there!" Ryker was bitter enough that Fontana thought one of the dead might have been a friend.

"What did you see at the Ratt?"

"Listen, if you want to get her off, you do it without my help. Three men are dead because of her and I'm not going to help out with any whitewash."

"You know as well as I do a big fire like that is a complex thing and sometimes it takes a long time afterward to unravel everything that happened. Diane wants the truth as much as you do. That's why she hired me."

Ryker thought about it for a minute. "We worked with her. Just once. Once was enough."

"What does that mean?"

"Just that I don't think she belongs in the fire department. As long as you're going to ask questions," said Ryker, his face turning red, "why don't you ask Cooper if she was hiding in a closet?"

"What does that mean?"

"O'Leary here's a good kid, but we've had women in the department hiding in closets at fires. This affirmative-action bullshit is for banks and insurance companies, not public-safety jobs. They make a mistake hiring here, somebody ends up dead."

"Just tell me what happened at the fire. That's all."

Ryker stroked his mustache. "Got called in off-shift. Spent most of the fire on the third floor, dismantling the place board-by-board, chasing fire in the walls. But when we first got there we were assigned to go up the stairway in the front of the building and check for extension, to see if the fire was in there. On the fourth floor we heard firefighters inside the door talking. We tried the door, but it was nailed or something, and we didn't have any forcible-entry stuff with us. One guy was say-ing, 'Well, how long are we going to keep looking for her?' or something to that effect. It was either Vine or Buchanan, because the other guy said, 'Until I say to stop.' That was Youngblood. I recognized his voice. The other guy said, 'You think she's hiding? We've looked everywhere.' And Bill Youngblood said, 'She might have panicked somewhere.' "

"This wasn't in any of the reports I read," Fontana said.

Ryker gave him an ironic smirk. "Makes you wonder, doesn't it? Everybody in the department, practically, knows about this. She went in there with them and must have got scared or turned around or who-knows-what. Those guys died trying to find Cooper. Everybody knows that. They were looking for Cooper when they ran out of air and then, knowing Bill, he probably kept looking until he got so hot in his bunkers or took in so much smoke he didn't know what he was doing. You had to know Bill. There was no way he would leave a fellow fire-fighter in a burning building the way Cooper did. No way."

O'Leary averted her wet eyes and walked slowly out of the room. Whether the topic was too painful or whether she was sick of hearing the same old litany, Fontana could not tell.

"See, while Ladder Three were getting themselves dead on the fourth floor, Easterman waltzes up to the fifth all by hisself and saves the two ladies. I never thought much of Easterman until that. Toward the end there were some scratching sounds upstairs. Near as I could figure it later, it must have been Buchanan, because I think the spot where they found him was pretty close to directly over us. He must have been clawing at the wall for help. Just sitting there, too weak to move, clawing at the wall hoping somebody would hear. We didn't know what it was. Gives you the creeps, don't it?"

Ryker's voice had begun to decay, for this wasn't a tale he told often, nor one he relished the telling of.

Fontana said, "The chief seemed to think they were searching the fifth floor. Ladder Three."

"Cheese is like that," said Ryker, contempt infecting his voice. "He's dumber than six fence posts. He won't even acknowledge they were found on the fourth. He said, 'It's my word against a dead guy's, who you gonna believe?' I swear his head is harder than God's elbow. Why they made him a chief...

"Somebody might have said he wasn't so bad a year ago and maybe I'd have agreed with you, but we've got dead firefighters now. We've had six officers transfer out of here to get away from that idiot. I've seen him argue over a basketball game on TV and say because he's 'da' chief that's the way it is. That's just how he sees things. I read something once that said it perfectly. 'A man overconfident of a misperceived universe.' "

"But the fifth-floor, fourth-floor thing," said Fontana. "I'm not sure I understand."

"You heard him talk. Could you understand him?"

Throughout the conversation with Chief Freeze, Fontana had had difficulty comprehending his inner-city dialect, had been forced to stop after many of the chief's statements and run them through his mind again and again, and each time he hesitated or asked Freeze to repeat himself, the battalion chief had become irascible.

"When he works in another battalion he gets madder than a wet hen because they don't know how to handle him. Freeze thinks it's because he's black, but it's because nobody can understand a word he says. The only thing with Freeze is, you gotta remember he only thinks about himself. Freeze wouldn't back you up if your front tire was on his grandmother's foot.

"The way I look at it the job was getting to be too much fun, so they handicapped it for us with women and minorities. But I guess we're still doing all right. Every fire I ever went to is still out." He laughed loudly.

Fontana found O'Leary in the hallway near the back door. "You were there too."

Smiling timidly, O'Leary said, "Is that a question?"

"Not really. I have a list."

"I should have figured." O'Leary was taller than Fontana and, from the look of her shoulders, stronger, a good thirty pounds heavier. She moved with the clumsy, deliberate posture of a dedicated weight lifter. O'Leary escorted Fontana to the back door, unlocked it, and, after assuring herself they were alone, whispered, "Can I tell you something?"

"Sure."

For a split second, Fontana thought she was going to ask him for a date. The end of the hallway was saturated with the smell of bleach from the floors, mixed with a tincture of her wildflower perfume. "First off, I don't think Chief Freeze is half as bad as everybody says he is. Ryker? He's a good fire-fighter but he gets bullheaded about certain things. It took me a long time to convince him I could do the job. He pretends to know about Cooper personally, but he only worked with her once and I was there too. Nothing happened and he never spoke ill of her until after the Ratt. She got on this new lieu-tenants' list and she's the only woman on it, so he knows she's going to get a job. He's jealous."

"What about the fire?"

"I heard one thing. But I don't want Diane to get in trouble."

O'Leary had a mannish face, chestnut hair pinned up reck-lessly at the back of her head, and wavering, watery brown eyes. "I had to go back to the rig to pick another hundred feet of line. Ladder Three was parked across from our rig, and they were there, Ladder Three's crew, and I guess they had all just gotten fresh air bottles. I didn't see what they were doing but they must have been ready to take the fifty-five out and haul it around the back of the building." O'Leary began to weep quietly.

"I'm listening," Fontana said gently.

"Well, Diane said something to Youngblood. Diane Cooper?"

"Yeah."

"I don't know what she said, but Youngblood gave her this awful look and said, 'You're not with me, cunt. You're not going in with me.' "

At the word *cunt* O'Leary's voice had lost so much integrity Fontana almost missed it. "Are you sure that's what he said?"

"I've thought about it a lot. But, yes. That's what I heard. I was only about five feet away." Two single teardrops began to trickle down her cheeks at different speeds. "I've gone over and over it trying to figure out if I might have misheard, but I know I didn't.

"I've always wondered what was going on. I mean, an hour later they were dead. Buchanan and Youngblood, anyway. I came in with Buchanan. He was a deputy sheriff down in Oregon somewhere before he came here. I liked him a lot. And his wife is a sweetheart."

"You didn't hear the rest of the conversation?"

"I couldn't stop and listen without embarrassing the hell out of Diane. I mean, at the time, it was just something I overheard. I didn't know anybody was going to die."

Twelve

▲

FIREFIGHTERS
WITH BLUE EYES
AND BIG HOOTERS

Cooper lived two blocks from Green Lake on Woodlawn
Avenue North in a tiny snail-green house with the chipped-
at-the-edges look of a rental. The lawn had not been cut for
a couple of weeks and a power mower stood in the scruffy
grass where it had last seen duty, reminding Fontana of the
Fricks, who deserted their Toro in the grass every week, never
quite returning it to the same spot, so that it seemed to creep
around the cars in the yard on its own as the year went by.

Green Lake was in the middle of the city and had a path
around it almost three miles long, clogged by walkers, joggers,
skaters, bicyclists, cops on horseback, and, in the summer
months, swimmers, sunbathers, and the occasional pervert. It
was popular enough that many nearby residents found it useful
only as an object of complaint.

In front of Cooper's house was a van with the right front
corner bashed in and the windshield starred where somebody's
head had slammed against it.

Diane Cooper answered the door in a robe that had been
pulled on hastily over a bikini, though it was hardly warm

enough for any except the most devoted of sun worshipers. She squinted at Fontana distrustfully, yet without fear, the relaxed smile wrinkles trapping the tan around her chalk-blue eyes. Her brown hair was in a bunlike affair behind her head, a small tail dangling from it. She had a fresh white bandage on her forehead. When she saw who it was, she belted the robe and cinched it tightly.

"Can we talk?"

"Yeah, sure. Come on back. I was just going to catch some rays? I was more or less expecting you." She led Fontana through a cluttered living room, the windows shuttered, past a startlingly immaculate kitchen and out onto a teal-blue sun deck overlooking a postage-stamp backyard. On the way past the kitchen she had picked up a personal check for three thousand dollars and handed it to him. The grass in the neighboring yard had been recently clipped, and the air was thick with the moist odor of it.

"I hope that's enough for a down payment?"

"Fine."

Paying little attention to Fontana, she rearranged her aluminum-frame lawn chair on the deck so that it was facing away from him, leaving him with the option of sitting in a wire patio chair behind her, or squeezing against the house plants on the railing in front with the added risk of capsizing one of them into the backyard. He chose the wire chair behind.

When she lay down and closed her eyes against the mottled sunshine, pulling her robe up to her knees, his view was reduced to her feet, kneecaps, the top of her head, and two breasts under her robe swelling with each breath. Cooper had immediately wrested control of the interview from him, a neat gimmick done effortlessly. She had begged him to help her and now she was pretending the whole affair meant next to nothing. He thought he knew why too. The whole thing meant far too much to her for her to allow her true feelings to surface, the way a kid who thought she might get a bicycle for Christmas had to pretend it was no big deal—just in case she didn't get it. She spoke to the yard.

"You going to tape this? It doesn't matter. My name is Diane Judith Cooper? I've been in the department six years." Fontana knew it was five years and three months, but in the fire service experience served as a merit badge of adequacy, so people took every chance to inflate their numbers. "At the time of the Ratt fire on King Street I was assigned to Ladder Seven. A detail house? I'm sure you know what that means? I took a lot of details and a lot of them were up at Sixes. If I got a chance I worked on Ladder Three. I like truck work. I had worked with Clint before. Buchanan was somebody I met for the first time that shift. He came into the department after me. If this all seems too easy, it's because I've said it a few times. Like about a hundred?

"That night when the alarm came in we were making dinner. Enchiladas, Spanish rice, and salad? Sixes was out of quarters on an aid run. You could sort of tell we had something because of the response. Four engines, two trucks, two chiefs, an ERS unit, and a medic unit."

It was almost as if she were divulging the story from a hypnotic trance, her voice subdued and emotionless. "You don't know what it's like to spend the day with three guys and then see all three of them under tarps by midnight."

"I'm afraid I do."

She hadn't heard him and didn't want to. Submerged in her own reality, Cooper was unwilling to dilute her own pain with heartaches from somebody else's history. "The fire was a disorganized mess, especially for the first few minutes when Freeze was running it. Freeze is a screamer. There's no way a screamer runs a decent fire. We came out on the street after the bells were ringing on our first bottles and Freeze was hollering, so Bill yelled right back and you should have seen the chief simmer down."

"Bill?"

"Youngblood. William Youngblood? He was only a firefighter but he was the acting lieutenant that shift."

"And your bottles were half-hour bottles? So the bells would typically go off after about twenty or twenty-five minutes?"

"That's right. I wasn't familiar with the building, but Bill seemed to think there was an awful good chance people were trapped somewhere. The time of day? The amount of smoke? We parked across the street, masked up, and took axes, bars, and a chain saw to the front door. But by that time Engine Six had been driven out of the basement and the flames were shooting up the front of the building, right next to us, all across the front door, which was next to the basement. We went to the west side and around to the back. Had to climb over a cyclone fence.

"There was smoke everywhere. The back door was a big steel-covered thing and we could tell when we hit it with our axes we could be there all day. Finally, Bill had Vine go back to the truck for a baby ladder and we got in by breaking a window on the west side."

"So it took a while? Getting in?"

"Everything took a while at that fire. Yeah. Once we got in we unlocked the front door from the inside, but the back door we couldn't get open. We found out later they'd had a bunch of burglaries and had bolted it top and bottom with padlocks on the bolts. We opened the front door, though, from the inside, and that's how everybody else got in. Later, I heard people griping that Ladder Three hadn't gone in the front door, like we had wasted time going around to the back. Well, when we first were at the front door, it was bolted from the inside and there were flames in our faces. The only reason anybody got in that door is because we opened it from the inside.

"Chief Freeze kept the air channels jammed by talking constantly on the radio, so there was all that noise from Youngblood's portable radio. Even though it wasn't that smoky in there I kept thinking we were going to stumble over a body. That whole fire was the creepiest thing?

"We changed bottles and Chief Wallace gave us the assignment of going around to the back and putting up a fifty-five to the roof. Ladder One had their aerial ladder up there from the street in front. They always want two means of egress. By the time we got around back, things had changed and we were assigned to search the fourth floor. Somebody had word of people inside. We actually had a stairway in front of the building, but we never did know about it because you couldn't get to it from the first floor where we had been. The stairs had their own doorway on the street next to the main front door and nobody found it until later. Screwy?"

"Who told you to go to the fourth floor?"

For a moment she stopped breathing, something he could easily monitor from his vantage point. "Youngblood."

"How did Youngblood get the order?"

"I've had problems remembering things since the fire? I took a lot of carbon monoxide and it kind of beat me up. This is what I think happened. We came around with the ladder, got it upright with Youngblood standing back behind us with the tormentor poles helping to hold the ladder up, and that's when the chief told him. I was securing the halyard when he came around and told us."

"How did he say it?"

"What do you mean?"

"Did he sound worried? Excited? Youngblood."

"At a fire Bill never sounded worried. He said, 'We're gonna search the fourth floor. The chief says there's someone up there.' "

"Then what?"

"There were two corridors running north and south in the building, one to the left and one to the right, with rooms in between and off each side. Vine and I took the right. It was so smoky I held the back of his coat. That's the way you do sometimes. A flashlight in one hand and the back of a coat in the other? We moved slowly, spread our arms out, and made wide sweeps with our feet. I kept trying to stay oriented but it didn't take me a minute to lose it. The first floor was so easy and that one was so hard. We kept tripping. There was junk everywhere. I put my glove into a toilet that was just sitting there on the floor.

"Vine had the right-hand wall and I was to the left of him. We kept calling out in case somebody was there? We met Youngblood and Buchanan toward the front of the building. Then the warning bell on Vine's mask started ringing. That's how long the search took.

"With all that smoke it wasn't anyplace we needed to be hanging around with empty air bottles, so Youngblood sent me and Vine back to the ladder."

"That left Youngblood and Buchanan inside?"

"They were going to search until their air bottles gave out and then follow us. It seemed to be an area nobody used. All the junk? I thought the whole thing was a wild-goose chase from the minute we got inside. After we went back, Vine and I got to the fire escape, which was on the same back wall where we'd put the ladder up. Our warning bells were ringing, but we left our masks on. I mean, even outside the building on the fire escape you needed a mask. Then, after a while, we heard their bells inside."

"So, when the warning bell goes off, how much air is left?"

"Around six minutes. We could hear Youngblood and Buchanan close, so Vine and I started down the fire escape. We got about a floor and a half when there was this crash. For some reason we thought it was Buchanan. So we went back up. We couldn't hear Youngblood at all. But he was like that. Bill was. It didn't matter how badly he was hurting, he would never say anything. Vine called out, but the thing is, it was so smoky, and their masks were empty too. The bells weren't ringing anymore. So they had to have taken their face pieces off. They were eating smoke."

"How far away were they?"

"The reports say the fire escape was thirty-five feet away from the room where they found a bunch of water heaters tipped over, which is what we figured later that bang must have been, but Youngblood was found down the hall, almost sixty feet from the fire escape." The first strains of emotion began dancing in her voice.

"When did Vine go back in?"

"Real soon. We kept calling so they'd know which direction to take. Then Vine went in."

"Why didn't you go too?"

She answered curtly, her tone effectively diplomatic yet implicitly rude, a ticklish accomplishment Fontana felt was probably the result of rehearsal. "Two reasons. One? As long as I was calling out to them they had a signal to work back to. I went in with Clint, we could have both got turned around. We'd already taken more smoke at that fire than I'd taken anyplace in my career. Vine was in when they didn't even mask up at fires. He thought he could handle it better than me. Two? Vine told me to stay out. He was the senior man. Plus, on the fire escape, I was taking almost as much smoke as they were anyway."

"Then what?"

"I could still hear Buchanan. He was going deeper into the building. I kept shouting but I couldn't get him turned around."

"Did he answer?"

"Nope."

"What about the PASS devices?" Seattle firefighters wore small battery-operated sounders on their masks that would, when the firefighter ceased movement for twenty seconds, emit a high-decibel beeping to announce the wearer was in trouble. The devices had been introduced after the deaths of two lost firefighters several years earlier.

"I have a feeling Youngblood never activated his. He was like that. He thought they were useless. Buchanan was probably too far away for me to hear by the time he sat down."

"Where did Vine go? Did you hear his PASS device?"

"I don't remember hearing anybody's. Clinton went back inside and I asked him if he was okay but he never answered."

"You had no voice contact with him after he went back inside?"

"None." She hesitated, tightening the robe at her neck in the event Fontana was staring down her neckline.

"Then what?"

"I waited. I yelled for Buchanan and Vine. All three of them. But nobody answered. After a while I started getting really sick from the smoke? I called down to Chief Freeze to tell him we were in trouble, but I couldn't make him hear me. I could barely see the fire escape under my feet, so there was no way I could see if he was even there. Then I threw up. The next thing I knew I was in the medic unit and they were asking questions I couldn't answer. It was so weird. I spent the night in the hyperbaric chamber at Virginia Mason, and the next day, after I got out of the chamber, the doctor told me I came that close to dying of carbon-monoxide poisoning. They give you straight oxygen under pressure. But it screwed up my memory. The CO."

"How about before?"

"Before what?"

"Did you and Youngblood have a squabble? I have a source who heard you and Youngblood exchanging harsh words."

"At the Ratt?" She was trying to sound incredulous, not quite achieving it.

"This supposedly happened before you went around back."

"I don't know about that. I don't remember."

"Why team up with Vine? Why not Youngblood? Or Buchanan?"

Cooper stretched her feet, tucked the white terry-cloth robe between her knees, and separated her painted toenails in the sun. "Just the way it worked out."

"And earlier in the day? You didn't have a beef with Youngblood?"

"I didn't talk to him earlier in the day."

"Isn't that unusual?"

"You're trying to say Bill and I had a quarrel and that's why he's dead. The whole department already thinks I'm the reason they're gone. Like I wasn't sick as hell myself. I was calling for help. Nobody answered. Freeze was supposed to be below, but he never answered. And there were all those chain saws going on the roof making all that racket.

"Vine went inside and never said another word. He stepped into the elevator shaft. I saw it later. All they had across it was a single two-by-four at waist height. I don't know why he and I both didn't fall in the first time we went past. It was on *his* side, but he never said anything. He obviously didn't know it was there. Four floors and then into the basement? Jesus Christ."

"Youngblood had a radio. Did he call out for help?"

"Nobody ever said anything about it, if he did. Not even the guy from Twenty-eights who got the two women down. The hero?"

"Were you back there when Easterman went up and got the women?"

"I guess not. I didn't see him."

"The reports say he used the fire escape. If you were still there, he would have had to pass you."

"I didn't see him or feel anybody else's weight on the escape."

Reviewing what they had discussed, Fontana palmed his clean-shaven face. The naked feel made him wonder at how smooth it was after a year of wearing a beard. Before he left, Cooper volunteered one last piece of testimony.

"These days nobody trusts the department. A guy gets lost in a fire and nobody searches for him. The administration is so busy running around covering their butts, they don't have time to run the department. All the experienced fire chiefs have retired and they keep promoting dummies on the basis of allegiance to the present administration instead of fire-ground ability. My family's got orders to sue the department if I die on the job."

A phone in the house rang, and Cooper got up, went into the kitchen, and picked it up off the wall over the sink. She faced away from Fontana, who stood in the doorway to the deck, and he thought he heard her say, "Who is this?" Her entire body had tensed. "Who is this?" she repeated. She was shaking. She put the phone down on the counter and stepped away from it. Her jaw was shaking and she kept clamping her teeth down in an effort to stop it.

Fontana snatched up the receiver and heard someone say, "And that's just the beginning if you think you're going to hang around, bitch . . . "

"Who the hell is this?" Fontana barked into the receiver. The line went dead. "Who was that?"

"How do I know? People call me all the time."

"Like this?" She nodded. "People in the department?"

"I think so?"

"Is that your van outside?"

She nodded. "I drove it home from work the other day. Somebody had loosened the lug nuts on the front wheel. I thought something was wrong, but I didn't stop. Then the wheel came off and I hit a tree."

"Lucky you weren't killed."

"I would like to think it was vandals. Only it was somebody in the department."

"Any idea who?"

"Does it matter? They all want to see me dead. We had a guy a few years ago walking across a roof after a fire, only most of the roof had burned away in this one section. Because of the roofing, the way it had been put on, there was still some tar paper laying across some of the holes. They forgot to tell this one guy about it and he fell through. That's what he said on the phone just now. That the next time they had a hole in a roof, I was going through."

77

Fontana considered the man at the river, the man who had pointed the gun at him. "Do you know anybody who drives a red Mustang?" She gave him a look but shook her head. She continued to shake her head, still shivering. He wasn't sure if he believed her or not, though she had no reason to lie as far as he knew.

Thirteen

▲

INDIGO RETURNS

*F*ontana spent the rest of his midday visiting two fire-fighters at their homes. The first refused to talk to him about the Ratt fire and the second was only marginally helpful. Then he went to Station 14 to talk to the department's training officers, who acted secretive and not the least bit interested. The training division had been responsible for one of the published reports he had read, so they were only guarding their own work by balking. He was sitting outside Station 14 in his truck when Laura Sanderson drove up in a huge gray Pontiac with rust spots, a door wired shut, and sagging springs.

Laura stepped out of her car, blinked against the glint of unexpected sunshine, and said, "You shaved your beard. You look good without it."

"Thanks."

"They told me at Eighteens you might be here. I hope you don't think I'm following you around. I thought of somebody you should see. He wasn't at the fire. But I think you'll find him interesting."

"Today?"

"I know he'll be in the building until three."

They took separate vehicles. In the heart of downtown Seattle Laura Sanderson's Pontiac swerved into an underground
parking garage beneath a brick-walled skyscraper. It was cool
inside, and when he got out, Fontana put his jacket on and
left Satan in the truck with the window down.

Laura bustled over from where she had parked, adjusted
Fontana's tie with a proprietary air, smiled, and said, "I just
wanted to make sure you saw Zellner. I met him the second
day I was in Seattle. See, *Sensation Plus*—that's one of the
magazines I write for—keeps an office in this building for their
correspondents. There was nobody using it, so they said I could
have it.

"Bennie Zellner's the head janitor for the building. His fa-
ther-in-law owns it. Or, I guess these days you call them engineers. He's crazy as a hoot owl and a little scary, but I think
you'll find him interesting."

There was an easy familiarity in Laura Sanderson's manner.
When she hugged Fontana's arm against her side, the motion
gave away the heft and feel of her breast, and while he had
enough mileage on him to think the movement accidental, he
also had enough juvenile conceit to want it not to be.

Fourteen

▲

DUMBER THAN
A CAT SKELETON
IN A TREE

"**F**irefighting used to be for men," said Bennie Zellner, grinning the lip-twisting, glassy-eyed smile of a man on medication.

Two flights up from the parking garage in the Belasco Building, Fontana and Laura had stumbled upon four men in a hallway littered with MSA air masks. Zellner was soberly instructing the three others on MSA procedures while Laura and Mac stood back and listened, partially because Zellner did not realize they were there—though he had looked directly at them twice—and partially because the scene was so bizarre.

When Zellner glanced at Laura Sanderson a third time, his squinting eyes did a little jitterbug of recognition, not realizing his three protégés, all tall, thin young men with what looked to Fontana like the abused veneer of a reform-school uprising, had been aware of the pair's presence from the beginning. None had uttered a word, deferring to the huge man.

One unshaven lad with hazel eyes that would have been pretty on a woman stared at Laura with a toothy familiarity that galled Fontana in both its intensity and its cheek, then gave Fontana a dismissing look. It was strange how swiftly one person could alienate another. Laura returned the young man's smile and touched his arm fondly. She introduced Fontana to Benjamin Zellner, then to the young man who'd been eyeballing Fontana. His name was Lee Viteri. "I just thought you might give Chief Fontana some background on the department. You have a rather interesting slant on things, Bennie."

Zellner had the bulk of a man who might have played pro football in his younger days, forearms like Presto logs, with puffy cheeks and squinty slit eyes surrounded by swollen lids. His salt-and-pepper hair fussed about his head like a storm cloud. He was probably in his late forties, but he could have passed for twenty years older. Bad genes, Fontana surmised. Add to that a life in the fire service. Probably add to that a couple of ulcers and twenty-five years of sucking cigarettes.

"Now, why would Chief Fontana need background on the department?" Zellner asked.

"He's investigating the Ratt fire. Unofficially, I guess you would say."

"Again?"

"For Diane Cooper."

Zellner began a slow burn, fusing his eyes onto Fontana's. "I'm not feeding information to some bleeding-heart pansy-ass liberal candy-butt trying to get her off the hook. Or that moron Freeze. Get on out."

A stunned silence settled in the hallway like dust. Laura stepped close to Zellner and said, "Now, come on, Bennie. Don't be that way."

"How would you like me to be? That fool woman's incompetence killed three men. One of them was my brother."

"I'm sorry. I didn't realize one of them was your brother," Fontana said, wondering why Laura hadn't warned him.

"She should be in jail, but from what I hear, they're fixing to make her a lieutenant."

"It's much more complicated than that, Bennie, and you know it. Chief Fontana is going to try to make sense of the whole thing. Why not give him a chance? There are all kinds of facts that need to be brought to light. He just might be the one to do it."

After a few moments, Zellner laughed wryly. Under Laura's aegis, he began slowly to radiate a reluctant goodwill, though Fontana had a feeling he was one of those Dugans who ironically radiated goodwill around any woman.

They were in the basement of the building, two floors below the lobby, in a stark hallway lit by fluorescent lights and surrounded by painted concrete-block walls. In navy-colored jumpsuits, Zellner's ragtag cohorts were picking up the equipment and leaving.

"Sure," said Zellner, grinning at Laura and revealing crooked, stained teeth that resembled small tombstones. He wore a bushy mustache much darker than his salt-and-pepper hair. "Yeah, sure."

"Which one was your brother?" Fontana asked.

"Bill Youngblood. Stepbrother."

"The acting lieutenant off Ladder Three. I'm sorry."

The shoelace on Zellner's scuffed left shoe was tied in a granny knot. His shoes had been for dress at one time. So had his slacks, blowsy now with two belt loops broken and flapping. His dark shirt was tucked in and buttoned high enough on his neck to look uncomfortable. He moved in a quasi-stoop, like a man who'd broken his back a couple of times and didn't want it to happen again; yet, his motions imbued the deceptive power of a lumbering bear. Fontana guessed Zellner weighed around 260.

Laura paired up with Lee Viteri, who was wearing a rhinestone earring, walking him to the end of the corridor where they stopped, he whispering, she giggling, he giving her intense looks and as much chiseled chin as he could muster, a move he had most likely refined in front of a mirror.

"Twenty-two years I was with the Seattle," said Zellner. "Until the chief of the department—Harcourt Thurmond—asked me if I wouldn't mind resigning, said if I didn't he would fire my ass, and I said fire away, and I'll sue you for every cent you're worth, so that's what we did. He fired me. I sued.

"See, I was publishing this newsletter anonymously. Before I got canned. The first issue came out, I only had about two pages, and one of 'em was part of the operating instructions written in jive. Even brothers were laughing. But the Black Firefighters Union got on their high horse, asked for an investigation, and after I put a few more issues out, it got into the local newspapers. Right across the front page it said, 'Racism in Fire Department?'

"And after a while, after they figured out it was me, the Black Firefighters Union started asking for my head on a platter. So Thurmond fires me, and he's the biggest racist going. I get fired, and there's a ton of blacks in the department using drugs. They're in and I'm out. Was a huge cover-up on that."

"So what do you know about the Ratt fire?" said Fontana.

"I know any report the department wrote is pure-dee bullshit," said Zellner, stroking his chin and propping one elbow up with a cupped palm the way Jack Benny used to. "Bill was a smoke-eating sonofabitch from the old school. But how he died? I've been trying to figure that out for months. I even got friendly with Diane and tried to draw her out, but the bitch not only killed him, I'm convinced she can't remember how she did it."

Zellner glanced around the now-empty room and Fontana wondered if he'd missed something when Zellner changed the subject. "You think this is a little strange? Drilling civilians on MSAs? I'll tell you what we're in. We're in a forty-eight-story building. As the chief engineer in charge of maintenance for the building, if something happens here, do you think I'm going to trust the fire department? Give me a break, bud.

"It's only a matter of time before one of these high rises downtown gets a good fire in it and incinerates a couple of hundred people. Simple as pie. Every department in the country is like a kid with his finger in the dike and we all know it. No way in hell we should be letting them build these things. Every chief in the department knows it. They'll admit it to you privately. A big fire would call for more units than Seattle and this whole area could supply. That's right, if they had a good fire in this building, Seattle doesn't *own* enough firefighters to put it out."

"I was under the impression you knew something about the Ratt fire," said Fontana, but Zellner was already far downstream.

"This here Belasco Building is in the family, and I want to keep it that way. Ruthie's father owns it, see. Course, Ruthie and me's on the skids, but she'll see the light shortly. We been on the skids before. She always sees the light. I guess it's this old Irish charm. Gets her every time." Zellner gave Fontana a halfhearted smile and raked a quartet of stubby fingers through his tousled hair.

"The truth about the fire department?" Zellner grinned puckishly. "The politicians tell them they have to have so many of this group and so many of that. You know, there's a sister in the department who will not go into a fire? The politicians plain don't understand. If they were cats there'd be cat skeletons in trees. There's nothing dumber than a politician.

"We're talking about a recruit the city hired they had up in West Seattle who couldn't tell his officer how much water a two-and-a-half-gallon pump can holds. I kid you not. Now, who was the moron? That kid, or the city who hired him?"

Zellner escorted Fontana up to the B basement level and into a machine room that did double duty as an office. Zellner's cluttered desk was shoved up against one wall, along with turnout clothing, pike poles, fire axes, and a stash of MSAs in a specially built wooden rack.

During the next twenty minutes Zellner chaperoned Fontana through the building, explaining that he had to make a general inspection three times a day, that there had been threats against the building by an unnamed organization. They could talk as they walked. The Belasco management had decided they needed more security, so now even the engineers and janitors were carrying guns. Zellner had a .38 pistol on his belt.

Laura's borrowed office was on the sixteenth floor. Fontana recognized the name on the door, *Sensation Plus,* and as they walked past it in the hallway, he thought he heard Laura's voice from inside.

Zellner was inspecting every fifth floor, the hallways, stairwells, and extinguishers. Scouting for suspicious activity, opening locked rooms and stairwells with his master keys, peering into offices. Everyone in the building seemed to be on fraternal terms with him.

On the roof, Zellner said, "Forty-eight stories. Seattle's got only the laddering capability to rescue people from the eighth or ninth floors. Every trapped victim above that is a write-off unless they can get them down through the internal stairways. The chiefs talk about calling in army helicopters to snatch people off the roof, but Seattle's never even practiced with helicopters. Maybe they need some of those big air-cushion pillows to lay out in the street. But tell me who's going to jump thirty stories? I don't even think a fireman'd do it, and they're all crazier than bat shit."

"I fought in a high-rise fire years ago," said Fontana. "It's not something I'd care to tackle again."

"Hell. The job was dangerous enough without having to work with people you can't trust. I was in this one fire and they told us to get our asses out of there, they were going to send another crew in. So I says I'll be right there soon's I pick up this here couch over by the door, but before I can pick it up the couch jumps up and runs out. It was a firefighter, been hiding out over there in the corner the whole time, sitting on his nuts while we were working our fannies off. A *guy*. A white guy. That was all I could see, he ran out of there so fast, or I woulda busted him when we got outside. They let so many weak sisters in the department, they accidentally let a few pansies in with 'em."

"What do you know about Bill and Diane Cooper?" Fontana asked.

"Well...I know this. Up until a couple of weeks before the King Street fire they were living together in his house out by Haller Lake."

"Diane and Bill?"

"See, Bill and Cooper studied together. It was the first promotional Cooper ever took—she flunked that one, but she kept studying and took the next—and now it looks like she's going to make lieutenant. She's way down on the list somewhere. Sixty, I think.

"The fucking deal was, he got tenth on the test and they were planning to make something like twenty-two lieutenants."

"Lieutenant is the first rank after firefighter in Seattle. Then you've got captain, battalion chief, and...?"

"Deputy chief. Bill wasn't real good at scholastics, so he studied two hours a day, six days a week for the first year. Then, during the second year he didn't do anything but live and breathe those cocksucking fire-department books.

"They took nineteen firefighters and made them lieutenants.

They take number one off the list, then they take the first minority, even if he's thirtieth, then the first woman. Then they go back up to the top and take number two, the next minority, et cetera. One, one, and one, they call it." A similar system had been in place in Fontana's department in the East and Fontana knew how much resentment it caused among white male firefighters.

"You know, if they had ever gone straight down a list, Bill would have made it four or five different times, but, as it was, he kept missing it by a cunt hair.

"Fact is, the month Bill died, I about lost it. Yeah. They had me under observation at Harborview. I guess I got acting unusual. A guy'll do that on you, you give him enough rope. I was just . . . you never want to spend any time in those lockup rooms at Harborview.

"There's a cot and a steel door with this little window in it, and every once in a while you look up and you see a face in this little window. Yeah, once I looked up and saw Bill's face. A little later he sat on the end of the cot and we talked, even though I knew he was dead. Even now, I visit with Bill. Yeah, you think I'm gonzo? Not very often, mind you, but Bill will be sitting next to me when I'm driving. I know he's there but if I look he won't be. And Bill and I drive along like that for a spell. And then all of a sudden he's gone. I tell Bill what I'm doing, what I'm thinking, but Bill don't say much.

"I've said too much already. I'll be seeing you a little later, Mr. Fontana. Me and Bill will be seeing you."

Fifteen

▲

NOBODY SANG
"DANNY BOY"

*I*t was less than two miles to the Ratt Building where Fontana finagled almost an hour and a half, some of it alone and the rest in a gossipy tour conducted by the building manager, an old coot named Knudson. Wearing a dark green jacket zipped to his neck, Knudson kept a claw hammer dangling from a loop in his coveralls, and when he wasn't grousing about the weather he was vomiting out a string of disparaging remarks about the construction company engaged on the remodel, about "them dumbbells."

The Ratt was a five-story building that, when it had been all apartments, had probably housed more than a hundred tenants. The fourth floor, where Al Buchanan's and William Youngblood's bodies had been found, and from which Clinton Vine had tumbled into the basement, was still vacant, the original partitions remaining, so that it was possible to pace off the death rooms from each other as well as from the fire escape, which had been removed.

Outside a surprise hailstorm played a medley on the windowpanes and pelted three black children walking home from school, books stacked on their heads as makeshift umbrellas.

Knudson delighted in steering Fontana from one fatality site to another, and, though he had left town before the fire and had no firsthand knowledge of it, assigned blame to black drug addicts who he claimed frequented the neighborhood.

"Fer a while there, some of the officials thought it was a tenant we had stayin' on the second floor. Real bad ass. You suppose you kick some bad ass out of his rooms and two days later the place burns all to hell, you suppose the two events are unrelated?"

"Were they?"

"Inspectors said the one had nothing to do with the other. I guess he wasn't anywhere around the night of the fire."

"What was his name?"

"It wasn't anything. Not even related. Shaddock, I think."

"If someone commits arson and a firefighter subsequently dies in the fire, or even responding on the alarm, by law, the arsonist is guilty of murder. So this Shaddock guy might be guilty of three murders."

"Well, this guy was just plain nuts. Had my son-in-law Lester with me 'cause I thought there might be some adversity. Lester used to be in the military police and Lester can handle hisself. But this guy got his skinny little ass all in an uproar and kept saying, 'You wanta die? Come on, fat boy. Come on. You wanta die? Come on.' Claimed he was some sort of judo ace or somethin', except Lester told me later he thought he was a fraud. I'm too old for such nonsense. Used to be you never ran into people like that. Now, it seems you see 'em every day."

"Seems that way," said Fontana. "So the fire was accidental?"

"That's what I heard. But I think them black drug addicts started it." Both the reports Fontana had read confirmed an accidental ignition.

It was easy to see how the first arriving units might have become confused. On the front face of the building were four entrances—to the far right, the basement door; higher and to the left, a stoop and a set of doors that led into the first floor; to the left of that, another door which led into a stairwell that accessed all five floors but not the basement; and still farther left, another entrance to the first floor only. Knudson said he believed a few of the doors in the building had been nailed shut at the time of the fire.

"When three guys die saving your building, you got no gripes. That firefighting is a hell of a sport."

"Ain't it, though?"

On the fourth floor, eight unused water heaters had been standing in a small room. The prevailing theory that William Youngblood had found his way into the room where the heavy cylinders toppled and broke his lower leg seemed to make sense now. Youngblood was found in the second room to the south of the water-heater room, and, though he must have been in agony, no one had heard any sound from him. If a water heater had snapped his leg, he had crawled or been carried in precisely the wrong direction to reach the fifty-five-foot ladder. His radio, discovered later next to Buchanan, had not been used, though it was operational.

One ongoing theory being handed around was that Youngblood had been in so much pain, he'd become disoriented and coerced a younger, less experienced Al Buchanan to go wrong with him. Youngblood had crawled twenty-two feet from the water-heater storage room, Buchanan almost forty feet farther along in the wrong direction. Both were discovered in small, enclosed rooms, each out of air, raccoon masks of soot blotting their nostrils and mouths.

Buchanan had removed his backpack, helmet, gloves, and bunking coat and stacked them neatly beside himself, had hunkered on his knees and succumbed from smoke inhalation. The portable radio, which Youngblood had carried earlier, was found alongside Buchanan, switched off and on the wrong frequency.

On the fifth floor were offices and warehouse-type storage, desks, chairs, and several dozen cartons containing typewriters. Two of the offices were in use. One belonged to an architect, the second to a young free-lance artist. Knudson sniffed and said, "This floor ain't changed. Looked just like this." When Fontana looked outside, the hail in the streets had melted, leaving white scabs of sleet across the sidewalks. Downtown, a dull rainbow impaled itself on the Columbia Center Tower.

In the basement Knudson unlocked a storage locker and, with a flashlight from his coveralls, guided Fontana into a small concrete-walled room where three giant steel bumper springs were stationed in a triangle on the grubby concrete floor, each pointing up.

"Still see the stains where they found that there fireman," said Knudson. Fontana hadn't been primed for the reverence and awe he felt standing at the scene of the deaths, this one in particular. "Squashed himself there on that spring. Ran it clean through hisself."

Fontana remembered Creed and the others so many years before, and as he went over the events in his mind, he knew the firefighters who had removed Clinton Vine from the elevator pit had had their memories vandalized forever.

Outside now, next door on the east side, an old warehouse housed a spaghetti-manufacturing company, its nearest wall twelve feet from the Ratt. Across the alley in back, on the north side, stood a two-story brick structure, part of a sprawling church. Fontana paced off the distance from the Ratt to the church. Twenty-three feet. There were wires overhead. If they'd put up a fifty-five-foot ladder back here in the smoke, they had either been lucky or very skillful.

On the way home he spotted the red Mustang in his rearview mirror. This time the Mustang stayed far enough back that he could barely see the driver. On Mercer Island, Fontana got off the freeway and parked. The Mustang parked half a block back and waited. After five minutes, the Mustang took off. Fontana didn't see it again.

Sixteen

▲

KLATOO BARADA NICKTOO

*M*ost of the cloud cover had lifted by the time Fontana and Brendan walked down behind their house to the river to exercise Satan in the damp sand and gravel, Brendan learning to skip rocks, Mac coaching lackadaisically from the bank. Stoked by the heavy rains, the milky Snoqualmie Middle Fork had surged in the past twenty-four hours. On the other side of the river, Mount Gadd had a penchant for sucking in clouds, and at certain times of the year there was an almost incessant drizzle in the area.

Sitting alongside Mary's ninety-two-year-old mother, Brendan had spent the afternoon beguiled by a black-and-white Alan Ladd movie, *Two Years Before the Mast,* and from time to time he would shout an observation about the film up to Mac.

Behind them in his driveway, Mac heard tires on gravel, a heavy car door slamming. A few minutes later Laura plunked herself down next to Mac, causing Brendan to roll his eyes at his father.

"You were supposed to come and get me after you were

done with Zellner." He shrugged. "Did you think he was crazy?"

"Is that why you wanted me to see him? Because he's crazy?"

"I'm not sure if he is."

"He's disturbed, is what he is."

It didn't take long for him to realize she hadn't come to talk shop. Her blouse was two buttons looser than when he'd seen her earlier, reminding him of a maxim his late wife was fond of: For every button a woman undoes, a man undoes ten points of IQ. Laura's movements were seductively languid, her laughter cloying, her body perfumed, her breath minty, and she bestowed worshipful consideration to everything he said, without forgetting to send occasional looks of adoration in Brendan's direction when she thought Fontana would notice. She had unlocked the arsenal, and he wondered if budgeting love into his life was ever going to be as simple as cashing in on sex. Not that he did much of the latter.

Laura explained that she had scheduled an interview on the other side of the Cascade mountains in Ellensburg, but that, after proceeding a third of the way to her destination, she had phoned from Staircase and was disheartened to learn from the wife of her subject that he had gone bowhunting for two days. Thus, on a whim, she had decided to drop by.

Some whim.

She had taken the time along the way to apply a rather startling shade of orangish eye shadow that was such a harsh contrast with her nearly maroon hair, Fontana had a hard time looking at her indigo eyes. She wore six rings—one on each thumb, three silver hoops in one ear, and one in the other. He was curious at how young she seemed. When he'd met her yesterday she was in her business pose, except for the shorts, but this palette was probably closer to the true Laura.

"You like Mexican food?" he asked.

"Love it."

She was amazed on the short drive to the Mexican restaurant when Brendan knew the words to "Wake Up Little Susie" and then again when she mentioned that Zellner was something of a UFO connoisseur and Fontana jokingly asked the boy if he still remembered the words that would save the world. *"Gort! Klatoo barada nicktoo,"* Brendan had returned, eyes big, asking Laura if she had ever seen *The Day the Earth Stood Still,* but she had never heard of the 1951 film.

They munched corn chips and ordered dinner, Laura a taco salad, Fontana a chimichanga, Brendan requesting *"Número uno, por favor."* He then turned to Laura, grinned, and said, "That's Spanish."

Laura gave Fontana a preoccupied look. "Are you hearing all the woman-bashing I'm hearing in the department?"

"These deaths are widely thought to be caused by Cooper."

"I think it's interesting the way men in the Seattle department are always saying these women are going to get themselves killed, yet three guys died and the woman survived."

"Yeah, well, I wouldn't crow about it until we know how it happened."

"You don't think women can do the job, do you?"

"Some women can. Obviously not all. I heard a physiologist lecture on it once and he said that of a hundred girl babies and a hundred male babies, around seventy of the male babies would grow up to eventually be capable of becoming firefighters. Of a hundred girls, only about eight would ever be capable. Maybe Seattle's finding the eight percent."

"There are a couple of things you might like to know, Mac. Rumors are sweeping the department that Cooper was lost on the fire floor and the others got killed looking for her. There's another one that Vine went for help, and that Cooper accidentally pushed him into the elevator shaft. One version has it she started to fall into the shaft and Vine saved her and lost his life doing it. Not only that, but there's this weird story going around that Cooper and Youngblood slept together."

"Yeah, well, according to Zellner, they were living together until shortly before the fire."

"That stinker, Bennie. I asked him and he told me he didn't keep track of his brother's love life."

After supper they drove to Snoqualmie Falls and watched the klieg lights play on the waterfall in the basin while a gaggle of tourists posed for pictures in the mist.

At home they invited Laura in, where she immediately began a slow tour around any room she was introduced to. Snooping or nerves, it was hard to tell. Brendan invited her to play a video game, Mario Brothers 3, and then looked up with his big, gray eyes at Fontana to see whether it was all right. Fontana smiled and nodded, knowing full well Laura had no interest in video games, though she enthusiastically lay on the floor on her stomach next to Brendan as he fired up the video monitor.

Later, Laura seemed more than willing to help put Brendan to bed. Afterward, she drank Fontana in with her fake indigo eyes and moved close with a seemingly inept klutziness that imbued its own deceptive grace. In the living room, away from the light, she fell into his arms and he kissed her. When she melted against him, he felt the heat of her breasts and her flat stomach against him. Without his beard, kissing a woman gave him a queer sense of vulnerability.

She breathed hotly into his ear and said, "I thought you'd never get around to that."

Fontana didn't have a reply. Two days? He'd known her two days. She took his hand and tugged him toward the master bedroom. "Not tonight," he said.

"The boy won't hear," she whispered. "I can be quiet." She stared at him for a moment, standing so close he couldn't focus on her, though her young eyes could easily focus on him. "What's wrong?"

"Nothing is wrong. I just don't think this is what we should be doing. My boy's in the other room and I just don't think this is what we should be doing."

Five minutes later, when Laura climbed into her Pontiac, she revved the motor and peered through the windshield at the dark house before pulling out from under the trees, wipers beating furiously at the drizzle. Her bald rear tires rocketed particles of gravel into the bushes on the way out of the driveway. He could still feel the heat of her against his chest. It took only a minute standing alone in the window to begin to regret sending her away.

Seventeen

▲

A SQUAT, FROG-EYED WOMAN

*T*he three of them were sitting in a kitchen alcove in a small bungalow off Meeker Street in Kent. So far the man had said nothing, sat listening to his wife make excuses, even though he had called the station in Staircase and left a message that he wanted to see Fontana. "It ain't easy for him to talk about this," said the old woman. "For months he wouldn't say a word. It's only been since he heard the rumors he's perked up a bit."

She was a barrel-chested, squat, frog-eyed woman who maybe combed her hair once every two or three days, and then with her fingers, which were so blunt her thumbs looked like big toes. Her clothing consisted of formless polyester pants and a man's Hawaiian shirt. Her feet were swollen, and she'd scissored the laces out of her shoes to allow for the angry bloat. A cup of steaming coffee sat in the cradle of her meaty fingers.

She was William Youngblood's mother, and by the look of her, she had been in her forties when she gave birth to him. Upon his death last March, Youngblood had been thirty-eight.

This was the person from whom William Youngblood had inherited gentleness, this woman who looked and sounded as if she'd worked half a century in a foundry. Shortly after he arrived, she referred to one of her neighbors as a "polecat motherfucker" but had been policing her speech since.

William Youngblood, Sr., sat across from Fontana, detached and grim, his tanned face pleated with wrinkles, his bearing stolid, unyielding. In seven minutes he had yet to utter a word. These people were as morose as two played-out bugs in a vat of turpentine.

Blistered by decades of cigarettes and arguments, Myrtle Youngblood's voice was an octave lower than Fontana's. "He heard you was investigating this fire, Chief Fontana. He appreciates your getting out here first thing. I appreciate it, and I know Bill here appreciates it."

Fontana and the old woman turned to the old man, who coughed and finally acted as if he might speak, clearing his throat three times first. "Worked thirty-two years in the department," said William senior. "Got my two sons in, Ben and Bill junior, and I thought I'd left me something to be remembered by. I fought up the ranks. Battled past that old sonofabitch Fitzgerald and made chief, and before I retired I was running the third battalion like it ain't been run since. Yeah, I worked my way up to fire marshal, investigated the fire that killed my own son, and retired the day we sent the report in. Hell of a deal."

"Yes, sir, I'll bet it was," said Fontana.

"The department tore him up," said his wife. "The longer Bill junior was in, the worse his attitude got. That last month he wasn't even the same boy. This man's fire department tore up all my men, one way or t'other."

"Maybe he came to his senses, Mother." Youngblood senior fixed Fontana with his obsidian-black eyes. Fontana had once arrested an arsonist who'd stared at him with the same unwavering and unnerving lack of expression. "Department's gone to hell. You got guys bringing their bunkers to work in stolen shopping carts. You got brassieres hanging from the flag poles. You got *Jet* magazine in the commode. You can bet Fitzgerald's rolling over in his grave."

"Women in the department," said his wife, nodding and hammering her blunt fingertips together. He was the melody and she the refrain.

"Why, do you know a good many of those females they got pretendin' to be firemen are lesbians?"

"Well, that's not what I'm here to talk about. The way I understand it," said Fontana, "the fire marshal in Seattle is in charge of the fire-investigation unit?"

"When the Ratt happened, I supervised the whole shebang. Got copies of most of the file right here," said ex-chief Youngblood, nodding at several manila file folders lying on the table.

"I understood you decided the fire was accidental?"

"You know as well as I do a body can make a fire appear accidental. But to the best of our knowledge it was an accident. No motive. No suspect. The owners lost on their insurance. We figured it was started with a space heater placed too close to a stack of newspapers. Nobody ever owned up to leaving the heater there or to turning it on. That's what kept us poking around as long as we did. There was some work bein' done on the room down in the basement, and it cooked down there probably an hour before anybody discovered it."

"Did you participate in the other investigation at all? The one trying to figure out what happened up on the fourth floor?"

"I knew what happened up there."

"And what was that?"

The old chief lit an unfiltered Camel, watching the smoke curl in front of his face and letting the paper match burn to his fingertips before casually dropping it. "Another of them lesbians let us down, that's what."

Fontana glanced at Mrs. Youngblood, who looked uncomfortable. It was a good guess that neither of them realized their son had lived with Diane Cooper. "Did you know Diane?"

"Who?"

"Cooper. The woman who was working on Ladder Three that day?"

"Don't recollect I did," said Youngblood senior. "Hell, during my career I can think of nine different times I had to be carried out of fire buildings. Tell me how many of these people could carry me out of a fire today. Some of them couldn't carry a bag of shit out of a nunnery. Hell, they don't know what fire is. We went in without masks. We ate smoke and we laughed about it."

"Yes, sir," said Fontana. "Things have changed. Some for the worse. Some for the good. On the phone you mentioned some evidence in your possession."

"The book," said Bill senior.

As obedient as a servant, his wife pushed herself up off the table and left the room in a tottering shamble.

"Naw, the bastards ain't done nothin' good for the fire service since I left. Thurmond, the chief of the department, is pretty much of a drunk. The reason we called you was 'cause he had one of his people phone me up the other day and tell me not to cooperate. That's when I got on the phone to you. My son dies, and he tells me not to cooperate?"

His wife shuffled back into the room and placed a stack of bound palm-sized notebooks in front of Fontana, then coughed hoarsely for almost as long as she'd been gone. "Got entries by the day," she choked out. "Right up to the twenty-third."

"It's Bill junior's diaries," said the old man. "His brother brought them over with his things after he sold the house. I ain't looked, but Ma has. Anyways, we thought if they ever got anybody to investigatin' who was serious, why, we'd want them to have a gander. We're going to get them published, you understand, as a literary property."

"I'll take good care of them."

"You know how he made chief, don't you? Harcourt Thurmond? Chief of the department? This affirmative-action bull started comin' down the pike and our union challenged it in court. When all the challenges run out, suddenly Harcourt was one-eighth Cuban. Thurmond is about as anti-black, anti-Indian, and anti-Mex as you can find anywhere. You name it, he's against it. But he declared himself one-eighth Cuban, which I guess he was, got it certified, and made battalion chief. Skipped a lot of people on that list, including me. Then there's that asshole, Rudy Freeze, another affirmative-action wonder."

"Your son was working directly under Chief Freeze at the King Street fire, wasn't he?"

"That's what they say. If you've met Freeze, you know he's a twit."

"What sort of relationship did you have with him?"

"When he's a firefighter you couldn't get him to do no housework around the station. At a fire he was always tangled up in something, tarps, hoses, whatever. We got him up in front of the Civil Service commission twice, but he squirmed out of it. Reminds me. You know what you call an attorney with an IQ lower than sixty?"

"I wouldn't know."

"Your honor." The old man laughed so hard he had a brief coughing fit.

"One thing you should know about Bill junior," said Mrs. Youngblood, taking up some slack in the conversation while her husband fired up another Camel. "You listen to Pa here and you'd think you knew how Bill junior felt. But Pa and Bill junior weren't alike at all. Bill junior always wanted to give everyone the benefit of the doubt."

"When I signed up, the city couldn't get anybody to take the job. It was dirty and unglamorous, and the pay was nothing. And people died doin' it. That's why we got the pensions we did. A pension was the only way they could induce anybody to take the work.

"I'd work a day shift, come home, eat dinner, and drive down to the Flying A and pump gas another four hours. Night shifts, I'd get off at eight in the morning, wouldn't even come home, I'd just report over to Isaacson Steel, get off in time to clean up, grab a shower and a bite to eat, and back to the firehouse. In those days, you had to work to put bread and butter on the table. Now, the last few years the pay got better, the hours too, and suddenly everybody and his little sister wants to be a fireman.

"Bill junior was a damned fine worker. And then he got into this horse shit and it killed him. I gotta hand it to Bill, though. For fifteen years he stuck in there and took the tests and bit his tongue and was a man about it."

"What are you talking about that killed him?" Fontana asked.

"Affirmative action killed him."

"Yes," said Myrtle Youngblood, tears scumming her eyes. "It hurt so to watch. His dad had a standing offer that anytime Bill made lieutenant, why, he'd give him a pair of season tickets to the Seahawks, and then, don't you know, they could go together. You know. Father and son. And Bill junior was always joking Pa better get his checkbook ready, because he was studying and he was going to make the next list."

"Sir, you say Chief Thurmond's office told you not to speak to me?"

"That was behind your back. In front of your back, he'll cooperate, or pretend to. He don't like nobody messing with his department. But, then again, Thurmond likes a good fight. It doesn't matter whether he's right, because he always thinks he's right. Thurmond's a man reaching out to shake your hand with a tack in his palm."

Ex-chief Youngblood knitted his hands together—one piece was missing off his little finger—puffed on his cigarette, and said, "Bill even thought there was a place for women in the fire service. That's how he thought. He liked all them lesbians."

"Bill liked people," said Mrs. Youngblood. "Everybody. He wasn't an old fud-a-dud like you."

"Chief Youngblood, I visited the Ratt yesterday and somebody mentioned that a tenant had been thrown out two days before the fire. Do you know anything about that?"

The old man began thumbing through one of the file folders in front of himself, pulled out several sheets of paper and held them at arm's length, then slipped a pair of reading glasses out of his shirt pocket and tried again. "Shaddock was the guy's name. Some sort of nut case. If he'd been around, we might have tried to fit a case around him, but he was in Tacoma getting rousted by the TPD. Had an ex-girlfriend down there he spent a lot of time scaring. Went into her place of work just about the time the Ratt fire was started and, in full view of eight or ten other women, pulled out his pud and dropped it smack into her empty coffee cup, then proceeded to fill it on up. He was a fruitcake, but he didn't start the Ratt."

"And you never found out who left that space heater next to the newspapers?"

"If this one was arson, they did a job. We thought it might have been the caretaker, a man named Knudson, but he wouldn't cop to a thing. We wanted to put him through a lie detector, but he got a lawyer and there was nothing we could do. Whatever, it was probably accidental. There was just no motive. We heard Knudson's been going around telling people it was some druggies did it with matches and gasoline."

"Was there anything else your investigation picked up? Maybe somebody with a grudge against the owner of the building?"

"I'll let you read through all these reports, you want. Can't take any of them with you, but you can paw through 'em. But there was one thing. There was a church next door. Behind the place, actually."

"I saw it yesterday. Big place."

"One of the biggest churches around. Somebody broke into it the night of the Ratt. Didn't take anything, just kicked in a door, and sat around in the pastor's office for a few hours, judging by all the pop cans and stuff laying around the next morning. We went in and took a look."

"What'd you decide?"

"Just some bum off the street looking for a warm place to watch the fire."

Fontana spent thirty minutes reviewing the fire investigation of the Ratt, then looked up from the table at Mr. and Mrs. Youngblood, who had sat silently throughout. "Thank you for your hospitality. You've been more than kind."

"No kindness to it," said the ex-chief. "If you can shed some light on what happened to my boy, why, it'll be worth it." They escorted him to the front door, and when they got there Fontana could see the tip of a purplish scar on the old man's chest. Open-heart, probably.

"How is Bennie doing?" Fontana asked at the front door. "I spoke to him the other day."

"He's my son by my first marriage," said Mrs. Youngblood. "I was married to Maury Zellner for two years before I met Bill. Maury was a ship's captain, but he was never around. Died at sea falling down a hole on shipboard. Six months later, I met Pa here, and it was love at first sight, wasn't it, Pa?"

"Bennie didn't do anything but say out loud what most everybody was thinking." The old chief shook his head and looked down at his polished work boots. "Insubordination, they called it. Told him to stop putting out that paper. Bennie always did have trouble keeping his mouth shut. It wasn't easy for him, losing that job and then losing his brother."

"Bennie takes after his natural father," said Mrs. Young-blood.

"You know," said ex-chief Youngblood, "Bill junior would have made lieutenant if he just kept at it."

"No, Pa. Bill was played out. You know that."

On the wall by the door were pictures of Zellner and Bill junior in uniform. Bill Youngblood was a handsome, blue-eyed young man with a dimple in his chin. There was also a black-and-white photo of Youngblood senior next to an old fire engine, a boy of about five sitting delightedly behind the wheel in the high rig. "Bill junior," said Myrtle Youngblood. Fontana looked at the little boy in the fire engine for a long time.

After Fontana walked out to the truck he turned around and surveyed the Youngblood house, which was in a commercial area in Kent that had once consisted of blocks and blocks of one-story frame homes. Theirs was one of the few holdouts that hadn't been flattened into a parking lot. Across the street was a K mart. A Kentucky Fried Chicken. A nationally franchised tire store. Two doors down was a bank. Their tidy lawn was green, their roses in bloom, but a blanket of auto exhaust had turned all the colors into grimy pastels.

Parking outside a pay phone down the street, Fontana called Pat Easterman in West Seattle.

"Pat? MacKinley Fontana here. I'm doing some interviews about the fire last March. You think there'd be a time you and I could get together."

"I'm busy."

"How about later in the week?"

"Busy then too." He hung up.

Next he called Seattle Fire Department headquarters and received permission to view all the videotapes they had stock-piled of the Ratt fire. He was mildly surprised and pleased that they weren't being more guarded.

Fontana sat in the truck and idly thumbed through William Youngblood's journals, pages and pages of cramped writing in ballpoint, all very neat. Bill Youngblood had been explicit, right down to the sound effects in one detailed account of love-making with someone named Carol Landrau. Clearly, the diary had not been written with a mind to publish, nor a mind for his mother to pore over it. Fontana canvassed the dates. March 23 was the last entry, the day Youngblood, Buchanan, and Clinton Vine gave up their lives in the bowels of the Ratt Building.

Eighteen

▲

THOSE AFRAID OF SMOKE, RAISE YOUR HAND

*T*he largest firehouse in West Seattle, Station 32 was home to a three-man engine company and a ladder truck as well as a medic unit. The ten members at Station 32 had been known to answer the third rail, "West Seattle Boy's Club."

Fontana parked on Thirty-Eighth Avenue S.W. in front of the station and walked into the empty watch office, where the ubiquitous portable television sat on a desk, the volume too loud. Moments later a firefighter in his dark blue uniform swaggered into the room, pushing a mop bucket on squeaky wheels.

"Yeah, man. Can I help you?"

"I understand Al Buchanan worked here. This shift?"

"Sure, man."

"I'd like to talk to a few people about him."

"About what?"

"The Ratt. His firefighting experience. Anything that comes to mind."

"And who are you?"

"Name's Mac Fontana. I'm the chief out in Staircase. Con-

105

ducting an independent investigation of the Ratt fire. I would appreciate your cooperation."

"I don't understand. Independent. What do you mean?"

"Diane Cooper has hired me to look into it."

"Sorry, man. No can do."

"It wouldn't take more than a few minutes. Anything you say would be confidential."

"No way."

"Think about it for a second. If you had died at the Ratt, would you want Buchanan to talk to me?"

"You think about this. I'm too nervous to steal and too lazy to work. This is my job. I'm not going to jeopardize it talking to you."

Only one man in the station felt free enough to relax with Fontana, behind a closed door in his office. Lieutenant Dimakis summarized what the others had thought of Buchanan. He said three of the firefighters at Station 32, including the one who'd liked Al best—they had been restoring an antique fire pumper together—thought Buchanan had probably been a marginal firefighter, partly because of his inexperience and partly because of his ingrained cockiness. He said they all believed it was hard to know because they got so few fires out of Station 32.

Dimakis went on to say that one man had criticized Buchanan for being in poor physical condition. Though he disapproved of it, Fontana knew plenty of firefighters who were not particularly fit. In fact, the sorry statistic was that, nationally, 25 percent of all firefighters were considered physically unfit to handle the job.

Al Buchanan was reputed to have been a know-it-all, as well as someone who took correction badly if he took it at all, qualities easily attributable to the fact that he'd been a deputy sheriff in Oregon and believed himself streetwise.

On the plus side, he was said to have been funny and garrulous and handled aid alarms like a pro.

His death was generally attributed to inexperience. These men had convinced themselves that because they had more time in the department, they were exempt from his fate.

They were ensconced in the lieutenant's office when Dimakis gave his personal views of Al Buchanan. Dimakis carried a belly that would have sounded off like a melon had someone thumped it with a finger, yet on the back of his locker door he'd taped a photo of himself in a sleeveless T-shirt paddling a kayak in what must have been a trial or a race. Dimakis wore his hair very short, had buttery black eyes, thick lips, and a cold smile that might have worked better on a man selling a litter of puppies he knew had distemper.

"Everybody by now knows the story. Ladder Three's crew was up there looking for Cooper. Somebody heard them talking. She got lost up there in the smoke and they stayed too long looking for her. Then she wandered out and they were dead."

"That's one theory."

"No theory. Fact."

"Buchanan was on your crew?"

"I taught him in drill school, so I know a couple of things I never told anyone around here until after he died. Probably something you should hear. Except it's not relevant."

"Oh?"

Strangely, Dimakis spoke in a meek and extraordinarily soft voice. "Al was scared of smoke."

"Pardon me?"

"This is hard for me to say, you know, because it makes the department look bad. And I love this department. But there's only one way to be scared of smoke. See, me and the chief of Training don't get along so hot, so he dumped Buchanan on me. I was down there working at Training when he came in. I had him maybe a month and a half, Buchanan, and then I wrecked my knee ice-skating and was out five months. When I came back, my battalion chief was retired and Buchanan had already passed his tests."

"What do you mean, he was scared of smoke?"

"Well, specifically, there were two Fridays in drill school when they had to go into the smoke room without a mask. Al came to me and begged me to get him out of it. I told him it wouldn't hurt him. He'd been a volunteer in Oregon and claimed he could do anything in a mask, but smoke made him toss his cookies. I was planning to watch him extra careful when we got in the smoke room, but I didn't have to. He kept a death grip on my arm the whole time. I wasn't writing evaluations on him that week, but I told the officer who was."

"What happened?"

"He didn't see fit to mention it. Justifying something he hadn't seen was going to be sticky. And if he mentioned me in his report, it was going to sound like we were conspiring against Al. There's a rule in drill school that the instructors don't talk about the recruits amongst each other. We're supposed to come up with independent evaluations. It's a rule that's helped more than one weak sister slip on through.

"I told him, 'Al,' I said, 'if you can't get around in a fire building without a mask for a few minutes, you're going to be in deep feces when you get out to the company. Maybe if smoke gives you this much concern, maybe you better give up the idea of being a firefighter.' But somehow he made the allotted time in the smoke room. Both weeks."

"You didn't tell anyone here in the company about him?"

"No. I was thinking he might have gotten better. If so, it wasn't fair of me to be holding it against him for the rest of his career. Whatever happened at the Ratt fire, I just hope Al didn't run out of air."

"Why?"

"I knew he had a problem and I let him slip on through. It might even be my fault all three of them are gone."

After he had finished with Lieutenant Dimakis, Fontana squeezed into the small phone booth in the watch office and dialed two numbers he'd looked up last night. No answer at the first. The second was picked up on the eighth ring. She must have been the older of the two women, because she sounded ancient, her voice as quavery as a reed in the wind.

"Mrs. Fitch?"

"Ye-e-e-e-s?"

"I'm investigating the Ratt fire on King Street from last March? Mac Fontana."

After a long pause, she said, "Why did you wait so long?"

"I was just approached to do this a week ago, Mrs. Fitch. I'm trying to get to everybody as quickly as possible. Any cooperation you could extend would be appreciated."

"Yes, I suppose. Everybody went home early except Anita and I. We were both coughing our fool heads off. Don't know why it took us so long to smell the smoke. Maybe because we were in that back room. Photocopying. We'd been working on a rush order all afternoon.

"We thought we were going to die, then this big firefighter just appeared in front of us. Yellow helmet. Heavy green gloves. Just like that. Said, 'Calm down. We'll get you down. It's no problem.' On that rickety old rusty fire escape. I sprained my ankle and Anita hurt her knee. Even the firefighter fell getting off. They kept us in the hospital all night and most of the next day. Said we had smoke inhalation, but it just felt like a heavy flu or something. For weeks I was tuckered.

"The fireman kept telling me to let go. Let go! Can you imagine? What on earth did he expect me to do if I let go? Flap my arms and fly? He said I was freezing on the rungs. Poking me in the ribs. I was all bruised up. 'I'm making you move for your own good,' he kept saying. And the papers and TV folks made him out such a hero. He was a snot-nosed hooligan." Fontana was beginning to think the same thing of Easterman.

"Mrs. Fitch, did you see anything on any of the other landings while you were coming down?"

"I didn't see anything. When they took my clothes off, why, I was just black and blue all over. I'll never forget. That fireman said, 'Get your fat behind on this ladder or I'll put it on.' Only he didn't say 'behind.' I understand it's their job, but when they're saving lives they should try not to be rude about it."

"When you got down to the alley, what did you see?"

"I don't honestly remember much of anything."

"Just the one firefighter? No chief?"

"Just the one."

"Thanks, Mrs. Fitch."

"Don't mention it."

Fontana made three more calls, but nobody was home. When he got out of the phone booth Laura Sanderson was talking to Lieutenant Dimakis. He was beginning to think meeting her was like stepping on a sheet of flypaper.

Nineteen

▲

INDIGO EYES, PALE SMOKE

Across the room, one leg tucked up as she leaned against the edge of the TV table, Laura Sanderson was deep in conversation with Lieutenant Dimakis and a tough-looking woman in a fire-department uniform wearing a small pack on her belt that held a tiny medical flashlight and a pair of bent-handle scissors in a scabbard. For an instant, Laura caught his eye, feigning surprise, though she could hardly have missed his 1960 GMC out front with the twenty-seven bullet holes lovingly patched with Bondo and touch-up paint.

Fontana let himself out the front door, but before he could close it, Laura, bare arms snaked around tape recorders, note-books, cameras, and the battered beige valise she carried every-where, had followed him outside. Dark gray clouds scudded under a skyline bedded with a high, pale overcast that had threatened rain all morning, teased to the north by a patch of sunlight.

She smiled, more chagrin than satisfaction, and said, ''I just dropped in to call a cab. Dropped my car off up the street. They're supposed to be good. Had to get a jump this morning, and it's not the battery. You busy finding out about dead people?" He noted that a Southern drawl had once again wormed into her conversation.

"Busy enough. Are you following me?"

"Of course not. You want me to?"

He would think about that later. "Get home all right last night?"

"Sure. Fine," she said in a tone that implied she had not.

"Where're you headed?"

"Just up near Seattle Central. I'm house-sitting an apartment. It's okay. I can deduct the cab fare off my taxes. Besides, a lot of these cabbies are going to make great characters in a novel someday."

"Nonsense. I'll give you a ride." The odds of his not offering a lift to a woman who had wanted to sleep with him the night before were slim, and she knew it. Her apartment was on Capitol Hill, a unique neighborhood famous for its bookstores, restaurants, trendy theaters, and an occasional queer-bashing. On Broadway, they stopped at an eatery called Eggs Cetera, and, as they talked, Laura seemed to have completely forgotten last night, her amnesia spurred by some lucky faculty of youth rather than diffidence, or so he believed.

After they'd assumed a window seat, watching the clusters of street people outside in the light rain that had started up, Laura said, "When we first met, you said you had a lousy summer. I just now this morning read more of your clippings. When we spotted you out there fishing it was hard to imagine your life being thrilling, but you killed a man a month ago."

"Not for the thrill."

"I didn't mean that."

"When I want a thrill I park in a 'load only' zone."

"How many people have you killed? I mean, it seems like an unorthodox thing to ask, but I'm curious."

He touched his teeth with his tongue. "Lifetime figures?"

"Sure. Yeah, sure."

He shrugged, watching the tension build in her features. "Seven hundred. Maybe seven-fifty."

She began to giggle in a sort of generic hysteria before slowly sobering. "I'm sorry, I guess I was..."

"Soup and salad, Laura? If we can forget the history, my day'll go a lot smoother. How about it?"

"Sure." He refused to dress the wound with an apology, and her face remained a blotchy pink throughout the meal.

They discussed Laura's book, Fontana's investigation, being a free-lance writer, travel, which Fontana liked but didn't do enough of, and which Laura abhorred but did all too much of. Afterward, Fontana drove Laura to her brick apartment building on E. Republican, hers a first-floor unit.

"Want to see my digs?" she said.

He glanced at his watch and saw that he had more than an hour and a half to kill before his appointment at Tens. "I'll just find a place to park," he said as she climbed out of the truck.

The apartment was on the right, door ajar, one of those efficiency units in which the rooms were spacious enough for one piece of furniture or a large man, not both, and in which you could light a candle and still smell the sulfur an hour later. A mother of four with half a brain would never serve beans in a place like that. Laura shouted from a distant room, "Just make yourself at home. I'll be out in a sec."

The apartment was tidy and Spartan and appeared to be the manifestation of an elderly woman. In the living room, Mac sat on a love seat before a coffee table on which he discovered a leather-bound scrapbook filled with published articles by Laura L. Sanderson: articles about a woman skydiver who'd set seventeen world records; a man who lived underground on a diet of bugs and roots; a commune for ex-porn actresses in New Mexico; a series on a woman whose husband was murdered by a tribe of Indians in the Amazon; and a story about the oldest madam in Nevada.

"I'll just get the tea," said Laura from the kitchen. She had doffed her shoes and taken her barrettes out, brushed her hair until it was stormy with static electricity.

Fontana rose and followed her into the kitchen, a phrase he'd read somewhere, "apple-assed young women," coming to mind as he watched her move. Laura stood in front of the stove, waiting for the water to boil, two tea bags on the counter in saucers. The place smelled of an electric burner, her perfume, and Satan, who had commandeered a strip on the carpet in the other room.

From behind, Fontana encircled her slender waist in either palm, stepped close, and pulled her body against his. She sighed and leaned her head backward onto his shoulder. Even as he held her he found it difficult to believe he was making a move on a twenty-two-year-old woman with hennaed hair and tattoos. Was availability the prime attraction? Hell, the longer he was around her, the prettier she became, yet that might easily be a function of availability too.

The firm feel of her body aroused him instantly. He kissed the side of her face, her warm neck, then her hot ear. Slowly she arched her back, turned her face toward his, and their lips met. She pivoted around in his arms, the fabric of her clothing sounding like a distant wind, and they kissed until the tea kettle whistled and then shrieked. He tried not to think about anything except the fact that she was warm and willing while she turned off the tea kettle, gave him a look, and walked heel-heavy in bare feet down the hallway to a tiny bedroom. Inhaling the scent of her hair and feeling improperly randy, he followed.

Candles had been lit. Incense was smoldering. The room was wavery with pale smoke, like something out of a B movie from the seventies.

Fontana found she was supple, as well as inept and heavy-handed, and they cracked heads several times on the waterbed just before she accidentally kneed him in the groin. It was over for her quickly, for she was eager and seemed to have little sense of where she was or what she was doing, while he finished at a slower cadence, sloshing and rolling on the waterbed, watching her face and knowing that he would recall the flushed pink of her cheeks for a long time.

There was almost something illicit in bedding a woman so much younger, a woman whose neck and cheeks turned roseate while staring him in the eye until she climaxed, at which time her eyeballs rolled up and showed the white on one side, the indigo contact askew on the other. Then, like a circus stunt, her eyes rolled back down and caught the loose contacts perfectly. Under different circumstances he might have laughed.

They lay together in the afterglow of sexual union while the heat dissipated off their bodies, while the waterbed rocked ever so gently, while Laura made a mild whistling sound breathing through her nostrils, while one of her small breasts rose and fell under his limp palm, and they both dropped into a short nap as if it were a bottomless hole.

Twenty

▲

EVERYONE IS STARING

You are sitting in the back of the chief's car, and they are parading past. It is six hours into the new shift, and nearly everyone who was here last night has returned: the police, the newsies, a milkman on amphetamines, even a cab driver who just happened along after the explosion, all of them wearing heavy frowns and hanging their heads like ignorant cattle in a chute waiting for the sledgehammer.

They simply *watch*.

They watch in a way that establishes there will never be a time when they will not be watching.

You are a sculpture in bronze, and the tourists are traipsing by at contrived intervals, ogling and thinking dark thoughts.

After all.

Six men are dead and you are not.

Six men have been rendered into pieces so small most of the bits cannot be found, and you are whole. Six families must be notified, and yours must not. Six funerals must be scheduled. Six station-house lockers must be cleaned out.

But not yours.

Nobody says it, but you know they are thinking it deep down in the recesses of their blaming brains.

You should have galoomphed through the icy night air in bite-sized chunks with the others.

Flashbulbs pop off and you squint. News cameras take endless footage of you, but you do not realize this until months later when some distant relative of your wife's writes a long letter listing all the different television channels she saw you on.

You have been up all night, and it is now closing in on noontime, but you don't feel weary. Truth to tell, you don't feel much of anything. Your friends are dead, but there is not much to do about it except sit in the back of the chief's buggy and let people come and stare. When you move, your wounds crack but you feel no discomfort.

The sun is climbing into a clear blue sky, cold, crisp, and filled with the odor of impending funerals.

There is a gaggle of new widows this fine morning.

You begin to wonder if you will be able to swim through the sea of crying women and steel-jawed men, if you can handle looking at coffins you know are mostly empty. What will you say to the starry-eyed children? How ever will you justify the life that is in your lungs? How will you answer the questions that are never asked.

A team comes in, but you do not know them. They are old-timers, with walrus mustaches, bowed legs, and beer guts, and ways about them it has taken years to define. These somber donkeys have come back with large black plastic bags, and it is clear they are carrying body parts.

You don't know why or how it is that you haven't noticed before, but you are shivering more violently every minute.

People are shouting.

People are staring.

The funny thing is they are staring *down* at you.

You must be on the floor. Or the ground. Because a helicopter flies over their heads in the distance. You try to push yourself off the earth, but half a dozen well-meaning sets of fingertips shove you back. You struggle, but you have no strength. Somebody is taking your blood pressure.

A woman parts the crowd, saying, ''Let me through. The

news. Let me through. The news." And incredibly, they let her through, and she leans over and points a camera in your face, a camera that is so heavy you pray she doesn't drop it in your teeth. The flash blinds you.

It turns out to be convenient. You close your eyes. You keep them closed.

Mac woke up thinking about Diane Cooper, wondering why he had been so cold toward her, and, even so, knowing that the next time they met he would be just as distant, regretting the future omission even as he regretted the past oversight. She was suffering as badly as he had so many years ago, maybe worse. She had lost a lover. She had a department tossing rumors back and forth. Blaming her for the deaths of three men. It was a wonder she could report to work.

"Who are you house-sitting for?"

Laura had been awake, unmoving but awake. "Friend of my aunt's. She's pretty cool for an old lady. Smokes grass. She once had two lovers at the same time."

"Bully for her." Fontana ran his fingers along Laura's belly. He'd noted a tattoo of a slipper with a caption that said, "Ginger danced backwards," above her left hip.

She smiled contentedly. "I thought you didn't like to fuck."

Mildly shocked at her casual use of the word and at the same time feeling stodgy because of his own reaction, he said, "Whatever gave you that idiotic idea?"

"You said no yesterday."

"Saying no and not liking it are two different animals."

She stroked his clean-shaven cheek with the backs of her fingers. "Did you shave this off for me?"

"What?"

"I hate beards on men. I mean, I kept staring at it. I have this feeling—and tell me if I'm wrong—that you sensed I didn't like it and shaved it off for me. You wanted to get me into bed that first day, didn't you? You wanted to fuck me when we first met."

"I shaved my beard because I was tired of it."

Laura gave him a look that indicated she knew what was going on in his mind, and even as she did so, her self-assured certainty made him uneasy. Even *he* didn't know what was going on in his head. He kissed her cheek and wondered whether he wasn't suffering from a severe dearth of female companionship, wondered whether he wasn't willing to bed the first woman who made herself available, because, had he outlined his ideal woman, Laura Sanderson wouldn't have come anywhere close. Was he slipping into that woeful juncture where a twenty-two-year-old a notch on the wrong side of pretty could blink and knock his trousers down around his ankles?

He glanced at his watch, pushed himself off the jiggling waterbed, washed up in the bathroom, and got dressed. "What are you doing?" she said, propping herself on one elbow.

"I have an appointment."

"What for?"

"At Tens. To view tapes of the King Street fire." Beginning to feel a vague resurrection of desire, he noticed her tan lines had been made by a scandalously small bikini, watched as the waterbed rocked her.

"I've never seen those, myself. Would you mind if I went with you? Oh, I'm such a bother. Forget it. I'll see them some other time."

"Get dressed." With a squeal, she catapulted off the bed, grabbed a handful of fresh clothing from the closet, and vanished into the bathroom, reapplying makeup, combing her hair, and climbing into black slacks, pumps, and a cashmere sweater. She seemed to have a split personality where clothing was concerned, as though she couldn't decide if she wanted to be a rebellious youngster or a conservative working woman.

In downtown Seattle at the edge of Pioneer Square, Craven, the public information officer for the fire department, was waiting in the foyer of Station 10, a restless look on his face. He appeared to be part Indian, and perhaps part Filipino. His thick hair was jet-black and slicked straight back. He was chesty and just a few inches shorter than Fontana's five-ten. His face had a slight sheen to it, as if he'd had ribs for lunch but hadn't been able to talk the waiter out of a napkin.

"Chief Fontana?" Craven clasped his hand as hard as he could. "Right in here. I've got it all set up. Actually, I'm in a pretty good position to tell you most everything there is to know about the fire. I did the same thing you're doing. I was the secretary for the department's review board, the people who wrote up the department's investigation? I ended up doing most of the actual footwork."

After setting up the machine, Craven unloaded ten minutes of official jargon about how well the fire had been fought. "You realize they could have lost the building and those two civilians to boot. What happened was a fire situation with a lot of confusion where one crew got in trouble and nobody found out about it in time. That's all."

"Nice of him to save you the trouble of finishing the investigation," said Laura after Craven left. "Has anybody said anything official to you, yet? About doing this?"

"Not word one."

The videos, news reports, outtakes, and home photography were all spliced together on one tape. It began with a home video a merchant from Chinatown had shot, twenty-two minutes of smoke, fog, noisy pumping engines, confusion, shouting, and very little of the actual fire. What became immediately evident from that first video, however, was the incredible density of the smoke in the street and the duress under which everyone involved must have been working. It was clear that for most of the fire the fifth story of the Ratt Building could not be seen from the street.

Channel 4's chopper started from around two thousand feet, began an intense search, camera and microphones running, but for the longest time could find nothing but dingy white puddles of smog tenting the city.

Finally the copter traced Jackson Street from near Lake Washington to determine the fire location. For an hour they hovered in place, and for an hour what they filmed was a surge of blackish smoke rising up into the night through the blanket of white smog.

At around nineteen hundred hours a very mild breeze picked up, and the Ratt Building was partially exposed from the air for a period of slightly less than five minutes. The Channel 4 helicopter took in a panoramic view of the action: the building, fire engines, ladder trucks, and chiefs' buggies with their rotating red lights. The aircraft circled, and Fontana could clearly see smoke coming from the walls below the gutters on the top floor. Fifteen firefighters labored on the roof with chain saws, having already opened two long trench cuts running north and south and several four-by-eight holes near the front. Smoke was coming out of only one of the holes.

At the fourth floor, smoke billowed very slowly from the west windows. In the front of the building and in back, north and south, blacker smoke was streaming out in heavy concentrations. The street in front of the Ratt was a spaghetti plate of hoses crisscrossing in every direction. Then the haze thickened and the fire building disappeared.

When the videotape ran itself out, Fontana pushed the rewind button on the VCR, stuffed his notes into his jacket pocket, and turned to Laura, who smiled sleepily and said, "Back to my place for a cup of coffee?"

"Don't drink coffee."

"Then, just come back and make my head ring, huh?" The second junket to her apartment was the wildest hour he had spent anywhere in years.

It was 9:45 before Fontana got home, driving the GMC through a misty September rain, turning on all the lights and the heat at his place, then tramping through the damp woods to pick up Brendan, feeling a sudden rush of guilt as he knocked on Mary's door, realizing he hadn't called and hadn't seen Brendan since early that morning.

"Hi, guy." Brendan had been sitting at the kitchen table playing a card game with Mary's mother, who wore, as she habitually did, her faded nightgown and a rose tucked behind one ear. The TV was on in the other room. Brendan gathered up his belongings and scurried outside to the dark path. Fontana bid a hasty thank-you to Mary, then caught Brendan.

"How's it goin', guy?" he asked, but there was no reply, just the top of Brendan's bobbing head. Fontana had seen the stiff-legged walk before. "Sorry I'm late. I should have called."

He knew Brendan was wary of losing him, the memories of losing his mother still vivid. Even now, closing in on two years after her death, Brendan continued to set three places at the dinner table.

"Look, Brendan. Next time I'll call if I think I'll be late. Forgive me?"

"Sure." But when he looked up at Mac, tears jeweled his eyes.

After tucking Brendan into bed, chatting up the day's events with him until they were pals again, and suffering Brendan's nightly ritual of cleaning toe jam from between every toe on both feet, Fontana took a shower, tuned the stereo to Patsy Cline's version of "Your Cheatin' Heart," flopped onto the living-room sofa, and thumbed through the notebooks William Youngblood's mother had given him.

Twenty-one

▲

A DEAD MAN'S
JOURNAL

*F*riday, **0034 hrs.**
I stink. I am ugly. And I don't give a rat's ass.

I shave only to come to work twice a week.

I look in the mirror and I see a bum with pale blue eyes and hollow cheeks and pepper in his teeth and blood in his gums.

I just came back from a walk around the station. It is dark everywhere. Martinson is asleep in the watch room bunk. There is popcorn on the floor in the beanery. I clean it up. Outside looks like frost. A hooker in a baggy sweatshirt works the bus stop in front of the library. I watch an old man in a station wagon stop, talk to her for a few minutes, then drive away with her. The old man looks straight ahead. Less than ten minutes later she is back. A ten-dollar hand job.

A line was drawn down the page as if something suddenly interrupted the entry.

0345 hours: *Just got back from a run on 31st. She got a ''no shock advised'' on the Lifepak so we knew there was no chance* *but it is in the standing orders to work on her.*

I like this job the most when the rest of my life is going to hell, because I am doing something nobody else on earth can do as well as me. Sarah Prudds.

God bless her soul. We walk in and there's her son home from the army and he's been doing CPR on his mama and there's a huge piss stain on her bed and we drag her out into the living room like a ragdoll, rip her dress open at the chest, take her false teeth out and toss them across the room and put the patches on. Then Harv bags her and Steve does his first compression and her ribs crack like a tree branch and then the medics come in and shoot the drugs into her heart, and this is how the man, Prudds, finds out his momma is gone.

All the neighbors were there and her two daughters and everybody looking at this 65 yr old woman we've stripped and broken. That'll be his last memory of her, with jelly on her chest and her breasts slapping the floor on either side. Hell, we knew she wasn't coming back the second we came through the door. But it wasn't our call.

Fontana thumbed a good thirty pages back through the journal.

Tuesday, 1203 hrs.

After my powwow with Thurmond I go back to Sixes. Just after lunch. The house is empty, everyone is out inspecting. I had driven downtown with every intention of accepting a job, getting my bars finally, having Chief Thurmond slap me on the back and hand me an assignment.

Lt. Youngblood.

After awhile, I can tell sitting outside the CHIEFS office in the waiting room that something funny is going on. The assistant chief walks by in shirtsleeves and gives me this funny look. As soon as he is past, I start sweating. I can feel it running down the small of my back and collecting at my belt line. Its tough when you know something you don't really want to know, tough when your brain won't let you believe it. I know that if you're on the fourth floor to get a promotion and the assistant chief walks by, he's going to stop and shake your hand, right? When he stares and walks right on past it means they're about to fuck you.

I'm not going to get any bars. Not today, little pardner. Everybody on the floor knows I'm there to get screwed. Everybody but me. And even after I figure it out, I'm too stupid to believe it.

Thurmond keeps me waiting twenty-nine minutes. This is his appointment. He has set the time.

And he makes me wait.

I go into Thurmond's office and he gives me this look—as if he's trying to figure out on the spot whether I deserve the lieutenant's bars, and I know good and well it's all settled, the paperwork, the chiefs notified.

Everything.

And the file clerks out in the halls giving me the look.

In fact, somebody else already has my bars.

Thurmond mentions Dad. Some old beef they'd had between them, and he goes on and on, telling me Dad was a tremendous firefighter, simply TREMENDOUS, and that he knew from all he had heard and seen of me that I was a chip off the old block, but all the while he's saying these nice things about Dad, you can see his blood is beginning to boil thinking about the hassles they had over the years (him usually coming out on the short end of the stick to hear him tell it) and he talks about a couple of them and there are others he hints at and it becomes crystal clear in my mind watching him that whatever he's about to do to me, he's about to do to me because of Dad—his way of squaring things. And here's this one last little thing he can do to the Youngblood clan. Take this up your arse, youngster, then go home and thank the old guy.

And all the while he's talking I know I'm number one on whats left of the list but he's going to give it to Carly Smith who is number 52 and it is well known that Carly doesn't have the strength to open a can of beans much less a hydrant because we all know she let a house burn down in the north end because she couldn't get the hydrant open and it's killing me to sit there and listen to all his drivel but I cannot get up and leave yet and he knows I cannot get up and leave because there is always the possibility that he really is going to promote me.

Thurmond talks on and on and finally I cannot take anymore and I say, ''Am I getting this job or not?''

Thurmond stares at me like I just broke through his office wall with an axe.

I back down a bit.

I'm embarrassed for my lack of balls when I know he's sitting there playing with me but I back down and I say, with a little smile that hurts when I'm doing it and hurts even worse as I think about it later, ''The suspense is killing me, you know.''

''Are you getting the job?'' he repeats, as if he needs to turn up a hearing aid to finish the rest of the conversation.

''Yeah,'' I says, more polite now. And more ashamed. ''I was wondering.''

Thurmond actually smiles and he says, ''I've decided to give the job to someone who's just as qualified but scored somewhat down the list.''

Thurmond is still talking but I'm not hearing him because I knew it wasn't going to happen all along, my whole life, I knew I would never be a lieutenant, that somehow I didnt deserve to be a lieutenant no matter how hard I worked and heres Thurmond confirming it with this little smile on his face, as if he knew my secret, that I didn't really deserve it. Dad always used to say everything I touched turned to shit, and now I know its true.

And so finally as I'm hearing some of the words Thurmond is saying, I start to think I am going crazy, because Thurmond is saying that a guy like me shouldn't really mind this minor setback—MINOR?????—

doesn't?

he

know

I'vebeenstudyingfortwelveyears?

I'll never get this close again.

And then Thurmond says from my political perspective, I probably won't mind that Carly Smith is going to take the job. My political perspective???????? What on earth is he talking about? Until now I haven't exchanged fifty words with Thurmond. And I don't know who the hell Carly Smith is except some woman from the north end who burned a house down trying to open a hydrant.

Thurmond is still talking.

MY POLITICAL PERSPECTIVE*!!!!!!!! And then I tune in again and I hear this.* ''Your old man wouldn't have taken up with a lady firefighter.''

Just like that.

I write the words down as soon as I get out of his office because I cannot believe them and I'm afraid my memory will play tricks on me if I don't write them down. I don't have paper so I write on my hand. Then he is saying he knows we worked together on the same shift, me, and without saying her name, Diane, and that he's sure everything was on the up and up about the night watch and everything and we've got a system of professionalism in the department etcetera.

Deep in his heart this old fart believes I was rattling Diane in the station.

On city time.

That's why I'm not getting the job. Because he hates my dad and thinks I got a piece of ass on city time.

This whole thing is a grudge!

And then Thurmond is walking around to his window telling me he is holding no prejudice against me and that he will be more than happy to consider me for lieutenant the next time. But he doesn't get it.

I explain and for once in this interview I surprise him.

"My name's not coming across your desk again," I say. He has been so full of himself he hasn't seen the effect of his words. He doesn't seem to know this is the end of everything for me. "What?" he says. "You're not taking the next test?" "I'm not giving you a chance to do this to me again. From now on I'm going to punch in at seven-thirty and that's all you're getting." "Don't you want to be a lieutenant?" he says. "Not anymore. And I'll give you a little clue. For every guy you see quitting here in your office, there's another hundred out there who quit a long time ago. The best people in your department aren't even taking tests any more. You've ripped the department to pieces. Maybe you better listen to me, because there's nobody left who'll tell you this to your face."

Thurmond actually seems surprised. Maybe nobody's ever said anything like this to this one-eighth Cuban. "You're a little hot right now," he says. "In two months, when you've had a chance to think about things, I want to have you in here again for a heart to heart. Will you grant me that?"

I go to the door. I put my hand on the knob. "Sure chief," I say. But we both know it will not happen. We will never speak again. He'll ask me back to his office when hell freezes over and

126

*every time he sees me he'll remember he was supposed to ask me
back and he'll know I couldn't have forgotten a thing like that
and he'll avoid me.*

*I get back to the station and both rigs are out and I am alone,
so I change out of my blacks. I just keep going from one mirror in
the station to the next, staring at myself and walking to the next
one, circling the station. A stupid promotion. People lose
promotions every day.*

*I want to call Diane. I want her to tell me something about this
situation I don't already know, yet I realize the odds of that are
zero.*

*Diane hasn't studied as hard as me, but she took the next test
and she was the only woman who passed everything. Diane is
going to get a job.*

*I don't want to think about her getting a job from the bottom
of the list and I don't want to think about the list and suddenly, I
don't want to think about Diane. I love Diane but I know I'm
never going to speak to her again. I was such a dope!!!!!*

*I studied with her. I helped her. Now she's going to be a Lt.
and I'm not.*

*So I get on the horn to Bennie, who says, ''That fucking
Thurmond. He just made the biggest mistake of his career.'' Geez,
those words made me happy. Nothing changed, but it's funny
how just having someone on your side can make a difference.
Bennie tells me we'll get even with the department. Together.*

Wednesday, 1123 hrs.

*When I took Diane's things out to the front yard, I found
myself crying.*

*She got home and it was raining and all her stuff was in the
yard and on top of the pile was the picture of us together, the one
she kept on the dresser.*

*I heard her van door slam in the driveway. Then she must
have been looking at all the stuff. Then I could hear her on the
porch. She waited a long time and then she tried the knob. She
walked around on the porch for a minute.*

*Ten minutes later the phone rang. ''Yeah?'' I said. ''Bill, this
is just so silly. You have to talk to me. I'm sick about . . . '' I
hung up.*

I don't care if she makes Lt. and I don't care if she gives it up because she thinks she's doing me some goddamned favor. I love her so much it hurts but I can't have her around.

She came back and left a thick envelope, jammed it into the mail slot, didn't bother to ring the bell. She must have been writing for hours to get that many pages.

It's still there.

I think it will be there when I sell the house. When she drives by she'll see it and know I left it but I cannot help myself.

Being mean to her is like a mental illness. It's like when you're a kid and you have a loose tooth and it hurts to push on it but it feels so good too, that's what it feels like hurting Diane. It makes me feel better about an absolutely bad thing, so that I can't stop myself from liking it. I can't stop myself from still loving her either.

Fontana was still poring over the diaries when Brendan wandered into the living room, sleepily rubbing his eyes and clutching a stuffed pig, his pajama bottoms twisted half around. Fontana noted a rather spectacular thunderstorm rocking the foothills and mountain behind the house. "For a minute I thought you were the diary police."

Brendan scratched his rump and said, "Huh?"

"Nothing, darlin'. Did the lightning wake you up?"

Fontana smiled to himself as a flash lit up the room and the lights whimpered and he and the boy waited, timing the interval between the atomic flash of white and the rumble.

He flicked off the lights, pulled up the living-room blinds, and collapsed into the easy chair in the corner. Brendan crawled into his lap and Mac pulled a quilt Linda had made over both of them, only their heads revealed. They watched for a long time, chatting, Fontana realizing with an acuteness so sudden it saddened him that had he stayed any longer in Seattle with Laura, he would not have had this with his son. Brendan would have been sleeping on Mary's couch and he would still be bumping skulls with a young woman he didn't love on a waterbed he didn't like.

"You think lightning could crack a rock open?" Brendan asked.

"I think so. It'd be hot afterward, but I think so."

Twenty-two

▲

TH-TH-TH-TH-THAT'S ALL, FOLKS!

*H*e was a short, stout man with a powerful and practiced two-count handshake: up/down. Bald as a tomato, he wore large wire-rimmed glasses that miniaturized his eyes. Though he wasn't particularly obese, everything about him was round—his stubby fingers, his palms, his sausage lips, calves, torso. He tried to pass off a grim twist of his lips as a smile. Fontana had once known a dedicated coroner who had a similar look, the bastard smile. With his upturned, blunt nose and tiny eyes, he looked amazingly like Porky Pig.

"I should have met you before this," said Chief Thurmond, exuding a blanket of civility that didn't quite cover the chill radiating from deep within his gray eyes. Fontana's first thought was ex-chief Youngblood's complaint that Thurmond had taken advantage of his being one-eighth Cuban in order to claw his way to the head position in the fire department. It was curious and, of course, unfair how gossip colored one's expectations. "I would have called and tried to meet with you yesterday, except I had a long business breakfast with Councilwoman Gregg. She's on the Public Safety Committee, and it's always useful to keep them on your side.

"Play football in school? You remind me of a guy used to be running back for the Panthers. We dusted them good my senior year. WSU was talking scholarship until they got the doctor's report on my knee. Played center."

"It's good to meet you, Chief," said Fontana. One of the phone messages that morning had been Thurmond arranging to see him at Station 28 on his way to work. It was Fontana's first meeting of the morning.

It was an overcast Wednesday, and on this, his third day on the investigation, he was beginning to get a feel for things in the Seattle Fire Department, a department still feeling the aftershocks of the deaths six months earlier. Whenever people died in a fire under less than normal circumstances, there was bound to be criticism of the department, warranted or not; it was part of the grieving process. Fontana had seen it back East and he'd seen it last summer when the volunteers began grumbling about the first death in Staircase.

An officer and two firefighters stood nervously in the watch office of Station 28, each waiting for a clean exit that would not attract notice. Chief Thurmond gestured Fontana into the first room off the corridor, an officer's room with a desk, bed, two chairs, and a partially open locker filled with uniforms and gear.

Thurmond snicked the door closed without saying a word, but the implication was, *"Don't disturb us!"*

"A lot of people think we're out to thwart your investigation, but they couldn't be more wrong. I welcome your investigation. If we have deficiencies in our department, we want to hear about them. I happen to think you're not going to find anything, but we want to help. Now, what can I do for you?"

"It's nice of you to offer, but not a thing."

"Everything going all right?"

"Sure."

The chief wore a dark tailored suit with a flashy yellow tie. He sat heavily in the wheeled chair behind the desk and gestured for Fontana to take the other chair, from which Fontana removed a pair of jeans and a plaid work shirt. Chief Thurmond's lips were wet, and he had a tendency to spray spittle when he spoke.

"My office has heard scuttlebutt to the effect that a few people weren't giving their cooperation. I believe you'll find *that* has stopped. Pat, for instance, in the other room."

"Who?"

"Pat Easterman? At King Street he saved those women Ladder Three was looking for. Pat and I came in together. Twenty-seven years, it's been. I was assigned to old Station Twelve and Pat was assigned right here. Funny how people choose different paths. He's been here ever since, and I've worked in almost every station in the city. I'm chief and Pat's a doggoned hero. Heh, heh. Good for him. The department needs heroes; good for the image. Good for old Pat, finally made out to be something."

Thurmond eyeballed Fontana. The harder he smiled, the more he reminded Fontana of Porky Pig, though his voice, instead of a stutter, was mellow and flavored with a tinge of hoarseness of the sort athletes get after an effort. Fontana thought he detected a whiff of alcohol on the chief's breath, along with a lassitude in Thurmond's movements, a slackness in his tiny gray-blue eyes.

"So, tell me, what do you think of our department? I just wish you would have the courage of your convictions in coming to me with it first. Whatever it is. I'm sure we can agree on that? Before you take anything to the media?"

"Whatever I find will be reported to my employer and no one else."

"I understand you've been keeping company with a reporter."

"What? Do you have people following me around? I'm investigating King Street for an individual, not for the press."

"I just want you to know we're a goal-oriented department. We've always been among the foremost in the country, and I intend to keep our record intact. Our Medic One program has been a model for the world. We get visitors every week from as far away as Japan. Now, it's our policy—if there's been a fatality in the department—to cooperate with any independent inquiries the relatives or others might launch. This particular inquiry is misguided, but that's another issue. We know what you're trying to do, Fontana."

"And what's that?"

"You're trying to prove Chief Freeze wasn't doing his job that night. You'd like to say he has trouble communicating. That would be a real blow to the department, if you could prove we had an incompetent chief, wouldn't it? Well, let me tell you something, *Chief* Fontana. The woman who hired you has some evidence against her too, or didn't you know that? We have good reason to believe she panicked and was up there hiding somewhere until her crew was killed looking for her. We could have written that in our reports, but we laid off. We laid off. Why don't you lay off?"

"I'm doing a job, Chief. Pure and simple."

"Is that why you spoke to Bennie Zellner?" Chief Thurmond gave off the sort of cherubic look that would have made him a swell St. Nicholas for a group of children too young to smell deceit. "A real piece of work, eh? That Zellner? Did he happen to mention when I fired him he threatened to burn down my house in Magnolia?"

"How did you know I spoke to Zellner? You do have people following me, don't you?"

"Don't be ridiculous. You realize, don't you, that you could very well end up subpoenaed and in court. You could be testifying under *oath*."

"I've been to court lots of times. It didn't give me hemorrhoids or anything."

"You haven't lived until you've been served a subpoena at five in the morning. Until you've been sued by one of your own chief officers." Suddenly Thurmond rose, his tone altering. "You know, if there was anything I could do about it, you wouldn't be tramping around our fire stations."

Fontana rose and stood half a head taller than Thurmond, who took a step backward and grabbed the doorknob in his pudgy hand. "I remember a chiefs' conference in Philadelphia where you gave a seminar. You are a very highly thought-of investigator, Fontana. There's no reason I should be trying to tell you what to do. I'm just saying it's self-defeating for you and I to be in an adversarial relationship."

"Chief, I don't see how we're in any relationship. I'll do this investigation and that will be the end of it."

"In the ten years I've been chief, we've hauled Seattle out of the cave. We've improved firefighting techniques. We've raised the social consciousness of our hiring policies. As of this year, Seattle is almost totally representative of the racial makeup of this city. How many fire departments can boast that?

"We have numerous black chiefs. Our balance of female-to-male firefighters is the highest in the nation. Seattle employs more females in its ranks than *any* department, even New York City. That's an accomplishment for a force of just less than a thousand."

There was something about Chief Thurmond's self-assured arrogance that begged for argument, a sucker trap Fontana didn't mean to fall into. "I don't want to be the devil's advocate here, but I understand your entrance standards were lowered to get this many women in."

"I'm surprised a man of your caliber is believing those kinds of malicious rumors. I've done everything within my power to make our entrance tests *fair* and *balanced*. Just yesterday I met with the chief of training, Zumwinkle, and we modernized another of our guidelines. It wasn't necessary, but we did it to stifle critics . . . "

"You don't have to get into this," said Fontana.

"Oh, but I assure you, Chief, you *faulted* my department, and I'm going to defend it, and you're going to listen. We're beefing up the test. Applicants do a single military press with ninety-five pounds. Get it up over their heads. Until now, it was pass/fail. We've changed that. In order to get a hundred percent on that portion of the exam, they have to press it five times now. So we've gone from one time to five times."

"So, if they only do it once, they flunk?"

Thurmond wrinkled his forehead. "One press will be seventy percent, which is passing. But we've beefed up the grading scale considerably."

Fontana considered for a moment. "So you're saying people who do only one press will still pass, which means that your affirmative-action appointments, who have only to pass to get a job, still do one press, as before, but those applicants who don't qualify for affirmative action will now have to do five presses because they have to be at the very top of the list to get hired. What you've done is to make sure the disparity between your recruits is greater than ever."

133

Thurmond laughed patronizingly. Fontana was obviously a simpleton.

Five minutes later Fontana located Pat Easterman at the rear of Station 28 in a large room with a long table running up to the inevitable TV. The beanery.

Easterman was a small, nondescript man who nursed a mug of coffee and held down a section of the want ads under his tattooed forearms. He had the bruised knuckles and the battered hands of a car mechanic. Without thinking too hard, Fontana realized Easterman would have been the last man in the room he would have picked as the hero, for among other distancing traits, Easterman had guarded eyes, avoided looking at anybody directly.

When Fontana introduced himself, Easterman frowned. ''Mind if we go outside? So's I can suck a butt?''

''Sure.''

Outside was a door on the east side of the room. There wasn't much out there, a view of a city engineering garage along with a couple of fuel pumps, a fence, and a parking lot. It was a rugged part of town, deep in the Rainier Valley. In the distance a boom box raged.

Twenty-three

▲

STEPPING ON SUPERMAN'S CAPE

"**C**an I do for ya?" Easterman said, popping a chrome-plated lighter under the cigarette that bobbed in his lips. Easterman was maybe fifty, with enough weathered facial lines and crow's feet to pass for seventy; not a handsome man, or a particularly agile-looking one, and Fontana wondered how simple it had been for him to effect a rescue of two panicky women at the top of a five-story fire escape while wearing full bunkers, though in his time he had witnessed plenty of less likely candidates performing even less likely deeds. A lot of these old firefighters were tougher than cobs.

"As you know, I'm questioning everyone, or nearly everyone, who was at the Ratt."

"Some state of affairs."

"What is?"

"You know what I'm talking about."

"Why don't you explain so we can be perfectly clear about it?"

"When you can be nominated for Firefighter of the Year one minute and get chewed out by the chief the next."

135

"Thurmond chewed you out?"

"He's not shit." Easterman shot a sideward glance at Fontana. "You talk to Cooper, did ya?"

"Cooper hired me."

"You're shittin' me? Now I've seen everything. You must need a buck awful bad, fella."

"Right now all I need is to talk to you without a bunch of sarcastic comments."

Patrick Easterman grunted, the phlegm in his throat catching and pulsating in an erratic and strangely musical warble. His therapist, in the unlikely event that he had one, would say he was smoldering with anger. It was typical for an out-of-condition smoker like Easterman to bitch about women in the department. In fact, Fontana was noticing that the more a firefighter lacked conditioning, the more apt he was to grouse about women. Fontana had observed the same phenomenon in Staircase with the volunteers.

"Missed you at your house. Your wife went to get you, and then you just sort of disappeared."

"Uh, hmmmm."

Apparently, that was as far as that was going to go, though Easterman was uncomfortable at the reminder. "What rig were you riding at King Street?"

"Always ride twenty-eights."

"Driver? Tailboard? Acting man? What?"

"I'm usually the driver."

"Were you that night?"

"I usually am. I said."

Fontana stood back from the tobacco smoke. "So, tell me what you did when you got there, what you saw. Who you spoke to."

"Nothin', really." Easterman shrugged in the chill breeze, drawing on his cigarette and staring off at the dark steel-colored clouds to the southeast. A gaggle of ducks was flying south. Easterman made a gun out of his fingers and, taking aim, whispered to himself, "Bang."

"Somebody must have given you some orders."

"I was in the back with Freeze."

"You were his aide?"

"Yeah."

"And?"

"I wrote down what he told me. He told it to me and I wrote it down. I never was an aide before. I didn't know how to do it."

"What about the women?"

"Which one? Cooper?"

"The ones you rescued."

"Well, Cooper ain't much of a firefighter, if you've seen her. I seen her tryin' to carry a ladder once and it was like watching a monkey fuck a football."

"What is it with Cooper? Did you see her do something at King Street?"

"I told it before. I didn't see her at all."

"The women you rescued?"

"Them. I seen 'em and went on up and got 'em. No biggee."

"How far into the fire was this?"

"I wasn't keepin' no stopwatch on things."

"So, what happened?"

Easterman finally looked over at Fontana, rolling his eyes slowly as if Fontana were nuts. *"Everythin'?"*

"How long could it take?"

"I hope you tested Cooper this bad. She didn't do *shit* at King Street. No matter what she tells you, she didn't do *shit.*"

"I thought you didn't see her."

Easterman sucked on his cigarette. "They sent me back to be the aide to Freeze. So, Freeze hands me this board with a bunch of name tags on it and says to keep track. Then goes inside."

"The Ratt?"

"In the basement."

"Did you go with him?"

"He told me to stay out there and keep track. Besides, it was shitty in there."

"I heard it was shitty everywhere." No reaction from Easterman. "How long could he have stayed in there? Did he have a mask?"

"I don't remember if he did or not. But he was gone a long time."

"Then what?"

"Then I saw one of them women upstairs. There wasn't

nobody else, so I got 'em. They coulda died."

"You *saw* them?"

"Or heard 'em. I don't recall. The smoke was so thick."

"I'm just trying to get it straight in my mind."

Easterman squinted against his own tobacco smoke. "I heard 'em. Then I went up."

"Where was the rest of your crew?"

"When we first got there Hathaway had me help Engine Thirteen put in another supply, and by the time I got to the staging area, Hathaway and the other guy were gone."

"Who was the other guy?"

"Some detail." A detail was an individual assigned to another station or unit for a shift, usually for reasons of manpower, but sometimes for training or because the detail's specific skills were needed.

"So, you were alone most of the fire?"

"That's why they made me the aide back there."

"Then what?"

"What else do you want to know?"

"Start from seeing the women."

"Okay. Sure. I heard that woman and I climbed up and brought 'em down. No biggee."

"Were you wearing a backpack?"

"No, I don't recollect I was."

"When you were on the fire escape, did you see anybody from Ladder Three?"

"Nope."

"You never saw anything of Ladder Three's crew?"

"Just their ladder standing in the alley in the middle of all those hose lines. It had a brick under one spur cause the alley was runnin' downhill."

"So, when you went up the fire escape, you didn't pass Diane Cooper?"

"I told you."

"Did you look inside any of the landings?"

"There was smoke billowin' out everywhere. I couldn't see nothin'."

"And she didn't pass you prior to that or after, while you were in the alley?"

"Told you."

"So, you what? You have to coax them onto the fire escape? The victims? There must have been a reason they weren't coming down on their own."

Easterman shrugged.

"Were they young women?"

"One was colored. One was older, 'bout my age. They were both coughing. They couldn't take the smoke. Didn't have the experience. Lots of coughing and shit."

"So, then you what? Took them around to the front?"

"Yep."

"Was Freeze there while this was going on? I mean, did you leave the alley in charge of Freeze?"

"He was in charge."

"But was he outside in charge? Or was he in the basement still?"

"Couldn't say."

"But Freeze was there when you went up?"

"I heard somebody ask him about it and he said he didn't remember it, so I guess he wasn't around just then."

"Where was he?"

Easterman fixed his eyes on Fontana. "You ever been to a fire? You know how confusing it is?"

"You knew all of them by sight? Vine, Youngblood, Cooper, and Buchanan?"

"Knew Youngblood's old man. He was sure a bull whacker. You didn't mess with him. Vine, yeah. And the splittail. Never seen Buchanan until his picture was in the paper with mine."

"So, if Freeze wasn't there when you got the women, there was a time when the alley was unattended, wasn't there?"

"I was on the escape."

"Yes, so except for the time you were taking the women around to the front of the building, you were in a position to have heard somebody calling for help off of that fire escape."

"Didn't hear nothin'."

"The funny thing is, I have a witness who says Cooper was on the fire escape shouting down to the alley for help." He didn't mention that the witness was Cooper. "Calling Chief Freeze. You didn't hear that?"

"You got a witness? What kind of witness? I never heard nothin' about this."

"Did you hear or see anything of firefighter Cooper in that alley?"

"Not until I took the two women around the front to the medics. Right after that, I heard somebody talking about Three Truck. I think she come around front about then. And later they started a search."

"How much later?"

Before he could reply, the station alerter went off and East-erman flung his cigarette to the ground and jogged into the station. The engine, the truck, and the medic unit were being dispatched, Easterman climbing into the cab of the engine. Fontana wandered into the watch office and sat in front of the television until they returned nine minutes later. The engine was backing in and the truck was still out in the street when they received another alarm. This time they were out of quarters for almost three hours.

Fontana made some phone calls, perused a clipboard piled high with departmental memorandums, and waited. Twice he called Laura, both numbers, but there was no reply at either.

When the units got back, Engine 28's crew spent twenty minutes changing hose and washing equipment, then ate a late lunch, the beanery resounding with shouts and cursing. Fontana drank a glass of water and joined both crews at the kitchen table, asking about their fire, a kitchen fire in a crack house. The police had been involved. The truck crew had been asked to cut open a small floor safe. Several wandering spectators had threatened firefighters. Two overeager truckmen had ventilated the living room by tossing a color television through a plate-glass picture window. A woman cop had slugged a suspect with her nightstick.

Fontana quickly noticed that Easterman was the least talkative man in the room, but, then, perhaps Fontana's presence had muted him.

After his meal, Easterman went outside, pulled a cigarette from his pack, and lit up. He seemed surprised when Fontana followed. "Got another few minutes?"

"You ain't done yet?"

"Not quite." It had started to sprinkle, almost a mist that didn't quite wet them under the eaves of the building. Fontana said, "Remember Freeze saying anything about Ladder Three's crew?"

"Ummmmm." Easterman drew on his cigarette until his mouth puckered to the jawline. "Freeze? That cocksucker. You know, they never should have let him into the department. He was runnin' around there like a stuck pig. Soon's they discovered Ladder Three was missing and that Cooper gal was in the aid car all smoked up, he started sweating bullets. He didn't know *where* they were. You shoulda seen him sweatin'.

"You know what they say, don't you? In the Seattle Fire Department? There's no pressure. No pressure at all. Because you only have to be as smart as the dumbest black and as strong as the weakest woman." Fontana didn't know quite how to answer that. He had a feeling from the lofty look on his face that Easterman had made it up himself, probably after a great deal of perplexing thought. Easterman excused himself and went back inside the building, leaving a strong odor of fresh human excrement in his wake. It took a few long moments before Fontana realized Easterman had crapped his pants, that, with all the rest of it, making it a most remarkable interview.

Twenty-four

▲

STRANGE MEN
WHO CARRY DOGS

*T*he grassy park at Rainier Avenue and Alaska seemed like a good place to park the truck and walk the dog. Satan had been trained in Germany in a *Schutzhund Klub,* had been a working police dog all his life and, as such, expected daily tasks, so the enforced idleness while recuperating from his wounds was taking a toll on his spirit.

Springing breathlessly out of the GMC and cocking his head around to regard his master, the German shepherd made tracks through the wet grass. Ten minutes later, when a man carrying a dachshund he called Earl tried to strike up a conversation, Fontana excused himself and left. Maybe there was something wrong with him, but he had never wanted to spend time around men who carried dogs.

He thought about Youngblood crawling toward safety with a broken leg, holing up in a small room and giving his radio and hopes to Al Buchanan, only to have Buchanan wander off in the smoke and eventually remove his bunking clothes and sit down to die in another room. Fontana could recall times in his career when the same thing might have happened to him. Waiting in a room for help. Inhaling smoke and knowing that every breath was dragging you closer to the grave. It was easy to see why Cooper felt the gravity of blame.

Fontana was suddenly overcome with an overwhelming feeling of detachment, from people, from the world around him; a sense of aloneness, as if for him, there were no more loved ones anywhere on earth. Perhaps the three bleak hours in Station 28 smelling the bleach on the floors and seeing the orderly memos filed away on clipboards on the walls and waiting for the units to return from their kitchen fire had precipitated these dismal thoughts.

Sensing an inexplicable and untimely loss of bearings in his pursuit of the case, Fontana drove to Laura's apartment on Capitol Hill, trying hard not to admit why he was there. He should have been in the International District while it was still daylight, once again exploring the burned-out rooms of the Ratt Building, canvassing the neighborhood. Nobody answered the bell at Laura's apartment.

He drove downtown to the Belasco Building, elevatored to the sixteenth floor, and rapped on the pebbled-glass door of *Sensation Plus*, waiting a moment after he thought he heard something stir inside. He loitered a long while before giving up, feeling ingenuous on the ride down in the elevator.

In the basement parking garage, he ran into Bennie Zellner trundling a welding-torch setup through the glass doors from the garage into the main body of the building. Bennie, dressed in coveralls with dirty knees, gave Fontana a furtive look, then, peering behind himself at a shabby pickup truck backed up tightly against the doorway, asked, "What are you doing here?"

"Mr. Zellner," said Fontana. Zellner wore an expression like a twelve-year-old caught with a pocket full of cherry bombs.

Crouching in the bed of the truck under a canvas canopy was the man Laura had spoken with the other day, in a navy jumpsuit. Lee Viteri.

After he had hopped from the rear of the truck, Lee fiddled with the canvas flap until the bed of the truck was buttoned up, then laced a rope through a series of metal eyelets, cinching it tight and knotting it. After long consideration, Zellner finally said, "You're not making me happy, Fontana."

"Ah, Chief. Back for a visit?" Lee asked. Before Fontana could reply, Viteri inexplicably leaped into the air and kicked at his face.

Mac dodged to the side, causing Lee's work boot to slam into the glass door next to his head. It nearly made contact with Bennie Zellner, who had moved closer.

Fontana was stunned, yet responded quicker than Lee Viteri thought he might. He shot a straight left at Viteri and knocked him onto his buttocks on the concrete floor. The punch had made a hollow drumlike sound against Viteri's bony chest.

Before he could turn to Zellner, Fontana found himself hurtling forward, crashing face-first into a concrete wall, bouncing, then sliding to the floor. When he turned around, Zellner was advancing. Lee was climbing to his feet and struggling to catch his breath. Fontana lashed out with his shoe and tripped him, then stood. Quick as an angry bear, Zellner reached out and slapped Fontana across the face with an open fist. The blow swung his head around and threw him off balance, almost knocked him cold.

"What the hell is this all about?" Fontana asked ducking a second swatting blow. He tried to move out of range, but Viteri was in a crouch off to his right, Zellner to the left, the wall behind. In his left fist Viteri had produced an open knife.

"*Eis! Eis!*" shouted Fontana. "*Eis!*"

"What? You want some ice for the shiner you're going to have?" Viteri asked, laughing. "He's talking Dutch or Chinee or something." From the beginning Lee Viteri had been the kind of man Fontana wouldn't have minded seeing with his testicles caught in a zipper. He had been conspiratorial and overly familiar with Laura. Thin and unshaven, he was six inches taller than Fontana, about the same weight, and was staring with a sort of boldness Fontana recognized from having been around petty criminals.

"What's this all about?" Fontana asked. "Are you guys nuts? *Eis!*"

Viteri stalked him, waving the knife, moving closer in the crouch of someone who had seen a lot of movies and thought he knew how to fight with a blade. While he was still feinting and flicking, Satan came out of nowhere, the only signal a telltale clicking of his toenails on the concrete walkway, snapped Viteri's arm, and dragged him to the ground, ripping and snarling. Viteri screamed, but the dog dragged him ten feet, working him like an old rag, Viteri kicking and shouting. *Eis* was a German phrase and Satan understood that it meant "take him."

Fontana kicked the knife under the pickup truck, but before he could do anything else, Zellner grabbed him by the collar. Out of the corner of his eye Fontana saw a flash of brown-and-black fur below Zellner's heavy arm, and then he was free and Zellner was yelping. Satan had hold of Zellner's buttocks. Zellner was reaching for the pistol in his belt. "You touch that gun, big guy, and I'll tell him to go ahead and have lunch," said Fontana. "Right now he's just holding you. You don't move, he doesn't move."

Zellner got very still. Fontana reached across and removed the revolver from his holster, walked over to Viteri, who was nursing a bloodied arm, and patted him down. Fontana broke open the cylinder of Zellner's revolver and watched six bullets slide out and bounce off the floor.

"What the hell was that all about?" Fontana asked.

"You gonna get this animal off me?" Satan still had a grip on Zellner, growling at his slightest motion.

Fontana glanced down at Viteri, who was sitting up now. "You make another move down there, and he'll let go of that fat butt and grab your nuts." Viteri paled and stopped breathing.

Zellner said, "Do me a favor, bud? Don't call the cops. Okay? I got enough trouble. Please don't call the cops."

"Two guys attack me, one with a knife, one carrying a gun, and you want me to let you walk?"

"Who's walking, man? I can feel the blood running down my leg. Get him off me. This hurts like stink! And look what he did to Lee. Just don't call the cops, huh? It would kill my mom. She doesn't need this right now. If it was any other time, man. But not now. Look, I admit we were out of line. I apologize, okay?"

"What the hell got into you?"

Viteri didn't say anything. Zellner said, "He's biting harder."

"*Fuss!*" said Fontana. "*Fuss! Fuss!*" In an instant, Satan was at his side, body alert, eyes moving intently between Fontana's two assailants.

"God, what is that?" Zellner asked bitterly. "An army dog or something? Where'd he come from?"

"Now, tell me what the hell that was all about. One minute we're standing here talking and the next minute you're trying to kill me."

"Nobody was trying to kill you. We just wanted you to think about what you're doing."

"And what am I doing?"

"For one thing, you're bugging my folks. The old man's had heart surgery since Bill died. We almost lost him. And you fandango up there and ask him all those dadblamed questions."

"Your folks called *me*. They wanted to talk. Besides, your dad was in charge of the investigation of the Ratt."

"You got no business conning my old man into talking to you. He hasn't spoken about it to anybody since it happened."

"He called me."

"My brother was killed in that fire and the bastards responsible should swing. And here you are running around trying to help one of them. I want her to pay. You're trying to make out like she had no part in it."

"I'm looking for the truth, Bennie. Whatever it turns out to be."

"My folks are half in the grave over this already. Both of them. It's killing them. Couldn't you see that, you self-righteous bastard?"

"I'm sorry if you're upset . . . " Fontana suddenly realized he was apologizing to a man who probably would have been stomping his liver flat if it weren't for Satan. "No, I'm not sorry. Fuck you, Bennie." "

"It was bad enough the administration threw me out like they did, and I'll get 'em for that, but when they killed Bill, it was too much. It grabbed my stepfather and just took all the bounce out of his step."

"What do you mean, they killed Bill?"

"You know what they do when they get too many drones in a beehive? In the fire department, they promote 'em. When he didn't make lieutenant, Bill was . . . busted up isn't *even* the word for it. See, he finally got high on the list, and everybody told him he was a shoo-in for lieutenant, and it just busted him apart when it didn't happen. If he hadn't gotten high it would have been one thing. Or if he'd gotten high and there had been no job openings. But he got high and there were openings and he should have gotten a job and everybody knew it."

Fontana noticed Zellner's shoes were tied in knots again. "What happened with him and Diane Cooper?"

Zellner reached behind and felt where the dog had bitten him, brought his hand around and stared at the blood, then gave a lugubrious look at the floor. "Bill thought he really found the one. I warned him when they were studying together he was cutting his own throat, helping a woman on the test, but he wouldn't listen. So, what are you going to do?"

"I'm still trying to figure that out."

"Yeah, sure. Did ya know the afternoon you saw him, my old man went back in for chest pains. You did that. That was just real sharp of you. If he dies over this, I'm coming for you. Don't think I won't."

"Me and everyone else, it sounds like. Listen, Bennie, you can't keep adding people to your list. You need counseling, somebody to help you get over all this."

Zellner grinned. "Don't rip your shorts over my psychological condition, Mr. Fontana."

"I'm going to let you off this time."

"That's mighty sweet of you, considerin' it'd probably be a death sentence for the old man if you didn't."

"Yeah, well, watch yourself."

"You come after me again and things'll be different."

"Who came after whom?"

"Just remember what I said."

Lee glared at Fontana as he walked away, then scooted backward on his rump when Satan sauntered past, backing himself up to a wall, face pale and sweaty. The dog stopped and gave him a hard look, his panting face not two feet away. After a few moments, the dog moved on and Viteri took a breath.

Fontana wondered if some of Viteri's antagonism toward

him didn't stem from a possessiveness he obviously felt toward Laura. She was so friendly with the guys she met, Lieutenant Dimakis, Viteri, Fontana. He was beginning to wonder whether she was *friendly* or just easy.

She'd been easy for *Fontana*, but when a guy runs across a woman like that his ego wants to tell him she is that way for him only. After all, his late wife had been easy too, but only for him. Fontana wondered that he had been dumb enough to manage to sleep with the first sure thing he'd run up against in a long while.

As he got close to the GMC, Zellner shouted after him. "You don't get it, do you? Some people were born to be firefighters. Bill was proud of his job and proud of the way he handled it. He didn't screw up. Something happened. The damned city and their watered-down fire department. They killed him. Them *bastards*. Piss on 'em. They look better underwater anyway."

Zellner was still yelling as Fontana drove out of the parking garage.

Twenty-five

▲

WHAT TO DO WHEN YOUR HEAD IS SCREWED ON BACKWARD

As Fontana approached Cooper's house he spotted her climbing into her white Plymouth van, where she disappeared, probably leaning over, picking up litter off the floor or securing an errant pop bottle at the same time as she accelerated away from the curb. He tailed her up residential streets to the west end of Green Lake until she pulled into the parking lot of an Albertson's supermarket. He angled the GMC close to the store entrance and got out as she strolled past behind a limping jogger, Cooper wearing faded jeans with holes in the knees and a raggedy puce sweatshirt. No makeup. Sockless feet and sandals.

"Diane? You were just leaving your house as I pulled up, so I followed you here. I hope you don't mind."

Though her tan was deep as paint, she looked haggard, pouchy half-moons of skin under her eyes. "What? Oh. You're *him!* Polite people call first." She pivoted and headed toward the store.

"Called half a dozen times. You don't answer. You hire me, but you won't talk."

She stopped and said, "What have you got?"

"I'm still piecing it together. I need some answers from you."

"Look ... I'm going through ... I go through these periods where I can't think."

"Whether you like it or not, there are rumors."

"I told you there were. That's why I hired you."

"I think you have some firsthand testimony you haven't given."

A breeze kicked up. She folded her arms and fingered the goose bumps on her forearms. It was September, and although there were only a few clouds in the sky, the air was damp and cool and smelled of incoming storms, the short Northwest summer having stalled. A small red Ford loaded with teenage males edged past in the lot, the boys gawping at Fontana's ancient truck.

Cooper made a gesture of resignation. He nodded toward his truck. Inside the GMC, she took note of the ancient tube radio he hadn't had the heart to remove when he'd had the new deck installed, then sat snugly against the passenger door, both hands on the seat beside her thighs as if bracing for an unpleasant carnival ride, the tendons across the backs of her deeply tanned hands standing out with the tension. Strangely, it reminded Fontana of the way Linda's hands used to clasp and unclasp the bed sheets when they made love.

Sitting sideways behind the wheel, Fontana kicked up one knee and spoke gently. "Diane, I spoke to Pat Easterman. I'm sure you're familiar with the story of him rescuing those women."

"The women *we* were supposed to rescue."

"He was below you in that alley. Yet he claims he never heard anybody shouting for help. If he was directly below, he couldn't have been more than forty feet away."

"You saying I didn't call for help?"

"I'm asking what happened. It's funny, because Easterman got uncomfortable when I questioned him about this. Same as you."

"No, if Easterman got uncomfortable, it wasn't the same as me. Three members of his crew did not die. It was not the same as me."

"I'm not going to pretend I know what you're going through, but I'm getting the feeling there is something unspoken between the three of us."

Her smile was grim as she turned from the window, glanced at him a moment, then looked out again at the parked cars. "Are you saying he's guilty of something, or are you saying I'm guilty of something?"

"Holding back, Diane. Nobody said 'guilty.' "

"Holding back what?"

"For one thing, you and Bill Youngblood."

"Damn you! I have a right to *some* privacy." The inside windows of the truck were beginning to steam over with hot words and body heat. Satan sat on the backseat watching Mac and panting noisily. "Listen, I've just gone through the worst year of my life. Half my friends think I killed the man I loved."

"You know Bill's brother? Bennie? He jumped me a few minutes ago. Him and one of his cronies down at the Belasco Building."

"I know him. After the Ratt, I worked down there at the Belasco doing a prefire for the department. I couldn't go back to combat. I was all screwed up from the carbon monoxide. So they had me go over some of the high rises in town and draw up prefires. You know, complete plans of the building and what we would do in case it ever went up. Bennie was a little wary of me at first, but we settled into a truce. I blew two weeks going through his building with a fine-tooth comb. I probably know it as well as he does. He's a bitter man. But what difference could all this make? Bill and Al and Clint are dead, and all the talk we can talk isn't going to resurrect them."

Fontana passed her a tattered newspaper clipping of a firefighter standing in front of an earthen crater, blood and dirt smudges on the firefighter's face, the photo taken by flash in the early dawn.

She held the clipping in front of her face long enough for it to stop trembling. "Who's this?"

"There were seven of us at the site. I was the only one who made it out." She stared at it for a long time. He explained what had happened. "After that, my head was screwed on backwards for a lot of years. I dreamed about it this week. Like

151

I was there again. Woke up sweating. I can't help thinking I'm one of the few people around who knows what you're going through."

Diane Cooper turned her blue eyes on him for a moment, then stared out the windshield. Wispy from inattention, her hair was piled on the back of her head, her ears standing out like handles on a jug. "We had an ammonium-nitrate explosion in town not long ago."

"I saw it on the news."

"So, how do you get over it?"

"Time. Everyone seems to need something different. One guy quit the fire service, saved his money, and bought into a potato farm. Me, I transferred to Arson Investigation and worked there the rest of my career in the East. I mighta stayed in combat, but a couple of months later we had a high-rise fire. I was on the line with a guy named Pratt. The eighteenth floor. Heavy smoke. Lots of heat. Every time you hit it, it would doughnut around up to the ceiling, and the heat would slap you in the face and drive you back out the door. But finally we got way in deep, to what appeared to be the seat of the fire, saw this round ball glowing up in the corner, kept pushing after it, crawling towards it and pushing, finally Pratt grabs my harness and says there's something wrong. I stop, just to tell him everything is okay, and just a second later a gust of wind blows all the smoke out of our faces.

"Now we can see we'd been squirting at the sun and were about to crawl right out the eighteenth floor, out one of those floor-to-ceiling windows the fire had busted out." Fontana laughed loudly. Now I'm a chief in the smallest town I could find that would have me. After a minute of silence, he said, "Diane? Did anybody know about the stairs? In front of the building?"

"I think, now, that Bill must have known. He and Buchanan got to the front of the building before me and Clint on our initial sweep. I didn't hear them say anything about the stairs, but with your earflaps down sometimes it's like you've got your head in a plastic bag and it's raining."

"You think it's possible when you were yelling from the fire escape that somebody answered you and you didn't hear because of your flaps?"

"No."

"You think with his leg busted, Youngblood might have been going for the stairs at the front of the building, rather than the ladder?"

"Maybe."

"Something else. If you were still there when Easterman went up the fire escape to get those two women, you could hardly have missed each other."

"Yeah, well . . . Maybe you're forgetting what the visibility was like. People were bumping into each other in the street. Chief Courier's car got a pike pole stuck through the back window."

"So what about Easterman?"

"Pat's had a long career. His dad was in. His uncle. They gave him an award. He saved those women and made us all look like fools. What's to tell?"

"Okay. You and Bill? I've got his diaries. You studied to-gether—you were staying at his place—and he got higher on the list than he'd ever gotten. Everybody thought he had lieu-tenant in the bag."

"Maybe we shouldn't have built up his expectations. Except at the time, it seemed like he *couldn't* miss. You don't know how much he wanted those bars. I suppose it's all in the diary? Bill trashed everything I owned. Dragged it out in the rain and stomped all over it. Even my books and albums had footprints on them. The most hateful thing . . ."

"Bill loved you."

"Yeah, well, he had a funny way of showing it." She was crying. "Thanks. You've been very kind. I have to go now. I just . . ."

"He had harsh words with you at King Street."

"After Thurmond turned him down for lieutenant, we only spoke once. I cornered him at the store. I told him he was feeling sorry for himself and that whatever happened with my career wasn't taking a thing away from his. I told him I knew he was going through a thing and that I would still be there when he came out of it. He said, 'Fuck off.' It was the first time I ever heard him say that word. It was like he was in one of those horror movies and he was possessed.

"At King Street he called me a cunt. Also the first time I

ever heard that word out of his mouth. Don't you get it? There were three firefighters with Bill that day. Bill didn't want me for a partner because I was a *woman*. He didn't want Clint because he was *black*. Bill had suddenly decided he was going to fight fire with white men only." Like small incandescent bugs, tears trickled down either side of her face.

"There's one other thing I have to ask." She nodded. "A guy named Ryker was on the stairs outside the fourth floor. He heard Youngblood and another man talking shortly before the three of them died. He said they were looking for you."

Cooper was silent for a long time. "You know my memory of that night is very limited. But what you're saying couldn't have happened. It couldn't have."

She choked back a sob and fled, trotting into the grocery store, sandals spanking her heels. On the radio, low, he noticed for the first time Gogi Grant singing "The Wayward Wind." He turned the sound up, but it didn't make him feel any better.

Twenty-six

▲

BLITHERING
FOR THE LORD

*T*wenty minutes later, Pastor Lionel Hill was exiting the Baptist Church behind the Ratt Building when Fontana parked on Jackson and walked toward the edifice. Fontana had driven there to get a phone number off the signboard in front, hoping he might set up an appointment for later in the week.

His wiry shoulder wedging open a heavy white door, briefcase in one hand, what appeared to be a bundle of laundry in the other, Pastor Hill waited in the doorway.

He was a man of indeterminate age, a tall, elegant, lanky black man with a bony face, rimless spectacles, bugged-out eyes, and a torso thin enough that it looked as if the door were going to crush him.

"MacKinley Fontana. I'm investigating the fire they had across the alley about six months ago."

"Ah, I guess I got a few minutes. I go jogging in the afternoons with a group of ladies from the choir here." Hill grinned, a man who spent his afternoons with ladies while others worked. "Lionel Hill. Actually, it's Lionel Brookings Hampton Hill. I been the shepherd of this flock for almost six years."

Hill wore black trousers, navy shoes, and a knit sweater over a button-down dress shirt. The teeth in his smile looked like toy piano keys. A lump of a potbelly belied his braggadocio about the jogging. The ladies weren't running him too hard. Here was a man with a false sense of charisma.

"Come on in. I'll show you where he was." Pastor Hill led Fontana into the shadowed church. Outside, they had been enjoying a brief campaign of mid-afternoon sunshine, so the contrast to the darkened vestibule was marked.

Hill led him down a series of corridors and up a set of stairs, chattering the whole time, explaining that nothing had been stolen during the burglary. "I found the door. Yeah, busted in. A side door downstairs off the alley. Coulda been a fireman, except the fire department said it wasn't. Was a footprint on the door looked like Michael Jordan's. And another one inside on the vestry, which we also keep locked, matched the first. That's where he spent his time, in the vestry. You didn't have to be a detective to figure that out. Over thirty cigarettes crushed on a picture of my wife and kids. What kind of person breaks into the Lord's house and defiles personal property? I ask you that."

They arrived at the vestry, a long, wood-paneled room overlooking the alley, and sporting from the center windows a full view of the rear of the Ratt. "They ever arrest anybody for the break-in?"

"The police told us he was probably some vagrant, undoubtedly moved on by now."

"You sure it was a he?"

"We did some detectin', me and Waldo, the janitor here for the building, and I don't see how it could have been a woman. The footprints on those doors. Bigger than mine." Pastor Hill held a foot aloft much longer than he needed to, showing off both agility and balance. His shoes were at least a size 12. "Couldn't have been a woman."

While Fontana walked around the desk and gazed out at the alley, trying to figure what someone might have been able to see that night through the fog and smoke, Pastor Hill burbled on about the women he jogged with down at Seward Park, about what their husbands did, about the two who were unmarried, about the one who might, just might, have her eye on him, and about the spotty rain they'd been having all day. Hill was a smiling kind of guy, full of good cheer and bonhomie, though he was burdened with an unfortunate attribute Fontana had read about in a Dave Barry syndicated column, Blitherer's Disease, wherein no filter was attached to the brain so that virtually every thought occurring to a person spewed forth in endless gibbering.

Fontana speculated about the odds of a random break-in next door to the Ratt on the same night as the fire. Then again, it was possible, as ex-chief Youngblood had theorized, that some homeless pauper had come in seeking a comfortable observation post. It was also possible that the intruder had come either before or after the fire and that the two events were unconnected. Or it could have been a firefighter hiding out, shirking his responsibilities. On the other hand, a lot of arsonists had a habit of sticking around to watch the results of their handiwork. The problem with that was Seattle had already decided it had not been arson.

The church would have been warm. It would have been convenient. Both Freeze and Easterman seemed to have disappeared for at least part of the fire. Or perhaps some chief officer who had long since forgotten had suggested the church needed to be searched for an extension of the fire and someone had come in, found the building clear, then decided to linger. Sit up in the vestry, watch your cohorts douse the flames. The doors had been kicked in. Firefighters almost always used their feet or a tool to breach a door, knowing full well that using a shoulder was for rookies.

"You wouldn't happen to have one of those broken doors laying around, would you?" Fontana asked. "Sometimes people leave things around."

"Funny you would ask," said Pastor Hill. "I replaced those doors myself, and I put the damaged ones downstairs."

On the way to the basement, Hill regaled him with stories about a funeral in which the hearse had caught fire, a bird in the building during one of his sermons, an old man in the congregation who had once sparred with an ex-sparring partner of a former sparring partner of Joe Louis, and a seminar he was planning on Christ and Insects, as well as future ambitions to learn Japanese and Cambodian, along with the fact that he hadn't had a cold in almost thirty years.

It was a small, musty room in the basement, with a dirt floor, a single light bulb dangling from the ceiling, boards stacked along one wall, a broken pew standing endwise, pieces of wood trim in a bin, and paint-spattered gallon cans of exterior latex house paint stockpiled in cardboard containers. The two broken doors had been pushed into a crawlspace that extended under the front porch of the church. One of the doors was painted white and had two footprints on it. The interior door had been broken in half.

"Do me a favor and hang on to these, would you?" said Fontana. "I might want to take pictures."

"They're not going anywhere."

"This the photo he ruined?"

"Picture of my family. I slipped the picture out and left everything else the way it had been."

Fontana counted thirty-two cigarette burns in the edge of the frame, one lone cigarette still squashed into the corner. He pulled it out and carefully unrolled it. An unfiltered Camel. He knew most cigarettes took around four minutes to smoke. At that rate, the intruder had spent at least two hours in the vestry, possibly longer. Or had there been two of them? Two prowlers? There was the additional consideration that your average burglar would have moved around the church and disturbed other rooms. This intruder had not moved.

"Me-o, my-o. I got to hustle on down to Seward Park. These ladies count on me to escort them on their daily outing. It's become a tradition. We even had one man—his wife used to jog with us—try to say I was just down there flirting." Hill smiled so hard his scalp retreated half an inch. On the way out of the building, the pastor told Fontana a wedding-night joke, something Fontana hadn't heard in years. He supposed only preachers told them these days.

Half an hour earlier, when Fontana had checked in with the firehouse in Staircase, there had been a message from Patrick Easterman, who wanted another meeting, this one at five o'clock in South Park. Fontana realized follow-up interviews, especially when requested by the subject, were frequently more important than the initial meetings, and he had a feeling Easterman finally wanted to talk.

Finding himself with some time to kill, he sat in the GMC and mulled things over. Chief Freeze had enormous feet and Chief Freeze had been unaccounted for during a portion of the Ratt fire, his post a mere twenty-five feet from the first broken-in door. The boot marks had been made with the right boot, which meant the burglar had probably been right-handed, since a man's predominant kicking foot was generally on the same side as his predominant hand. Was Freeze right-handed? He couldn't remember.

After a while, he picked up Bill Youngblood's diaries, figuring now was the time to read the entry penned on the last day of Youngblood's life, the one written sometime between one o'clock, when his lieutenant took ill, and the time the units were dispatched to the Ratt. Mac had been avoiding it, but now he was interested in what Youngblood was thinking an hour before he died.

Twenty-seven

▲

LAST JOURNAL ENTRY
OF A DEAD MAN

*M*onday, *1646 hrs.*

Buchanan from Thirty-twos came down here to fill in. I know nothing about him except he is not part of the Great Government GIMME Program.

Working here all day with HER does something to me I cannot explain. She will soon be a lieutenant. Fifty-seven on the test and she makes lt. I've been higher than that on five tests.

She tries to smile at everybody and make small talk but she does not fool me. Everybody knows we were living together.

I can see by the way her breathing changes when I come into a room and the look in her eyes she still loves me as much as I love her. She almost cries when I leave the room as she is entering. I do it often. I am afraid I will lose my mind if I stay.

I fixed a quick lunch and fed myself downstairs in the teevee room. Clint came and asked me why I was hiding out, but I gave him a look and he said, 'Okay, be dat way.' The thing is, the blacks are always the first to piss and moan about how unfair promoting women from the bottom of the list is. As if they came from someplace else. Welcome to the club—GUYS!!!

I haven't much talked to anybody all day.

Diane has a look these days. It's the look somebody might have if they were about to get whipped across the face. She has it whenever I am around.

This whole thing has a part to it that I cannot put into words.

Diane cannot help it that she took the test and is going to get a job. She knows if she turns down the promotion it will do not a thing for her in my eyes. My anger has nothing to do with her accepting or not accepting. My anger has to do with the fact that I STUDIED with her. I helped her.

This morning when we were putting our boots on the rig there was a moment when Diane and I were the only ones out on the floor, and we stopped for a second passing each other, and she knew I wasn't going to talk to her but she stopped and gave me this look, like, 'Gee, it's just you and me. Don't you want to say something?' What I wanted to say was, 'I love you. Come back,' but I kept my mouth closed.

Here I am, thirty-nine years old, and suddenly I wake up one morning and I'm a bigot.

Every time the thoughts come to me I fight them, but it's like I'm one of those crazy people who hears voices. Like Carl Nebenfuhr over on Twenty-ninth South who hears voices and they tell him to kick his mother, his poor old mother who's taken him in off the street so many times, and he fights the voices and he fights and they don't stop and so he kicks his mother. Then the voices say to break car windows in the street. He breaks car windows. Six of us pin him down and strap him to a stretcher and I realize I am as crazy as he is.

I should be strapped to that stretcher.

Clint works with me wrestling Nebenfuhr and I think to myself, Clint, you didn't earn this job. This is not your job. And the next run we get, Clint throws a twenty-five up to the bedroom window and scrambles through into the smoke and I think, damn, I am proud to be working with that guy. And we go to the Thriftway for dinner and two little black kids get all big-eyed when they see Clint marching through the store in his uniform, competent and most of all, black, and they trail along behind him and follow him and giggle. They do not look at me. They have eyes only for the black firefighter, and this is as it should be. And again, I am proud to be alongside Clint.

161

Still, I turn more and more into a bigot every day, just like my father and my brother.

There is rot in me and it is growing like a cancer.

One day if Diane still loves me, maybe I will tell her I went crazy and . . .

Here, the journal was abandoned. Fontana's guess was that Youngblood had been writing when the Ratt alarm came in.

Twenty-eight

▲

DOES PINOCCHIO HAVE WOODEN BALLS?

*T*he appointment was for five, but Fontana found himself slogging through rush-hour traffic on First Avenue South slightly after four-thirty, moving along quicker than he'd anticipated. It was a stark area of automobile-repair joints, small factories, tool and die plants, tire stores, and the odd house sandwiched somewhere in the mishmash. The sunshine had vanished, slate-colored clouds scudding across the sky. Every once in a while the windshield wipers on one of the automobiles coming from the opposite direction would be pumping. When Fontana was a child, he had called this earthquake weather.

It was a small business off Kenyon called Midcontinental Operations. There was a modest door factory across the street, along with a garbage transfer station up the road and several smaller one-horse businesses on either side.

Clogged with commuters, the flat roads were grimy with exhaust, though a rainy week had plastered most of the dust to the ground.

Easterman's message had said, "Need to talk. Meet me at

Midcontinental Operations on South Kenyon. Five o'clock P.M. Office. P. Easterman.'' When he'd phoned Station 28 to confirm, they'd told him Easterman was at the doctor and most probably would not be working the rest of the shift. It wasn't until he paged through the Seattle phone directory that Fontana discovered Midcontinental Operations was a junkyard.

It was on the north of Kenyon with a cyclone fence around it and two large drive-through gates. A sign said that because of a death in the family they were closed and would reopen next week. Fontana noticed that the padlock was not snapped shut but was set up to look as though it were. Through the gate he could see several fifteen-foot-tall stacks of wrecked automobiles, a large open space with thousands of flattened bits of colored metal on the ground, pounded down from trucks and cars passing over, and a two-story building made of corrugated tin. It looked older than sin. In front of the building he caught sight of the rear end of a late-model carmine-colored Buick. A red Buick had been parked in Easterman's driveway in West Seattle.

Fontana swung the gate open, got back into the truck, drove inside the yard, pushed the gate closed again, and parked near the Buick. In the right rear window of the Buick he spotted a red-and-white IAFF sticker, International Association of Firefighters. The trunk was open, and inside the immaculate boot he saw three pieces of aluminum trim from a junked car, the screws carefully taped to the trim in small plastic bags.

The front door to the building was closed but not locked, and, when Fontana knocked, there was no reply. Apparently Easterman had come early with the intention of picking up parts. The guy was probably just too lazy to forgo the rest of his day to meet Fontana, mixing business with business.

"Pat?" Fontana called, entering the building with Satan at his heels. It was dark and cool inside, like the shell of a little-used airplane hangar. Silence gloved the rooms.

It was a large, open building, the walls lined with dismantled engines on huge, grease-stained wooden racks, dozens of them. A rack near a set of crude wooden steps held car windows, all sizes and shapes. The place smelled of dust, car oil, weed killer, fertilizer, and rubber tires sitting in the sun. In the center of the largest room was a mountain of wheels without tires. The only artificial light in the building spilled out of a doorway at the top of the stairs.

"Pat?" Fontana went up the stairs, his shoes scraping on tiny bits of metal ground into the wooden steps, noticing for the first time how much scrap was lying around the place. As Satan trotted beside him, Fontana hoped the dog wouldn't cut his pads.

Easterman was sitting at a desk under a girlie calendar in the first small office. He wore Levi's with the cuffs rolled up the way he'd probably worn them in high school; sturdy low-cut work boots that he'd greased the day he bought them, right before he went next door and showed them off to his neighbor; a Buck knife in a tiny black holster on his belt; and sideburns of a length that had been in style fifteen years ago when he had refused to wear them because they were newfangled and worn only by young people, who had long since moved on to other styles. A practical man above all else, he didn't want to try something unless he knew it was going to last.

Satan whined at the silence. "Easy, boy."

Easterman wore nine bullet holes in his chest as if he'd meant for them to be there, centered and oozing just the tiniest bit. From the look on his face, it had been as much of a surprise to him as it was to Fontana.

"*Suche!*" said Fontana to the dog, although he was almost certain nobody else was in the building. When the dog came back a minute later, panting, looking curiously at Fontana, twisting his head from side to side, Fontana said, "*Suche! Suche!*" and sent the dog downstairs. This time he was back in a little over two minutes.

"It's okay, Satan. I was pretty sure we were alone." The dog seemed winded and fidgety, though clearly, had there been someone hiding downstairs, he would have signaled. Satan was having a busy day. First Zellner and Lee Viteri and now this.

The dead man sat in a green, wheeled office chair, his face directed at the ceiling, both hands limp on the chair arms, the chair pushed back a bit from the desk as if the impact of the bullets had shoved him backward. Nine holes that could have been covered with a man's palm. The assailant hadn't been nervous at all.

165

Fontana decided the shots had come from a large-caliber weapon, probably a handgun, since only one of the nine shots had bothered to exit out the victim's back, and then it hadn't broken all the way through the light windbreaker and plaid shirt he wore, remaining under his clothes. Nine rounds. They made pistols these days that held fifteen rounds. One had a magazine capacity of twenty-seven. Nine rounds from across the desk. Fontana glanced at the floor and noticed empty .380 shell casings.

The scarred desk was clear except for a stapler, a closed Seattle phone directory, a telephone, a dog-eared desk appointment calendar still on last month, a tin can full of pens and pencils, and an open bag of M&M's. Fontana looked around on the floor to see if anything had been dropped in the excitement. What he found was another .380 shell casing, a coffee mug on its side, and three yellow M&M's.

The dead man's eyes were half open, and Fontana had the mystical feeling that the corpse was watching him as he moved around the room.

Without displacing the bag, he pulled out a green M&M, popped it into his mouth, popped a red one into Satan's mouth, then lifted the phone receiver and pushed redial, watched the digital readout print out across the top of the phone body. He hung up before it rang, scribbling the number down on a pad he kept in his breast pocket.

Then he went downstairs, drove the truck to the gate, opened it, parked across the street, walked back across the road, closed the gate, then went into a window-blind company office and watched the whole office stop dead in its tracks when he picked up the phone, dialed 911, and said, "I'd like to report a murder."

Cops love murders, and less than two minutes later the first cop, a blond, fleshy-faced man with a crewcut, arrived in one of Seattle's blue-and-white cruisers. Fontana displayed his ID and said, "I had the dog do a search of the building. Just the dead man."

"He police-trained?" the cop asked, glancing across the street at Satan, who sat alertly in the backseat of the GMC.

"Yes. He's very good."

"Sure the guy's dead?"

"He's got enough holes for a golf course."

"You know him?"

"A gentleman named Patrick Easterman. Lived in West Seattle with his wife. Seattle fireman."

"You see anybody else when you got here?"

"Nobody. The gate was like that. One car inside. I drove in, found him, and drove over there about five minutes later."

"Okay. We'll wait until my sergeant shows. It shouldn't be more than a few minutes." A few blocks away a single siren coursed through the neighborhood on the other side of the highway, a mechanical siren, which meant a fire engine. Nobody else in town used mechanical sirens anymore. The cop said, "You got any background on this guy? What was your meeting about?"

"He was involved in that fire on King Street last March where the three firefighters were killed. I'm investigating the fire independently. We were to meet here and talk."

"Yeah, a bunch of us went to the memorial services. Grim. I never saw so many uniforms in one spot in my life. You guys got a bad job. I wouldn't go into a burning building if my life depended on it." The cop put a leg up on his fender and leaned his backside against the car.

When the blast came, it knocked him off the fender and onto the ground. Fontana was knocked to the dirt, facing away from Midcontinental Operations, and, without thinking, he found himself cradling his head, wondering if he'd been knocked down or had flattened himself. His ears were ringing. He could hear the dog barking. Pieces of flotsam hitting buildings all around the area. Pieces of corrugated tin sailing through the air. The windows across the street were mostly shattered. Several large, heavy objects rolled in the fenced yard and banged up against the cyclone fence, now canted outward. Fontana glanced back over his shoulder. Midcontinental Operations's office and warehouse were gone. He looked at his watch: 5:02. If he'd arrived at the appointed time, he would be dead.

"You all right?" The cop was standing over him.

"Yeah."

"You're shaking. Sure you're all right?"

"I'm all right!"

"Yeah, don't get pissed. I'm shitting little green nickels my-self." Fontana got to his hands and knees and looked around. All the windows in all the buildings across the street had been broken. "I just want to make sure you're all right."

"I'm all right."

"Man, I think that concussion knocked the crap out of me."

Fontana stared at him and smiled. "It kind of surprised me too."

"What the hell was that? A gas leak?"

"I didn't smell gas inside."

"Well, what the hell? If I hadn't decided to wait out here, we could have been killed."

"Tell me about it."

The officer jogged across the street, talking on his portable radio as he moved. The windshield of his cruiser was cracked. Across the street, Satan was jumping over the seats in the GMC, barking. None of the windows in the truck had any visible damage. Fontana dusted himself off and straightened up. The cop had been right. The building in the yard was almost com-pletely flattened. The second story was gone, as was any trace of Easterman.

Half a dozen cars on the highway behind the junkyard had stopped, citizens standing on the grass or on their hoods for a better look. There was no fire, just rubble and a little steam from a ruptured hot-water tank. Two of the huge stacks of crushed automobiles had tipped over. Their bulk had protected the buildings across the street, as well as Fontana and the officer. The buildings across the street had disgorged dozens of people, though everyone remained on the other side of the road.

Blue lights flashing, two more police cars careened up Ken-yon and screeched to a halt. Fontana noticed a jagged metal sliver embedded in the right front tire of the Seattle police car that had partially shielded him from the blast. He could hear air hissing out.

The first cop came back, told his co-workers what happened, then moved over to Fontana. "You okay now?"

"I was okay before."

"I didn't know if a chunk of something hadn't struck you."
"It reminded me of something, that's all."
They surveyed the flattened building together. The cop said,
"Were you as scared as I was?"
"Does Pinocchio have wooden balls?"

Twenty-nine
▲
TECHNIQUES FOR DUMPING A LOVER IN PUBLIC

*I*t was Friday and Fontana was exhausted from a sleepless night and a lazy morning talking to the cops on the phone. According to the police, Easterman's grieving wife could supply no helpful information. They strongly suspected a bungled robbery, surmising that Easterman had been robbed while waiting for Fontana, or that he had surprised a burglar in the act of ransacking the junkyard office. It turned out that Midcontinental Operations was owned and operated by Easterman's wife's brother, who had been off tending to the details of his mother's funeral. All in all, a bad week for Pat Easterman's wife.

Detective Macklin of the Seattle Police was in charge of the investigation. He phoned Fontana at the fire station Friday morning. Claiming pain from an old knee injury, Easterman had signed off duty to see his doctor shortly after Fontana visited him that afternoon. "You touch the body?" Macklin asked.

"He was warm."

"Stiff?"

"Not a bit."

"So he'd been there less than a couple of hours?"

"An hour or less. My unprofessional guess."

The explosion had been centered directly below the offices of Midcontinental Operations, so not a whole lot of Easterman's cadaver had been recovered, and that not in chunks large enough for an autopsy. The foundation around the building was intact and most of the scattered engine blocks inside the building were still inside, everything else blown into the yard, the street, or the highway behind the junkyard.

The explosive agent had been an undetermined quantity of ammonium nitrate, the same stuff Fontana had been involved with back East.

Detective Macklin said, "It went off at two minutes after five and you say you had an appointment in the office on the hour? Think that's some sort of coincidence?"

"I'd like to think that, yeah. I thought that last night before I went to bed, but I didn't sleep much thinking it."

"Anything else odd happen lately?"

"I had a run-in yesterday with a couple of people I'd talked to about the Ratt fire, but I don't see how this could have been them. I mean, technically there was enough time, but I don't see how they could have got their act together fast enough or why they would have wanted to kill Easterman." Fontana gave Macklin the full names of Zellner and Viteri.

"What about anybody else?"

"Got me," Fontana said, suddenly remembering the number he'd taken off the redial on the phone in front of Easterman's body. He gave it to Macklin.

"Was it actually Easterman who called you to set up this meeting or could it have been someone else trying to set you both up? Who would want to kill both of you and for what possible motive? Or maybe it was Easterman who set up the whole thing to kill you but then was coincidentally killed by an unrelated intruder. Did he have any reason to want you dead?"

"I can see how Easterman may have been annoyed with me, but not enough to kill me. As for who called the station, I don't know who it was. Somebody claiming to be Easterman left a message. It's not like I haven't been thinking about it, but I haven't come up with any answers," Fontana said.

Before leaving Staircase that morning he had phoned Laura from the station and arranged a luncheon date. Yesterday when he'd gotten back to Staircase, he discovered eight messages from her on his desk in the fire station, yet he hadn't returned the calls, preferring to spend the rest of the evening with his son, some old-time rock 'n' roll tunes, and a few strange thoughts.

Although he lost twelve minutes wrestling the GMC around looking for parking, he still arrived early for his appointment with Laura.

The Columbia Center was the tallest building in town, seventy-eight stories, the gargantuan mezzanine rimmed with shops and eateries. The centerpiece was a bank of tall escalators. Fontana found an empty table in the public eating area, pulled up a chair, and perused a derelict *Seattle P.I.* The explosion and dead firefighter were front-page news. A pipe fitter working twelve blocks away told of seeing a fifty-five-gallon drum rocketing a quarter-mile into the air. Fontana was thankful his name had not been mentioned.

"Hey, Dugan? Where's that lifesaving dog of yours?"

A broad smile prettying up her face, Laura Sanderson strode across the mezzanine, hips swinging, voice booming so that several women eating deli lunches nearby stared. She stood over the table looking hopelessly young, and Fontana wondered what quality he had seen in her besides availability. The thought disheartened him, made him feel old and foolish and not a little fickle. "He had some excitement yesterday so I thought it was better to give him a rest."

"You two don't seem kosher without each other."

"Brendan'll run around with him this afternoon. Give them both something to do. Course, he was upset when I wouldn't bring him along."

"Your dog was upset? What'd he do, take you off his Christmas card list?"

"Oiled my hubcaps."

Laura laughed, leaned over, and kissed Fontana hard on the lips, then sat across from him, gazing at a woman trying to maneuver a stroller through the quick-striding lunch-hour

172

crowd, most of whom were too important to be polite. Laura wore impossibly tight jeans and a white sweater, open at the throat enough for a view of the pale tops of her breasts, a faint blue vein visible along the slope of one. She crossed her legs and wiggled a sensible walking shoe in the air.

"What'chyoo been up to?" she asked.

"Interviewing."

"Anybody I know?"

"Bennie. The gang up at Station Thirty-two. Lieutenant Dimakis. You knew that. Easterman. Twice. He didn't say much the second time."

Laura looked at him curiously, bobbed her foot, and touched her tongue to her lower lip. "Would it surprise you if I told you Dimakis said we could have a drink in the back of his van? He said there was a cot back there. He said he would wear a safety. Is that gall, or what?"

Fontana watched her foot as the rhythm increased. "Maybe. Would it surprise you to find out Pat Easterman was murdered yesterday afternoon?"

"What?"

"I guess you haven't been watching the news." He explained.

When he had finished, Laura said, "They were trying to kill you."

"Who was?"

"Whoever murdered Easterman. Hey. Mac, if that explosion took place at two minutes after five, how can you have any doubt? You would have been there. You would have been finding the body at two minutes after five. The only thing that saved you was you got there early and went across the street to use the phone. They were trying to kill you too. It's obvious."

"That's just in the movies," Fontana said without conviction.

"If you'd used the phone in the junkyard the way I would have, you'd be dead, don't you think?"

"You know, Satan was uneasy in there, but I thought it was because I gave him a search command for the first time in a long while. He was trying to tell me something. But whether it means somebody was trying to get me or whether it means they were trying to wipe out the evidence of a crime . . ."

"It's also possible . . . oh, God, Mac, have you thought of this?

What if Easterman was setting you up? What if he went down there and rigged the explosives and then, before he could get out of there, somebody shot him? Maybe, like you said, somebody came in to rob the place?"

"There's a million what-ifs to this one."

"Be careful, Mac. I don't know. That run-in you had with Lee Viteri? Mac? Stay away from him. Okay? He's bughouse. I went out with him a couple of times, and he decided he owned me. You know? One of those Froot Loops? He calls ten or twelve times a day. He thinks you're the enemy."

"He looked at me funny from the beginning."

"All he talks about is revenge. What he'd do if he caught some guy with me. He's not all there, Mac."

"What did you tell him about us?"

"I told him we were an item, but that was before I realized how jealous he was. He was pestering me to go out with him again, and that was the only thing I could think of to get rid of him."

"Great."

Her indigo eyes were watery, hot, and heavy-lidded. "What do you say we blow this joint and go up the street to my office in the Belasco? They say I give great couch."

"Who's they?"

"Every swinging dick around." She grinned at him, straining to be bawdy, but succeeding only in looking young and dim-witted. It pushed a switch in him, but not the one she wanted.

"Thanks, but I have to work." He stood. "Something to eat?"

"You know, Mac, I'm not sure I understand you."

Fontana took Laura by the arm and walked with her to a deli along the outer wall of the mezzanine. "You're always so offended when I turn you down. Why is that?"

"I don't often get turned down. Can't even remember the last time. Don't you like fucking?"

"Nice question. People are listening. I like it just fine, Laura, but life has priorities. Once I start with you, I'd be there all day."

"Yeah . . . " She sighed. "You fuck good." A woman in line spun around to look Laura up and down, then turned back. Fontana paid for avocado and sprout sandwiches, soft drinks, and a wedge of carrot cake for Laura.

Back at the table, she pushed some bills at him for her share and said, "I spoke to Rudolph Freeze this morning."

Fontana pushed the bills back. "What'd he say?"

"He thought you were judgmental of him."

"That's silly. I asked questions is all." She pushed the bills back.

"He said you were being judgmental when you asked them."

"Maybe he was feeling uneasy about something."

"You *were* being judgmental. I can tell from your tone."

"I don't believe so, but I've heard things about him since that make me wonder if he was telling the truth."

"Mac, there are *things* being said about every black in the department. You believe them all?"

"Where are we going with this, Laura?"

"I don't think you're giving Freeze a fair shake. I like him." She waited for confirmation, but when he said nothing, she went on. "Why are you like this, Mac?"

"Maybe he is a terrific firefighter."

"And then there are all these rumors about Diane Cooper. Everybody seems to think she is in some way responsible for those fire deaths. I suppose you agree with them."

"Have you forgotten I'm working for Diane Cooper?"

"Doesn't mean anything." Laura's voice began to speed up, the Texas twang rounding off her words. She was slowly getting frantic about the direction their conversation was taking; at a loss to stop it, yet propelling it single-handedly. They were sliding down a chute together and neither of them had brakes. "It's all rumors. Dirty rumors. She told me so herself."

"What do you expect her to tell you?"

"I can't believe you're taking *their* word against hers. I can't believe you think she's a coward because she's a woman."

"I didn't call her a coward, for godsakes. And I haven't taken anybody's word for anything. You've got some sort of chip on your shoulder."

"I have a chip? I'm not a man whose macho territory has been invaded by women. You don't like women in the fire service. Admit it. None of the old-timers do."

"Now I'm an old-timer?" Fontana smiled. "Laura. There are people in the department who don't belong. Some of them are men, some women. Every department is like that."

"Yeah, but most of the ones who don't fit are women, right?" Laura wiped her mouth with a paper napkin. "Because it suits your sexist view of how women firefighters behave? Because no woman has as much courage as a man? You men don't even call it courage. You call it balls. *Cojones.* That's because you know *we* don't have them. You define courage in biological terms that disqualify women."

"You're trying to turn this into a male-female issue with me, and it's not. In fact, it's not an issue. I don't even know what we're arguing about. You're going off half-cocked . . ."

"Half-cocked. Another male term."

"Nice try. Half-cocked comes from the early firearms. There was a half-cock setting and a full cock. A gun wouldn't fire if it was only half-cocked."

Laura stared at him, her eyes wet and glimmering. She'd thrown her sandwich down on her paper plate, where it had broken open. "Cooper told me people were making up rumors about her. And about the other women in the department. That they're all lesbians. There's even a rumor about one of them having a sex-change operation and turning herself into a man."

"I think you think the only people capable of telling the truth about women in the fire service are other women."

"It certainly looks that way to me."

Fontana took a deep breath. "Laura, we don't need to squabble."

She gulped and tried to keep her eyes obstinate and cold, but he knew he'd punched a button. "I knew you were going to be trouble, Mac Fontana, as soon as I saw you sitting on that rock grinning at me."

"I never grinned."

"What was I to you? A one-night stand?"

"Was?"

"You're getting ready to dump me, aren't you?"

"What makes you say that?"

"When I kissed you a few minutes ago. That's what. And you turned down the couch. So answer the question."

"*Dump* isn't a word I would use. I am thinking an affair isn't something that would fit into my life just now."

"Oh, bullshit. . . . You're thinking I'm not pretty enough is what you're thinking."

"You're attractive in your own way. You're comely."

"Hah. Now I've heard everything. Laura Sanderson is comely."

"And intriguing. And sexy. And bright. Laura, it's got nothing to do with you or what you look like."

"You don't want to be around me, but you'll give me references?"

"I don't know if you're going to believe this, but it's my son."

"Are you trying to tell me you're throwing me over because screwing me would take time away from your kid?"

He knew this was sounding like horse manure, but he could think of nothing with which to replace it, even though he was becoming more and more ashamed of the idiotic way he was handling it. A smart man would shut up.

"I don't want to get involved just now because it robs him of my attention. He deserves as much as I can give. At least for the next few years. I know it sounds dumb." Lord, did it ever.

"Oh, it's just as noble as hell," Laura said. "I can hardly even believe you're telling me the truth, but I guess you are. Just as noble as hell. Thrown over by a saint. Now I've had everything done to me. Well, anyway, what say let's go have a farewell couch job? One last bang. I owe you that much. What do you say, Tiger? Tell me the truth. What was I to you?"

"I don't know. I couldn't help myself."

"And now you can? Well, hooray for self-control. And chuck you, Farley."

He watched her walk across the polished floors of the mezzanine and out the front of the building. The floppy dollars she'd pushed at him for lunch were still on the table. So was her lunch, which she had demolished during the argument. "Golly," he said. "That certainly went well."

177

Thirty

▲

RECAPITULATIONS

On Saturday Mac drove to Everett, which was a little less than an hour north of Seattle on I-5. Everett was a dying mill town desperate enough for new commerce that the city had recently, over a squall of protest, acceded to a navy facility.

A stunning woman with brown hair, a huge oval face, and intense eyes so dark as to be nearly black, Anita Jannsson greeted Fontana in her living room, her husband in the far corner with a newspaper blocking him out. Anita was a large woman in slacks and a pearl-colored blouse with a small coffee stain in the shape of a baby's bum on her lapel that would have given her apoplexy if she'd known about it. Fontana supposed she had been athletic as a schoolgirl. Her chocolate skin was as flawless as a piece of freshly glazed pottery, yet it was her composure that overwhelmed him.

"There was that inversion layer we had been living with all week. I mean, there were warnings on the radio for old people to stay indoors. At first we thought the fire was on our floor. It didn't occur to us it was downstairs until we got into the stairwell."

Fontana said, "I'd like to know about the firefighters you saw. Each of them."

"Remember, I had my hands full keeping Grace calm. First she wanted to race down the stairs in the smoke, but we got into the stairwell and it was so hot we became worried we'd be walking into a fire. And neither of us could breathe. I don't understand how you firemen can work in it. It was *so* hot. Then, when our floor started to get *really* smoky, Grace was talking about jumping. I mean—really. Sooner or later they were bound to find us."

"How *were* you found?"

"We heard a voice in the back of the building. This fireman came up the fire escape in back. It made me feel really dumb for not thinking of it. Worked there eight years, and it never occurred to me there was a fire escape to use back there."

"The firefighter say anything?"

"All I remember is he had his helmet not on his head but slung on the back of his neck by the strap. His face was all sooty, so I don't know that I could recognize him again. Not for certain. I do know this . . . "

"What's that, Mrs. Jannsson?"

"Well . . . he was not the one they showed in the papers or on the news."

"Say again?"

"The fireman who saved us wasn't the one on the news."

Fontana glanced over at her husband, who hadn't moved from behind his *Wall Street Journal*. "Mrs. Jannsson, let me get this straight. It wasn't Pat Easterman who brought you down the fire escape? Is that what you're saying?"

"That's the name. Easterman. No, it wasn't him."

"Easterman claims it was." Fontana was thinking how frenetic Anita Jannsson and Grace Fitch must have been, so jumpy neither one of them had even remembered the fire escape.

"Maybe he brought us around the front, but he didn't come up for us. That was someone else. And whoever it was, if he hadn't been on Grace like a duck on a June bug, she would have slipped off that ladder. He came down with his arms around her."

"Mrs. Jannsson? Who brought you down that fire escape?"

"All I know is he didn't have a mustache. That guy on the news had a mustache."

"Did he have an L-Three on the front of his helmet?"

"Now, that I could not tell you."

"In Seattle, firefighters wear yellow helmets. Lieutenants, red. Captains, orange. Chiefs, white. Do you recall the color of his helmet?"

"I didn't pay attention. I'm really quite afraid of heights. It might have been white or yellow."

"Was he black?"

"I realize several firemen were killed that night, so I studied their pictures in the newspaper. But it was so smoky and Grace was making such a to-do. I don't know if he was. I don't think so."

"Why didn't you say anything before?"

"I did. Months ago. After I saw this other man on the news, I called the fire department and got transferred around a whole bunch of people until I spoke to Chief Thurmond personally. Thurmond said he would take care of it."

"Officially, Easterman's still the Dugan who saved you two."

"The one with the mustache?"

"He had a mustache."

Anita was upset. "Well, that's just . . . the chief said he would handle it."

Fontana didn't want to tell her that Easterman and Chief Thurmond had come into the department together, that they had known each other for more than twenty-five years. "What happened that got you separated from the firefighter who brought you both down?"

"Were we separated?"

"You must have been. The photo in the newspaper showed Easterman escorting the two of you around the front of the building. Yet you say Easterman is not the one who brought you down."

"I don't know what happened there."

"Could there have been two firefighters escorting you down?"

"There was only one."

Fontana had been lugging around the fire department's centennial yearbook, brought it from the truck and splayed it open for Anita Jannsson, pointing out photos of Easterman, Clinton Vine, Bill Youngblood, Al Buchanan, and Diane Cooper, but she failed to identify her rescuer. On a hunch, he showed her a picture of Chief Freeze. She studied that photo longer, but claimed another blank.

Around noon on Saturday, Fontana phoned Diane Cooper. "I'm glad you called," she said. "I've been trying to reach you."

"I didn't get any messages."

"I don't like leaving messages. Easterman was killed. Somebody from Engine Twenty-six said you were there. They got called in to lay lines."

"I don't know why anybody in the department needs phones."

"What happened? What does it mean?"

"I don't know, Diane. But I would like you to come clean. Tell me everything you remember. Everything."

"But Easterman? Who would want to hurt him?"

"You tell me."

"It's beginning to get a little frightening, don't you think? I could understand if somebody wanted to hurt me."

"It might not be relevant, Diane. But there was one little thing."

"What was that?"

"There was a phone in front of Easterman's body, on the desk."

"Uh, huh."

"I pushed redial. Your number was the last one dialed from that phone."

There was a long, pregnant silence, long enough that Fontana began to have serious reservations about Diane Cooper. Almost any firefighter would be able to rig up an explosion. If she had done it, why had she hired Fontana in the first place, only to have him discover things she would kill to hide? "The police talked to me for a long time about my phone calls that day, but they wouldn't tell me why. He called here?"

"Did you talk to him, Diane?"

"I don't know. I got a call. It wasn't all that different from other calls I've been getting. I've gotten, I don't know, half a dozen since you started. Even Chief Thurmond tried to pressure me into letting you go. Thursday afternoon. I was working in the yard. Some man phoned and said, 'Back off.' That was all. Just two words. I hung up on him. I've probably gotten fifty calls like that in the past six months."

"Was this Thursday?"

"Around three or four. I'm not sure."

"Would you recognize Easterman's voice on the phone?"

"I'm not sure that I would."

Next, Fontana telephoned Mrs. Easterman and explained who he was, told her they'd met once before. She didn't seem to remember. "I'm the one who found your husband," he said.

"The police said you might be calling."

"I apologize if I caught you at a bad time."

"All times are bad right now."

"Maybe later?"

"No, I find distractions prove helpful. Any distractions. I suppose you want me to tell you what I told the police? Pat had very few friends, but I don't think he had any enemies. Once a year he'd go fishing with two of our neighbors. He'd come home from work, putter around in the garage, work on one of his projects, and then watch TV in the evening. He very rarely had anyone over."

"Did he ever say anything to you about the Ratt fire? Anything at all? I have reason to believe Pat was worried over something that happened at the Ratt."

"Of course he was. I knew right after the fire. Pat told me something. Let me see if I can remember. Something about if the fire had been an arson that meant something special about the deaths. Could that be right?"

"In this state, Mrs. Easterman, if someone sets a fire and a firefighter dies fighting it, the arsonist is guilty of murder."

"Yes. That was it."

"Did he think the Ratt was a set fire?"

"Well, I don't know. He was restless because he'd seen something he hadn't thought he was supposed to see. And it made him rather apprehensive. But then, after a week or so, he stopped talking about it, and I forgot it until now."

"What was it he saw, Mrs. Easterman? This is very important."

"Pat never said."

"But you knew there was something upsetting him?"

"It had to do with the fire possibly being an arson. I'm sure of that. I remember the day he read the official cause of the fire was accidental, he breathed a sigh of relief and just never said another word about it."

"Mrs. Easterman? What did Pat see at that fire?"

"I'm telling you, Pat never said. He just never said. But I had the feeling he saw somebody or something he shouldn't have. Somebody he knew. But he wouldn't tell me about it. You saw how Pat was."

"Mrs. Easterman, if you think of something else, would you give me a call?"

"Certainly. But I do have one little question. If you don't mind. You found him?"

"Yes."

She hesitated. "Did he suffer?"

"It was instantaneous, Mrs. Easterman."

"Are you sure?"

"Instantaneous."

Fontana spent a few lackadaisical days making more phone calls, organizing information, typing up notes, outlining the beginnings of a report, walking in the woods and thinking things over. When all was said and done, he had spoken to more than a hundred Seattle firefighters, in person and on the phone.

It was difficult, if not impossible, for Fontana to hold people to the topic of the King Street fire. Affirmative action, downgraded hiring standards, and inferior firefighters crept into conversations. Most often women and minorities were singled out, quite possibly for no other reason than that often a white male was doing the talking.

The serious racist language had come from the mouths of Bennie Zellner and ex-chief Youngblood, stepson and stepfather, as if being out of the department gave them leeway to turn malevolent, yet he knew that bigots were not only clever at using the "politically correct" language these days, but that they were not prone to think of themselves as bigots. Whatever the case, when it came to race, Seattle firefighters were careful about what words they chose. When it came to women, *split-*

tails and other derogative terms were used without thought, providing there weren't any women within earshot.

Another week passed, during which Fontana spent more time with Brendan and less time in Seattle quizzing firefighters. The red Mustang did not reappear and Fontana had to wonder whether the man in the Mustang was an irate firefighter, upset over the fact that he was working for Diane Cooper, or someone else with some other motive. Either way, Fontana was not happy about being followed or about having had a pistol pointed at his gut.

On the phone he spoke to the chief of services in Seattle, once again to an irascible Chief Thurmond, who wondered aloud why Fontana had not completed the investigation, and to twenty-seven more firefighters. It seemed the Ratt had metamorphosed into a mythical elephant described by an army of blind men.

Half a dozen nasty rumors about Diane Cooper were sliding along on the dirty grease of resentment. Yet there were unanswered questions. Had it been strictly personal when Youngblood cursed her after they changed bottles, or was it a result of something that had happened in the fire? And why had neither Freeze nor Easterman heard Diane's shouts from the fire escape? Freeze claimed someone had been there at all times, and Easterman had vowed that, aside from rescuing the two women, he didn't leave his post. Was it possible that there had been no cries from the fire escape? That Cooper had been so weakened and delirious from the smoke, she had just imagined calling for help? And what had caused Easterman to be so vague and squeamish when discussing the Ratt? Was it possible that he had not rescued the women, that Youngblood or Vine had and he was taking the credit?

Laura Sanderson left a message at the fire station saying that in the event he needed to give back the materials she had loaned him, she would be in Toronto for a week but would return Tuesday. She left a phone number in Toronto.

Fontana had listened to the tapes of the radio transmissions and discovered people weren't exaggerating Chief Freeze's inadequacies. He cut off the beginning of more than half of his transmissions. Thirty percent had to be repeated to the dispatcher, and several were plainly never received by anybody:

dispatcher, fire ground commander, or other officers at the fire.

At the time Ladder 3 had been in trouble on the fourth floor, Freeze had made a transmission that was so garbled, Fontana could make out only, "This is C sector command . . . " Then a bunch of static and clicking. Fontana had a sick feeling that Freeze had been addressing Ladder 3's portable, but, if so, Freeze hadn't persisted, had not obtained a reply. None of the official investigations had mentioned the cutoff or the garbled message. None of the official reports had mentioned Freeze's problems on the radio, his problems being understood.

Mac thought long and hard about something else in the reports. There had been two flashlights discovered in the basement with Clinton Vine's body. Both were the small, personal flashlights Seattle firefighters clipped to the front of their bunking coats. While they found a larger battle lantern alongside Bill Youngblood, his personal flashlight had not been recovered. Mac wondered if Clinton might have borrowed Youngblood's flashlight, and, if so, when? Could it have happened after he went back onto the fire floor, after leaving Diane Cooper on the fire escape? Or could the extra light have belonged to Cooper? Nobody had bothered to inventory her equipment.

Mac made a list of people he hadn't been able to contact, making phone calls and waiting for people to return from Reno, weddings on the East Coast, sailboarding vacations in Mexico, and, in one case, a burro expedition in the Grand Canyon. Northwesterners were frantically trying to snatch up the last slim strands of summer.

When the muse struck, Fontana drifted into Station 1 in Staircase and gave advice to Kingsley, but Kingsley had come up with a new procedure for Thursday night and Saturday morning training sessions, displaying a sudden independence and cool efficiency.

Now that he was not driving into town every day, Mac took advantage of the extra time to resume his hikes up Mount Gadd, the mountain still salted with the random autumn hiker.

As much as possible, he spent the afternoons with Brendan, walking him home from school, and, while he was at it, catching the eye of one or two mommies waiting in the parking lot to round up their brood, engines idling.

Brendan's baby-sitter, Mary, caught Mac up on the latest town gossip. For the third time that year the rumor ("Gospel truth. I know for a fact this happened, and they want it secret to keep us from panicking . . . ") circulated that a man-woman team was kidnapping, raping, then murdering beauty-parlor customers in back of Vale Sorenson's parlor. Mac laughed at that one. Bud Caspeneau fell out of a tree and was ambulanced to Swedish Hospital in Seattle with a concussion. Bud had, in the past, fallen off his roof and out of his moving Jeep. He'd been injured by his own dog after putting on a disguise and a hood as he tried to train the dog to attack strangers. He'd tumbled backward off his tractor and been dragged a quarter-mile through a field dripping with fresh steer manure. And one time he called the FD for a hysterical child when one of his daughter's hamsters died. Bud figured it would be easier for his daughter to accept if she thought the hamster had *wanted* to die, so he strung the already-dead critter up in his cage with dental floss and told her he'd hanged himself. Bud came from a broken mold.

Friday night Mac left Brendan with Mary and drove to the Bedouin, the local dance hall, unofficially the slow-dancing capital of the Northwest, where beer and ballads had become a Friday and Saturday night rite.

Thirty-one

▲

SLOW DANCING WITH
A WOMAN WHO STRADDLES
A BROOMSTICK

*M*ayor Mo Costigan loved to dance almost more than she loved to bicker, a better dancer even than his late wife, and she had been good. After another tune or two she would loosen up and be herself, but right now she was as preoccupied as a skunk in a kindergarten.

Patsy Cline wrenched out her rendition of "I Fall to Pieces" as Mo moved casually but affectionately with Mac in the crowd of dancers at the Bedouin, holding him closer than seemed appropriate given the fact that she had been backbiting since they arrived. Awash with rain, this particular Saturday night at the Bedouin was slower than normal.

Despite weekly requests, Velma, the owner, refused to tolerate square dancing, although it would have gone over big in a town where a good 20 percent of the males wore cowboy hats to church and where the electric guitar had replaced the organ in at least one congregation. Stocking her jukebox with Sinatra, Johnny Mathis, Roy Orbison, and other balladeers, Velma claimed square dancing was for people with smaller brains, prompting one dissenter to answer, "Well, we need a place to dance too."

Neon-pink and green, her sunglasses looked too young for Mo, who was only thirty but who usually dressed in no-nonsense business attire. She'd obtained the sunglasses from her father, the druggist, who gave them to her because they had a chip in the left lens and he couldn't sell them. Mo's mistake was in believing they concealed her black eye.

She had driven to Fontana's house shortly after dinner and found Mac and Brendan playing ball with an aluminum bat and an oversized softball, Satan shagging the runs when they bounded down the driveway.

It took Mo only a minute to cajole Mac into dancing.

It was the first time they had driven together to the Bedouin instead of "running into each other," but she didn't seem to place any import on it, thumbing through a *Firehouse* magazine on his coffee table while he took a shower and climbed into slacks and a new shirt. Brendan went over to Mary's before Mac was out of the shower, carrying along a jar that housed one of the summer's last grasshoppers, which they both knew Mary would fuss over.

When they got into her Porsche, Mo studied him long enough to apply lipstick, bartering for time as she peered into her rearview mirror. "What needs to happen, Mac, is you need to help me hire a couple of women and a minority for the Staircase Fire Department."

"Uh, you're getting a little confused again, Mo. I'm doing the hiring. You and the council agreed on that."

"Sure. Sure. But I'm not going to have anybody saying we weren't fair about this. We're going to have women in the department, Mac. Professional women firefighters. I'm not going to be the last little town on the Eastside to catch up. You get done with your project this next week, and you hire these people. I don't have any idea how to pick out a fireperson."

"Then why meddle in it?"

"Just make sure you hire two women and a minority. I was thinking Asian or Mexican this time. We already have a black. You can just toss all the black applications. Actually, most of those Asians are pretty smart and probably don't need hand-outs either. Throw out the Asian applications too. Make it a

Mexican. Then he won't have to pick apples or wait tables. And, actually, I have a cousin who works at the Mountain Hardware. She might be interested. So, there you go. I got two of them for you. A beaner and my cousin."

"Mo, do you know what that sounds like?"

"I'm a politician. Do you think I'm stupid enough to say what I think in public? I'm telling it to you, Mac, so you'll understand the situation. We're going to have a black, two women, and a beaner. Then nobody can criticize."

The Porsche's rear tires fired pebbles across the yard as Mo manhandled the car out of his driveway. When Mac's head slammed against the seat, the glove box flapped open. In his lap and on the floor he found a brassiere, two open packs of cigarettes (Mo didn't smoke), five match folders from local motels, half of a pair of handcuffs, a broken flashlight, a cracked coffee cup, four pairs of defective sunglasses, an unopened package of Polaroid film, an open package of lubricated pastel condoms, a tattered *Newsweek* magazine featuring an article about the nation's small-town mayors (Mo had been mentioned), and a single man's shoe. Mac wasn't able to fit it all back into the glove compartment.

"Done snooping through my stuff?"

"It popped open."

"You were snooping."

"It popped open, Mo, I said. I always wondered who threw all those shoes out on the highway. Everywhere you go, it seems like you see a shoe by the side of the road. You're the one."

"I can explain that."

"You got a beaut of a black eye, Mo. Can you explain that?"

Mo glanced in the rearview mirror and cocked her head at different angles, trying to figure out how he had guessed. "Well, don't worry about it. I popped her a good one back my own self."

"Her? You were in a girl fight? You should have called me."

"That's sweet, but I didn't need any help. I met up with a gal who was putting up posters of me that said, 'Ladies, keep your man away from this woman.' "

"You should have called me."

"I didn't need help."

"Who said anything about help? To watch. I like girl fights."

"You're hilarious. Save me the last dance, huh?" she said as they pulled into a parking space behind the Bedouin.

"You got it."

He danced alternately with a pair of visiting backpackers who had decided to stay in town and make a weekend of it, a roly-poly, foot-sore pair who looked enough alike to be sisters. In their early thirties, the first had been divorced twice, the other once.

As he was dancing, a slim forearm reached up and tapped his partner's shoulder, cutting in.

Laura Sanderson slid into his arms effortlessly, her indigo eyes imbuing the look of someone who had been making plans. "She your new lover?"

"I don't have a lover, Laura."

"No one since me? That's hard to believe. I wish I could say the same."

"Even if you could, you wouldn't. What is it, Laura?"

"Just a dance with one of my favorite guys. Is that all right?"

They were quiet for a minute. Laura had a mismatched assortment of earrings in each ear. Her hair was wild, wind-tossed. She wore a black motorcycle jacket, raggedy holes in both shoulders, jeans patched with leather, rips in the knees, and, under the jacket, a black corset/bra affair. She looked as though she had spent a paycheck on makeup and was determined to wear it all at once. Everybody was staring at her and she loved it.

"Look. I went out to your place, but nobody was around. I asked the neighbor lady."

"It's nice to see you, Laura."

"Really?"

He smiled and lied. "It is."

They danced. Since the explosion at Midcontinental Operations he had felt like a different person, definitely not the sort to fool around with a twenty-two-year-old journalist who asked him how many people he'd killed. The murder and the explosion had put a kind of shock through his belief system that had him in a constant state of reevaluation. People went around thinking they weren't going to die. That was part of life, thinking you weren't going to die, yet the explosion had reminded Fontana of all those years after the "incident" back East when he'd been wondering why he didn't die. Wondering why you didn't die is a whole different mental atmosphere from thinking you won't.

The number ended and another began. Mo Costigan drifted through the crowd holding hands with a man in a suit, and began dancing. When Mo spotted Mac with Laura, her look lingered curiously before she turned away. Laura leaned back, a move that ground her pelvis into Mac, and looked up at him, her tinted contacts shimmering in the shadowy light. "Did you know Cooper was promoted to lieutenant? She's working at Station Forty. So, how are you doing on the investigation?"

"I think I need a beer." Fontana spent twenty minutes watching Laura dance with other men. After a while, Mo Costigan, who had been talking to a woman with a beehive hairdo, skipped down four stools at the bar to sit next to him. "That's not the reporter, is it?"

"Just flew back from Toronto."

"On her broomstick? My, my, she's popular. Listen, Mac. You've been putting Staircase into kind of a high profile lately."

"I thought you liked a high profile."

"Yeah, well, all that trouble last summer. The thrust of what I'm trying to say here is, you're causing problems. You bring in a cheap, snoopy reporter. Look at that getup. And you knoooooow those aren't her boobs. Who knows what she'll write about the town?"

"Yeah, maybe she'll find out about your black eye."

"Chief Thurmond called. Seattle isn't real pleased with the negative attitude you're bringing to the investigation."

"Putting pressure on me through you was highly unethical, Mo."

"Thurmond said you were asking unorthodox questions. Being generally uncooperative with his administration. Mac, the way I understand it, they've already written a report on the Ratt. All you have to do, really, is copy theirs."

"Did he suggest that?"

"It only makes sense."

"I hope you told him to go jump in a lake."

"Actually . . . "—Mo sipped from a beer stein—"I told him we'd have a chat, see if I couldn't settle you down. Thurmond and I are having lunch Monday to discuss it, and I promised I would bring you along." Fontana snorted and laughed, trying not to aspirate a mouthful of beer. "You will be there, Mac. That is a direct order. Do you know how it will make me look if you don't show?"

"One, I'm on vacation. Two, even if I wasn't, this has absolutely nothing to do with you or Staircase. Three, Chief Thurmond has no vote on how I perform."

"You're beginning to upset me, Mac."

"Good. I like it when you're upset. It means you're thinking."

Mo glanced across the space between them, her face running through a catalog of expressions before eroding into a weak smile, the smile she would wear if she smashed her car into another vehicle at an intersection, then won the resulting argument with the other driver. Mo had priorities, and being right was at the top of her list. She was one of those keenly intelligent people who were right about a lot of things, but whose primary complication in life was that they assumed they were right about *everything*. "You *will* be at lunch with us on Monday."

"Actually, I've scheduled a bowel movement for noon Monday."

"Good Lord. I can't tell that to Chief Thurmond."

"Want me to write him a note?"

"Your job just might be on the line over this, Mr. Fontana."

"Mo. Watch real careful. If I start getting smaller, it means I'm walking away."

"You always say that. Mac? Mac?"

Fontana was already across the room cutting in on Laura. They danced through the end of that tune and into the next. Finally, Laura said, "Any more attempts on your life? Any more bodies?"

"Life's been pretty dull the last week."

"Just the way you like it, huh?"

"Exactly the way I like it."

"I need to tell you something. Lee Viteri's been after me. I had to call the police last night to keep him away from my apartment. We slept together, what, three, four times, and suddenly he thinks he owns me. Anyway, I wanted to warn you to watch out for him. Mac?"

"Yeah?"

"When we broke up . . . I just thought it might last a little longer. You realize, because of you I spent two days shacked up in a hotel room in Toronto with a guy named Fritz. We're going to correspond."

"Charming story." As soon as he had the time, he decided, he was going to get a blood test.

"Anyway, Mac, first thing Monday morning, I'm going to the Belasco and get all my stuff out of the *Sensation Plus* office. I think Lee's been snooping in there when I'm not around. He scares me, that's all. Last night he called and asked me to go to Tahiti with him on his yacht. I said he didn't have a yacht. He claimed he would have one shortly. He's crazy, is what he is."

Thirty-two

▲

SMOKE IN THE CITY
AS A BASIC
TOURIST ATTRACTION

Monday, the foothills were smothered in fog, and in Staircase the drizzle was punctuated at irregular intervals by thunder rolling down from near Snoqualmie Pass. According to the truck radio, it was raining everywhere in the state.

The investigation had dragged into October, and Fontana was hoping he could begin typing the final draft of his report tonight, though it bothered the hell out of him that he hadn't come to any real conclusions. There were so many things missing.

He went to the fire station in Staircase for breakfast and found Pettigrew in the beanery chewing a cud of sunflower seeds. "You got messages waiting," said Kingsley.

"Yeah?"

"One from Chief Thurmond. One from that young lady you was seeing a couple weeks ago."

Thurmond he didn't need to hear from. Nor Laura, who had spent Saturday night alone in the Staircase Motel after her car had broken down outside the Bedouin. He knew she had wanted to spend the night with him, suspected she now wanted him to oversee the car repairs. He left without reading either message.

When he crossed Lake Washington on the new floating bridge, the water on the north side of the bridge was like molten glass measeled with raindrops while the south side had a slight chop to it. He drove to Station 40 in a nice residential area in the north end of town. Fontana parked and discovered the engine was out and the back door unlocked.

When he thumbed through their daybook, he saw they had been dispatched to Station 25 on Capitol Hill to fill in. There was a 211 going on downtown, and uninvolved companies were being reassigned to cover the city more evenly.

Twenty-fives was a glass and concrete monolith at the corner of Thirteenth and Pine. When Fontana parked in back and walked around to the front, a short, stumpy man in chinos and a pale yellow windbreaker zipped to the neck opened the door from inside, nodding and grinning and nodding some more. There was a name tag safety-pinned to his jacket: Mike. He had Down's syndrome. Fontana supposed he was the station mascot, similar to Claude in Staircase.

Engine 40 had signed in ten minutes earlier, though they were gone now. A few minutes later, Ladder 3, also filling in, pulled into a stall after the man with Down's syndrome galloped over and opened its door. "Heeeey, Mikey," said one of the firefighters, who went directly to the beanery in the rear of the station and tuned in the monster television.

It was another ten minutes before Diane Cooper showed up on Engine 40, wearing a shiny-new red lieutenant's helmet.

When she came into the watch office, she glanced at Fontana, murmured, "Sons of bitches" under her breath, signed into the daybook, then went into a room off the corridor and wrote something in a green notebook. When she came out she dropped her helmet and peeled off her bunking boots and pants, leaving the equipment in the doorway. Underneath she was wearing a lake-blue officer's shirt and dark navy trousers with the creases pulled out of line on her muscular thighs.

"Wanna talk?" she asked, wiggling her stocking feet.

He followed her into the office, where she closed the door and stepped into a pair of black uniform brogans. "Congratulations on the promotion. When did that happen?"

"Few days ago."

"Do you have time? There's a 211 downtown, isn't there?"

"Doesn't seem to be too much going on with it. There's almost no radio traffic. Maybe an electrical vault, something, because I heard City Light getting called. Most of the units are on standby."

Fontana shifted his weight. "I think you're a good firefighter, Diane. I think you went to the Ratt and you had the whole crew against you . . ."

"Clinton wasn't."

"I think Youngblood encountered a hazard of the profession. The water heaters fell over on him in the smoke and broke his leg. If somebody could have got him out, he would have been okay. But two people tried, Buchanan and Vine, and they failed. Buchanan was afraid of smoke. Didn't know that, did you? I think when Buchanan's bottle began running out, he panicked. I can't prove that, but that's what I think."

Cooper became very still, eyes unblinking.

"I think Youngblood gave the radio to Buchanan because he was in too much pain to use it, not realizing how wired Buchanan was. I think the hero of the story here is Clinton Vine. He went back in alone looking for them. I don't know if that was the wisest move. I think you did what you were told throughout the fire. I think you took a hell of a beating in the smoke."

Cooper's blue eyes were beginning to grow watery.

"I believe Chief Freeze was derelict in his duty. One of the crews he was supposed to keep track of was Ladder Three. He seems to have forgotten them completely. And now he tries to blame the tragedy on Ladder Three itself. I think the department could officially exonerate Chief Freeze because they had all these unofficial rumors about you to fall back on.

"So you've been taking the rap. Unofficially. I think Easterman was lying about something. One of the women he supposedly rescued says he wasn't the man who saved them. I'm telling you these things so you can know what I'm thinking. Also, Easterman's wife says he was worried about something after the Ratt fire. He seems to have thought it was a set fire. That would mean the deaths were murder."

"What did he know?"

"Whatever it was, he didn't tell his wife."

Cooper had tears in her eyes. "You don't believe I choked? That I could have saved them but saved myself instead? You don't believe they were looking for me? That I was hiding somewhere?"

He shook his head.

Cooper turned toward the wall and tried to compose herself. Fontana remained standing, hands in his pockets.

"When we were up there, on the fourth floor, I heard something, footsteps or something, above us. Like a woman's high heels. I tried to tell Bill, but he wouldn't listen. I told Buchanan, but he followed Bill's lead. I told Clint outside on the fire escape, but by that time we had Bill and Buchanan to worry about."

"You're saying you realized you were searching the wrong floor?"

"That's exactly what I'm saying." Cooper slapped her thighs with both hands, cupped her palms to her face, then spoke through a knot of fingers. "All I remember after that is being in the aid car and then in the hospital. I had a lot of weird dreams the weeks after that fire. After a while, the dreams began twisting the memories."

"Freeze claims he sent you to the fifth floor, yet your crew went to the fourth. Later on, when the search started up, Freeze told his superiors you were on the fifth. That mistake caused an additional delay in finding Buchanan and Youngblood."

"Maybe Freeze and Youngblood each made an honest mistake. I don't know. When they began their search I'd been in the hospital, probably fifteen minutes. They didn't initiate it until they talked to me. By then Bill was already dead."

In the other room the scanner had been squawking, mostly radio messages from Six Avenue Command, which was what the chief in charge of the fire downtown was calling himself. Now Six Avenue Command said, "Turn off the repeater."

Cooper held up her hand. "They do that when something happens that they don't want the press to hear. See, actually our radios don't broadcast very far by themselves, but our transmissions are picked up by repeaters all over the city and rebroadcast. When they turn off the repeaters, only the dispatcher can hear what we're radioing."

"Okay, Six Avenue Command," said the dispatcher. "Repeater off."

"That's the fourth time in the last thirty minutes," Cooper said. "I'm beginning to suspect what's going on down there is bigger than I thought." The whole station grew silent. In the beanery the TV had been silenced.

Cooper nodded.

Fontana said, "It's funny about this job. You can go months without anything serious. A whole career, sometimes. And then in one minute all the stars fall to earth."

The captain and a firefighter were already outside in front of the station staring toward downtown and scanning the horizon for smoke plumes. When Fontana and Cooper followed them, they saw only a thin column of black smoke spiraling up from the skyscrapers in the distance.

"I have an ugly feeling about this," said Cooper. "The Belasco Building's got all those fire-suppressant systems. How could they have a fire?"

Thirty-three

▲

LOVE NOTES FROM
A SCARED WOMAN

Before anybody could say anything, the bells in the station clanged, and Engine 40 and Ladder 3 were dispatched to the Belasco Building. After they left, Mike shut the apparatus doors, overseeing the automatic mechanism until the station was silent, then, dressed in authority, he strode into the watch office. Fontana waited at the silent radio scanner for a few minutes before reaching beneath the watch-office console and switching on a TV.

Microphone in hand, a reporter in a double-breasted raincoat stood several blocks up the street from the Belasco, speaking urgently. "Police and firefighters are on the scene here in downtown Seattle and will continue, apparently, to be on the scene for quite some time. It is unknown at this time precisely how many terrorists have taken the building or just what demands have been made, if any, but the FBI has been called in. What we have to realize here is that, of course, all the problems here are compounded by the fact that the building seems to be on fire.

"Just a few minutes ago the fire department put a ladder up

in an apparent attempt to rescue some of the trapped victims. Immediately after the ladder was extended to the building, we here, at our location, heard what sounded to this reporter like gunfire. It is not yet exactly clear what has occurred. Whether Seattle Police Department sharpshooters wounded one or more of the persons holding the building, or whether one of the uniformed personnel here in some official capacity was injured. We do not know if any bystanders were injured. We *do* know that just a few minutes ago the fire department took several apparent victims away from the scene in aid cars. We do not know who these people were."

The man in the raincoat pressed a finger to an earpiece. "The condition of the building? The condition of the building, Hal? All we know is this. It is a forty-eight-story skyscraper. There are an undetermined number of workers still inside. Apparently, at this point in time, neither the police department nor the fire department has been able to gain access, although we have had some reports of the police SWAT teams entering and leaving. These reports have not been confirmed.

"The SWAT team, by the way, was supplied with fire-department oxygen tanks, but apparently the team, although they have been trained in their use, had some trouble in the smoke and had to leave the building. The inside of the building, at least the lower portions, Hal, oh, I'd say the first four or five floors, seem absolutely charged with very dense and very black smoke. At one point the fire department attempted to place blowers at the entrance of the building, but those attempts have been abandoned and we've seen no further physical attacks on this fire. We have no word about the fire-suppression systems inside the building or what, in fact, those systems may include.

"And there's another interesting point about this emergency here in downtown Seattle, Hal. Nobody seems to know exactly where the fire is.

"You can see, if you look carefully, people waving what appear to be pieces of drapery in the windows of the Belasco. As far as we can tell from our viewpoint—and the Seattle Police Department won't let us get any closer—almost no one has left the building. At least, not since we've been at this location.

"We were told earlier by witnesses who said they had been inside the Belasco visiting a merchant shipping company on the thirty-eighth floor that as they were leaving they saw two men in coveralls welding something to the front doors. Apparently, Hal, the building has been sealed from the inside."

The in-studio newsman asked, "John, does the Seattle Police Department have members inside the Belasco at this time?"

"Hal, they may have personnel inside the Belasco, but we don't have any confirmation on that. What we do have from one of the people who works across the street and who was just evacuated a few minutes ago is that the SWAT team did enter through an undetermined entrance at the front of the building, through that very dense and very foul-smelling black smoke you can see from here, and they were wearing what appeared to be fire-department breathing devices. There was some gunfire from inside the building at that time, or what appeared to sound like gunfire, and our witness says that after only a very few minutes inside the building, all of the uniformed personnel withdrew."

"Does the situation seem to be getting any worse, John?"

"Hal, as near as we can tell, the amount of smoke has remained constant since early this morning, oh, around eight forty-five or so, when this incident seems to have begun. Also, there really have been no flames reported, as of yet. In fact, the very nature of this problem is in dispute by members of the fire department itself."

"John, the fire department tells us they got their first call at eight forty-seven—"

Fontana switched through the three major news channels until he found one with a view from a helicopter showing the Belasco with black smoke coming from two roof vents. A cluster of fifteen or twenty unhappy-looking people in business dress were standing on the roof, waving coats and scarves at the news chopper.

Fontana's stomach was beginning to feel as if he'd swallowed a quart of cold dishwater. He went down the hallway to the phone booth and made a call. "Kingsley? Do me a favor. Read that message to me. The one from Laura S."

"Just a minute, Boss." The line was silent a moment. "Here.

It says, this is what it says, Mac. 'I'm in the *Sensation* office. Call immediately. In trouble. Your everlasting wonder, Laura.' Zero nine ten hours.''

"That's all?''

"It's Pettigrew's crabby little handwriting. He told me after you left she wanted to know if Claude could patch a call to you through the county dispatcher to find you. I thought you knew.''

"Claude sat all through breakfast and didn't say a word?''

"Maybe he thought you already got the message. It *was* taped to the wall over your desk.''

"Maybe he has shit for brains. Or maybe I do. The TV on?''

"We've been watching. Are you in town?''

"Until I can get out, I am.''

Fontana hung up, riffled through the telephone directory in the booth, dialed the office of *Sensation Plus*, and got a recording. At the beep, he said, "This is the jerk who doesn't have a phone and doesn't read his messages. I'm in Seattle about . . . a mile from the Belasco. If you're there, Laura, give me a call.'' He racked the receiver after leaving the number.

Fontana recalled Bennie Zellner's speech that first day, about how easy it would be to burn down one of Seattle's high rises, and the talk in his brother's journal about revenge. Zellner, if he were behind this, had been planning it for a very long time.

He dialed *Sensation Plus* a second time, left another message.

"Trouble,'' said Mike, elongating the word. Mike was ensconced in a chair beside the desk in the watch office watching the television.

"Big trouble,'' said Fontana. "I'm wondering how many people are in that building.''

"Ten?''

"Probably more, Mike.''

Fontana dialed the *Sensation Plus* offices again. In the other room Mike was watching a woman reporter explain that an as-yet-unnamed terrorist group was demanding ransom for the Belasco, fifty million from the city or everybody inside would die before nightfall. "Hello?'' Her voice was remote, tenuous.

"Laura?''

"Mac! Where have you been? I've called everyone on earth trying to track you down.''

"You all right?"

"I'm scared. You know who's doing this?"

"Zellner?"

"Who else could have got the building ready without anybody knowing? Somebody on our floor tried the elevator, and when the doors came open there were two bodies inside. We ended up dragging them into the men's restroom down the hall. One of the dead guys had false teeth that fell out. This lady stepped on them and they exploded all over the place. She went hysterical for a few minutes. Somebody slapped her just like in the movies. Just like in the movies, Mac. Except she slapped him back and stayed hysterical. Mac, what are we going to do?"

"You checked the stairs?"

"Full of smoke. Both sides. Mac, you've got to get me out."

"How much smoke is on your floor?"

"It's not too bad on any given floor. There's a guy here came up from twelve. The doors are locked. You get in the stairs and you're locked in. It was lucky we heard him banging or he would be dead now. There's two cellular phones on this floor, Mac. One was the one from my office. All the other phones are out. There are some men down the hall using the other one to keep in touch with the police. Mac, I'm so scared I've been running to the john every ten minutes. I got in here early, just after six. There were trucks downstairs in the parking garage. I saw Bennie Zellner and I think Lee Viteri. Mac, I think even if they pay him what he's asking, and you know they won't, I think he's going to blow us to rubble."

"What are you talking about, Laura? Blow who to rubble?"

"Me. All of us. Explosives. Tons of the stuff. In the basement all around the building. Tons. I went downstairs with an armload of stuff, leaving, and they wouldn't let me out. Bennie was there with two of his apes. And across the hall was a room full of sacks. Wires all over. They made me go back upstairs. I didn't know what else to do. The front door had bars welded all across. Mac, I'm scared."

"Laura, there's got to be some connection between Zellner and Pat Easterman. There were two explosions in Seattle in the last couple of weeks. One I saw on the news. Remember? A house blew up. I was at the other one. Zellner was practicing at the first. The second one, the junkyard, was a warm-up to this.

"Laura, I'm guessing they haven't really set the building on fire. They're generating smoke somehow. If they set the building on fire, there'd be a possibility of losing control. This is a controlled evolution. They've got access to the fire control room too. They've flooded the stairwells with smoke to keep everybody pinned."

"The TV claimed they want fifty million dollars."

"I heard."

He had seen them unloading a truck the other day in the garage. He had seen a welding rack, and the floor had been gritty with what he had taken to be dirt. Ammonium nitrate was easy to get and easy to pass off as harmless. He'd walked in on them unloading supplies for the assault, and now he wondered what they would have done to him that afternoon if Satan hadn't come to the rescue. The phone was slick in his sweating hand as he contemplated how close he must have come to getting cold-cocked and folded away in a storage locker.

"Laura, have they disabled every system in the building?"

"Only in the last few minutes. There's no water anywhere. The toilets are starting to reek. No electricity. And there's no air movement in the offices. One of the guys noticed that. He's got asthma. We tried to break out a window in the other office with a fire ax one of the guys found. The ax just bounced off the glass."

"They're controlling the pressure on all the floors, Laura. You can be thankful there's no air movement, because if there was, it'd be charged with smoke. Don't break out any windows unless you absolutely have to. Smoke would creep up the building from the outside and get into your floor. Every fourth or fifth window will have a white dot down in the right-hand corner. That's a pane that'll break. Tell them not to do anything unless they have no alternative."

"Mac, I wish you were here."

It would have been cruel to confess to her how glad he was not to be. "My guess is the building has ammonium nitrate in it. A lot of it."

"I think Bennie said forty tons."

"How long did you talk to him?"

"Just seconds. He was giving lots of orders. He had a walkie-talkie."

"How many people did you see with Zellner?"

"In the basement I saw Bennie, Lee, and one other. Then, as I was leaving, four other guys. Mac, I'm only twenty-two. Don't you think that's too young to die?"

"Laura, you're not going to die."

Zellner and his roughnecks had the building in a net, and for three hours now, nobody had been able to cut through. It seemed implausible, but any high-rise building was a natural bottleneck, two or three small entrances at the base, with hundreds, possibly thousands, of people stacked on top of that. In fact, the taller the building, the more likely the strategy was to work. A seven-story building could be evacuated by aerial ladder. A forty-eight-story building . . .

"The TV guys keep saying the building's on fire, Mac."

"They have to assume it is. You always plan for the worst. Does the city know about the explosives?"

"We called and told them. I guess we should all plan to die."

"Don't say that."

"You know, it's so funny, Mac, because some of us are so nervous we're about ready to keel over, and the others just think the fire department will take care of it. Bennie liked me. I know he did. And he gave me this real funny look when he told me to go upstairs, you know, like he was sentencing me to the electric chair. All morning I've been thinking about that look, and it's been giving me a hell of a headache. I have this feeling I'm going to die, and I don't like it."

"We're all going to die, darlin'. But not today."

"The department let me ride an aid car a couple of weeks ago, and they got a run to this older guy who was having chest pains. He kept saying he thought he was going to die and his wife kept telling him he was okay and he kept saying he thought he was going to die and you know what—he died. They told me . . . I guess you know this already . . . one of the main symptoms of a heart attack is a feeling that you're going to die. Like you know something. And then you die. I feel like that, Mac. Like I know something. Mac?"

"Laura."

"Can you figure some way to get me out?"

"I wish I could. I'm going to stay here, keep in touch with you, and if something develops, I'll be nearby. Deal?"

"Geezus, Mac. I've been trying to get you on a phone all morning thinking once I heard your voice I would be safe. And now you say there's nothing you can do. You've always been nice to me. Except when you dumped me. I really appreciate this, Mac. I'm going down the hall and check in with the others and tell them about those windowpanes, then I'll come back and call you in a while."

As soon as Mac cradled the receiver it jangled.

"Keeriste, don't you guys ever get off that phone?"

"What do you want?" Fontana asked.

"Peter there?"

"Peter's out."

"He be back for lunch?"

"Real doubtful."

Thirty-four

▲

DEATH AS YOUR BASIC APHRODISIAC

*T*oward evening it stopped raining, though the streets remained wet and slick and the heavy gray clouds shouldered away the daylight.

For half an hour around noon the building had filled up with sweaty officials barking orders as the fire department and the police toyed with the idea of using Station 25 for their command post. In the end, they vanished from the station in silent unison like a school of fish making a sudden turn.

When he came into the building, Harcourt Thurmond spoke to some flustered fat men in suits, then approached Fontana. "Yeah? You think I'm worried about your silly little report? About putting the finger on some chiefs? Think again, buddy. We've got a situation here. A situation. I've got ten million dollars in cash in a bank car. We're trying to get the rest together to wire out of the country. This sonofabitch is going to get away with it. The thing I don't understand is, we've got him trapped. How's he planning to come out of that building without getting caught?"

"Have you seen him?" asked Fontana.

"What do you mean?"

"What makes you think he's inside?"

"Oh, Christ. We haven't even thought of that. We're trying to hold off on turning the money over until the last minute. Maybe he'll surrender before then."

"And maybe you'll lose some people, Chief. Ever think of that?"

"You still dithering with that stupid little case? Is that why you're here?"

"Easterman got murdered. You knew that."

Thurmond wiped his pudgy palm on his face, squashing his nose flat and then releasing it. "Pat was a good man. We just lost another firefighter downtown. The terrorists shot two of my men off an aerial ladder and one of them's dead."

"There's some doubt whether Pat thought the Ratt fire was accidental."

"What would Pat have known about it?"

"That's what I'd like to find out."

"You stay away from whatever caused the Ratt fire, Fontana, or we'll sue your ass."

"I talked to one of the women he supposedly rescued from the Ratt. She says somebody else rescued her."

Another chief came into the room and Thurmond, without turning away from Fontana, said, "Frank, what if they're not even inside? What if they're running the whole thing from a remote location?"

"Good thought, Chief. I'll talk to the commander about it." He bustled out of the room.

"Now, what was it you were saying?" Thurmond's city was in danger of being blown off the map, but, like a dog with a rat, he'd found a quarrel.

"One of the victims Easterman supposedly rescued says he wasn't the one who rescued them. If he wasn't, who was? I think maybe Youngblood was on the fifth floor after all."

"Yeah, I heard that bullshit. But we're talking hysterical women, here, Fontana. Hysterical women." Thurmond began walking away, as if what he'd given was the definitive explanation.

"She said she called and told you."

Thurmond turned around, his mind on other things already.

"I might have spoken to her. So what? Just a hysterical woman. You don't believe her?"

"I think I do . . . "

At six o'clock Fontana could resist driving downtown no longer. He got within two blocks of the Belasco, which was as close as the police barricades would allow. His truck had fire insignia on it, as well as a light rack on the roof, but it was so rickety and beat up it nullified any impression of authority.

A Japanese film crew stood twenty feet from Fontana, using the distant Belasco as a backdrop for their reporter. Canadian, British, and Swedish newscasters had all passed him in the few minutes he'd been downtown.

Fontana had watched the evening newscasts from Station 25 alongside a somber fill-in engine crew from Bellevue. A great deal of time and film had been devoted to the "Situation in Seattle."

A videotape had been messengered to the fire department, then played on local newscasts before the networks picked it up.

Manufactured by the terrorists, apparently over the weekend, the tape revealed rooms stacked high with bags of ammonium nitrate, the bags stained with something that easily could have been the fuel oil the narrator on the tape claimed it to be. Fuses. Detonators. The videotape showed small, open-ended mortars constructed from steel pipe and set up in hallways with trip wires. It was impossible to discern the locations of either the ammonium nitrate or the booby traps, but they were clearly inside the Belasco, for the Belasco logo of a four-leaf clover with a *B* inside it was visible in many of the shots.

Experts estimated the quantities of ammonium nitrate at not less than thirty tons.

Oddly, though the phone lines were out, there were a number of cellular phones in the building, and the police department had put out a statement saying they knew by actual head count that there were 450 people on fourteen of the floors, and who knew how many exactly on the rest. Quick calculations placed the possible aggregate for the building at around 1,500. By the time the early evening news had come on, there were three known dead, including one firefighter who had been shot with a 30-30 that morning while trying to enter the building via aerial ladder. No more attempts to enter the building were made by either the fire department or the police.

Structural engineers at the university stated that if an explosion occurred, the building might not actually collapse, though the likelihood was good that it would. Experts from Philadelphia and Los Angeles gave predictions claiming that even if the building survived an explosion, the resulting fire and concurrent shock waves inside the structure were apt to precipitate a staggering loss of life.

City and fire-department spokespersons said the negotiations with the terrorists were continuing by phone. Nobody, aside from the city negotiator and the terrorists, knew how far the talks had proceeded. Nobody knew for certain how many terrorists there were. Fontana was guessing at seven or eight. Sources close to the city administration said the arrangements for depositing fifty million dollars in foreign bank accounts had obviously been prepared by a finance specialist.

Police cars, motors running, blue lights washing dimly across the nearby buildings, were situated in a pattern around the Belasco that extended five blocks on one side and five on the other, so that twenty-five square blocks were cordoned off. Virtually all traffic and commerce in downtown Seattle had ground to a halt at noon when first the mayor, and then the governor, declared the city to be in a state of emergency.

The downtown district was a ghost town.

The Space Needle and other viewpoints around the city had been crammed to capacity since early that morning. People waited with sandwiches, binoculars, video cameras, and children in prams.

Fire apparatus trundled into town from every county in the state to fill in at the empty Seattle fire stations.

On hand in the downtown area were eight ladder trucks, twenty-one engines, seven battalion chiefs, eight officers from the fire marshal's office, and all the ranking officers from the fire department's administration. Off-duty members of the Seattle Fire Department had been mobilized into a special task force to help clean up after the incident, and were congregating south of the incident site at Station 10. A gargantuan force of paramedics, nurses, ambulances, and doctors was on standby up the hill at Harborview Hospital, where the downtime fueled a party atmosphere. Experts from City Engineering, City Light, the water department, and Washington Natural Gas huddled on an hourly basis with fire department officials to figure out ways to minimize damage to the rest of the city.

It didn't take the media long to work up a profile of Zellner, dispossessed firefighter, grieving brother of the fallen William Youngblood, Jr., and racial bigot gone bananas. Quotes from the underground newspaper he had circulated were read on the radio and television.

Various news sources interviewed his grown children, estranged wife, ex-neighbors, bartender, and two former co-workers.

Earlier that afternoon at four o'clock, inky-black smoke began pouring out the twenty-second story of the building. It was later determined that that floor had probably been chosen because there were only four people on it. Four and a half minutes after the floor began to take on smoke, somebody succeeded in smashing out a window on the north side of the building.

Fontana had been on the phone to Laura, Laura sitting alone in the dark in the *Sensation Plus* offices, her imprisoned cohorts down the hall mustered around a battery-operated television.

"Omigod!" shouted Laura.

"What is it?"

"I think I just . . . let me see. I think I just saw a woman fall past my window. I just caught a glimpse. Oh, shit, Mac! There's goes another one. I could see the look on his face! . . . Oh, my God! Oh, my God! Oh, my God! There're two bodies down there in the street. There's medics running toward them."

The phone was silent for a long while. Fontana had no idea what to say, so he said nothing. A news camera caught the action live, and a few minutes later with Mike, Fontana watched a replay on television in Station 25. Soon thereafter, Mike went home.

Even before all the glass had been cleared from the frame, a woman stepped out of the window through the billowing smoke and fell in agonizing calmness to her death, her long hair pointing straight up, landing on a car parked in the street, the ripping wind from the fall pushing her jacket up around her face, the impact on the roof of the car scattering parts of the windshield onto the street. Seconds later a man stepped out of the same window, whirled his arms, and shouted on his journey to the sidewalk.

Just as Laura said, he fell facing the building, giving anybody who happened to be glancing out a window a glimpse of his protruding eyes as fleeting as the click of a camera shutter.

These few grotesque frames of film became the lead-in and close-out on nearly every national and local newscast. By the time Fontana got downtown, he'd viewed the clip twenty times, each one anesthetizing another small portion of the horror, numbing some of his compassion.

Fontana had borrowed a cellular phone he'd found in Station 25. Now, downtown at the roadblock, he sat in the truck under the deepening darkness and dialed the Belasco.

"Laura?"

"Mac? I haven't had anything to eat since last night. We found a bowl of hard candy on one of the receptionists' desks, but that's gone. We emptied the soda machine. We ran out of change, so one of the guys broke it open."

"I'm two blocks away. Listen, I've been thinking about this. You been watching the news?"

"Mac? Those people . . . they just jumped out like it was nothing. Christ, I close my eyes and feel like I'm falling. I got the dry heaves for five minutes after I hung up with you." Her voice was hoarse, her intonations ragged, slurred, and unpredictable. "I wish they'd just pay the ransom and get us out of here. Mac? You think maybe impending death is like an aphrodisiac or something?"

"What are you getting at?"

"The longer I've been up here the hornier I've been getting. Is that weird, or what?"

"You can put it in your book, Laura. Hang on. Drink lots of fluids if you can get them—to keep yourself hydrated. Keep rested. You don't know what you're going to be called on to do."

"I wish I could think straight. I'm so tense. I tried to take a little nap an hour ago and couldn't even get my eyes closed. Like they were on springs. I'll tell you one thing I'm learning. I'm not as tough as I thought."

"None of us are, darlin'."

"And Mac?"

"Yeah?"

"If I don't get out of here, would you tell my mother I said I was sorry."

"You're going to get out."

"But would you tell her? She'll know what I mean."

"I can do that."

Thirty-five

▲

PEOPLE WITH AXES CHASING A LONG-NECKED WOMAN

After spotting Engine 40 up the street, Fontana donned his turnouts and decided to go inside the perimeter established by the police. He noted two squad cars at every intersection, staging areas for fire-department vehicles, army trucks in front of the Belasco, and thirty-five or forty news vans with microwave dishes and assorted news-bureau automobiles.

If the Belasco went up, most of these people would be injured and the rest would be dead. They were all way too close.

"More questions?" Cooper asked. She was sitting on the sideboard of Engine 40 with an older firefighter who had a sparse mustache and steady black eyes. Another group of about fifteen Seattle firefighters, including four officers in red helmets, stood on the corner sixty feet distant, chatting quietly, masks and tools at their feet, paying scant attention to Fontana and none to Cooper. Engine 40 was a block and a half from the Belasco. Wearing turnouts, Fontana had bluffed his way inside. "We have orders to keep nonessential personnel out of the area."

"You kick me out, I'll go."

Cooper shrugged. "I really should." She wore her full bunkers, coat unbuttoned, but her helmet was on the back of her
neck. Her hair was mussed from wearing the helmet all day.
Cooper walked with him to the middle of the street, where
they could see the main entrance of the Belasco about seven
hundred feet away. "I have a friend in the building," he said.

"Close friend?"

"Close enough I'd rather she didn't get blown to smith-
ereens."

"I'm sorry."

Cooper pivoted and glanced up the flat street. Dense smoke
drifted along as if it had a mind of its own, some of it picked
up by a snatch of wind and some of it skulking along the
ground. The smell of burning rubber permeated the evening
air. People had been in the windows all day, waving at news
cameras. Now a few could be seen slumping against the glass
in a posture of defeat.

"Tell me about Bennie."

"He was one of those incredible guys who the officers hated
to have around the station because he wouldn't lift a finger,
but get him to a fire and he was the one you wanted next to
you. He called me one night after midnight a couple weeks
after the funeral and said the city was going to pay."

"He's got burn barrels in there," said Fontana. "That's what's
been burning. Has to be. Not the building. Course he gets
enough hot gases in a confined space and he'll get a flashover.
I'm sure he's disabled the sprinkler system and standpipes so
that even if you guys pump water it won't get to the barrels."

"That thing in Philadelphia? It didn't go out until they let
it burn freely for two floors and then . . . what was it?"

"In Philly? Nine little sprinkler heads put out a fire a couple
of hundred guys couldn't. Three firefighters died in that one."

"I hate him," said Cooper.

"I see you wear your helmet on the back of your neck. Is
that common in the SFD?"

"Well, it's easier, sometimes."

"I don't know that I've ever seen anybody else do it." He
stared.

"What are you driving at?"

"The two ladies who got rescued at the Ratt told me their

rescuer wore his helmet like that." Cooper looked down the street at the Belasco again. "I don't know why you didn't want anybody to know."

"Know what?"

"Want to tell me about it?" Cooper stared up at the tiny figures in the windows of the Belasco.

Thirty-six

▲

WOMAN AS SCAPEGOAT

"*T*he day of the Ratt we're together at Station Six and Bill is steamed. He's staring at me—making me feel like a bug. And the thing about Bill is, he's so sincere, so I know he's not acting. Sincere hatred. Somebody can do something bad to you and that's the wound, but when you know they really hate you, that's the salt in the wound."

"After you got to the fire, what happened?" Fontana asked.

"We search the first floor, run out of air, get fresh bottles, then get assigned to go around to the alley with a fifty-five. We are already tired and hot and that's one heavy ladder. It's around this time I foolishly try to break the ice with Bill and he calls me, yeah, okay, a 'cunt,' and says from now on when he partners up it will be with somebody he can trust.

"It rattles me. We're walking with that sonofabitchin' ladder around the building, and I'm not thinking about anything but Bill.

"So we ladder the fourth floor in the back of the Ratt, and when we get halfway up it's so smoky we can't see the ground. We're in teams. Bill and Buchanan go left. Me and Clint right.

217

We're being thorough because we've been told there is a woman up there. It's not like we're guessing. There is a woman.''

''Then what?''

''Bill turns around and says to us if she's up here, she's probably unconscious. She's been in the smoke a spell. Look everywhere.

''We look everywhere. Crawling mostly.''

''And you're with?''

''Clinton Vine. And we get all the way to the other end of the building, the front end, and neither team has seen anything. I mean it's pretty obvious from all the junk lying around that this floor is not being used.

''And me, I'm hearing footsteps above us. Like high heels. Somebody walking around up there. I'm the only one who's hearing the high heels on the ceiling. I'm the only one who cares. I tried to tell them but they wouldn't listen, none of them. I was the 'cunt.' We make kind of a half-assed search on the way back. At least I do. Because I know they're one floor up.''

''And you don't get lost?''

''No, I don't get lost.''

''On the way to the front of the building with Clint, I am on the left and Clint is on my right. On the way back to the ladder, again, I am on the right with Clint on my left, so we both search the same area we each already searched. Coming and going. Clint passes by that open elevator shaft twice without falling in. Go figure. So we get not to the ladder but to the fire escape, Clint and me, we're waiting there, and we hear all this racket off inside the building where Bill and Al Buchanan should be coming. And we're calling inside to ask if everyone is all right. Nobody answers. We hear them going wrong. We shout but they keep going wrong.''

''And they're looking for the fire victims, not you?''

''Of course. They know where I am. I'm yelling at them. Around that time we run out of air. Clint and me. So we have our face pieces off, and we're taking a pretty good beating on the fire escape, and we hear the bells on their backpacks inside, so we know they're about out too.

''We start hearing all this loud talk between the two of them.

218

I can distinguish the voices, but I can't tell what they're saying. Bill is sounding pretty calm when you think later about how bad his leg is busted."

"So they're running out of air too?"

"Almost out. Buchanan sounds like a pig some boys are chasing with sticks. I get embarrassed for him, and I don't even like him. We're talking the kind of panic I never thought I would hear in the fire department."

"Buchanan?"

"Buchanan. And Clint's getting jumpy listening. I mean, we're calling out to these guys, but they keep going deeper into the building, getting more and more lost in the smoke. They're not even going particularly fast. Just dead wrong, paying no attention to us whatsoever. And now their bells have stopped. Both of them. I guess you know your bell stops ringing, your tank is down to zilch, because it takes some air to make the bell ring.

"So Clint says for me to stay and be the beacon. He's going to make a dash, tell them they're wrong, lead them out.

"Makes sense to me. Both of us go in, we could all four end up lost. I mean, even in the rudimentary search we had just done, we got turned around. It pays to have at least one person in the crew totally oriented. And Clint's a lot more experienced than me in those situations. It made sense for him to move and me to stay. Besides, he's in charge."

"Makes sense," said Fontana. "Then what?"

"I stay put. Inside of ten feet Clint goes bassackwards. I yell, 'Clint, this way. They're up the other hall.' Clint doesn't answer. Of course, I can't hear his bell or his regulator because we've sucked our bottles dry. In the smoke he might be standing a foot in front of my face.

"The whole floor is in a horseshoe shape and there are two hallways, the one we took and the one Bill and Buchanan took. I call for about fifteen seconds and then I really start to worry because Clint just now told me how we had to keep in constant contact.

"So, in I go."

Fontana said, "Back in the building? Neither of you has air, right?"

"Both out. I keep calling, and in I go. Yeah, I know. Stupid?

I've got my flashlight and I'm crawling, shining it along in front of me, and when it gets real close to my face I can see a glow, but otherwise, everything's black. I'm sweeping my hands along in front because I figure something weird happened to Clint just a few feet inside. I find this space, the uncovered elevator shaft is what it is, but I don't know that. I think it's a room.

"I put my light in this hole, kind of lean my head in, and something flutters in front of my face. The visibility is better in the shaft than anywhere, but still, it isn't until later I figure out what is fluttering.

"For a split second his hands flutter in front of my face as he is falling.

"Clint must have been hanging on the edge, and as I shined my light his strength gave out and down he went. For the first few weeks afterwards I felt so guilty, like I knocked him in. But I didn't. I didn't touch him. He's the one who should have felt guilty. He never said a word. I could have gone right in with him. All he had to do was say, 'Look out.' Anything. He almost got me killed. It was his job to warn me. You don't step in a hole and then just sit there when help is coming and don't tell them about it.

"Anyway, I don't know how he held on as long as he did. I dropped my light after him. My light. His light. Him. They all fell in together.

"And then I hear a thump. Way the hell down. I can't believe how far down it is. And the sound. Everything at the fire seems to get quiet for that one instant. It takes me, I don't know, a few seconds, me there coughing and spitting and crying, to start back to the fire escape, but by this time I have taken a ton of smoke. And I guess you can figure I am shook. I keep thinking, it couldn't have been Clint. It was just something hanging against the wall fell when I leaned in and looked. Trying to convince myself. Except where was Clint? And how did two lights fall in?

"Maybe you can figure now why I didn't tell any of this before. Buchanan in a blind panic. Clint not saying a word so that I almost fall in with him. I don't know. I don't think it's going to do the families a bit of good, all this floating to the surface."

"There's more, isn't there, Diane?"

"I don't remember anything that happened after that, not until I was in the aid car."

"You went up and got those women and brought them down the fire escape, didn't you?"

She sighed. "I thought . . . I have these weird dreams about it. But how could I have? Easterman brought them around the building. Easterman did it. He even said he did. Why would he lie?"

"You brought them down and you sprained your ankle getting off the escape. That was when Easterman took them around."

"My ankle *was* sprained."

"One of the women said her rescuer wore their helmet slung on the back of their neck, the way you wear yours. Did you say anything to them on the way down?"

"I dreamed that I said . . . I think I might have yelled real bad at one of them. The older one. The way I dreamed it, I told her to get her fat ass on the ladder and then I went down with my arms around her. In my dream, I was yelling at her the whole way. She was real shaky."

"That's the way the women tell it too."

"It is?"

"But that's not the way Easterman tells it. The way he tells it, it was easy as pie. He went up and got 'em. 'No biggee.' Your version is the truth."

"My God. I thought . . . I thought . . . "

"That smoke screws you up, doesn't it?"

"I remember this decision I had to make. Nobody would answer me from below, so I had this decision. Go in and look for Bill? Go down and find Chief Freeze? Or go up and get those women?

"I stand on the fire escape for a second. I have been in this sort of a squat, and when I stand I get dizzy and have to grab the rail, and even then it feels like I'm falling. So that decides it. Those women are probably not going to make it if somebody doesn't clue them real quick they've got a fire escape they can go down.

"So I head up.

"The women. Two of them. I bring them down, but when

221

I'm getting off the fire escape, I jump and twist my ankle in the alley, an excruciating pain shooting up my leg.

"I'm disoriented.

"I'm so tired I can't lift my own arms.

"Sweating so bad I feel like I've been oiled inside my turnouts.

"By the time I get up, I am by myself in the alley thinking I'm at the department picnic, which they hold in August. Pat Easterman is around the front becoming a hero. The next morning I wake up in the hyperbaric chamber.

"When I get out I see the morning paper and there is Pat Easterman with one of these women on either arm, pushing them along all uncomfortable-like, the way he is, and I think I imagined saving them. Below they have yearbook photos of Bill and Buchanan and Clinton Vine.

"That's when it really hits me.

"Those bad newspaper photos.

"The accompanying article says I am in the hospital and they are not sure if I am going to pull through. My head feels weird, and I am wishing I won't. Pull through.

"My family spends time with me. Somebody from the union spends time with me. I don't remember what anybody says. I just keep thinking about how I should have saved Bill. In fact, for months and months that's all I can think.

"Chief Thurmond comes to the hospital. We are deep into the questions and answers when I realize Thurmond does not have my best interests at heart. Thurmond is trying to build a wall around me. I am the scapegoat.

"I tell him how I called down to Chief Freeze and how nobody answered. He keeps asking why we were on the fourth floor. How did we screw up and get on the fourth floor? Did we go up the ladder and come down the stairs in the building? What the hell were we doing on the fourth floor?

"When I tell Thurmond that Chief Freeze ordered us there because that's where he thought a trapped victim was, Thurmond starts getting riled. I can see right away there's only one place level enough for him to put his bucket of blame without it tipping over and spilling on him. On somebody who is dead . . . or on me.

"I start crying.

"It is all I can think to do.

"I go on crying jags for weeks. It is a real bad time for me. I've never been as chronically exhausted as I have over the past six months. Sometimes I'm so tired I feel like laying down and dying.

"I was crying because Thurmond didn't believe what I was telling him.

"My sister-in-law, Cherish, happened to be there when this was going on and threw his ass on out of there. I guess I decided right then and there nothing I was going to say was going to bring anybody back. And I wasn't really sure of all the facts. I believed I had brought those ladies down, but Easterman said he had, so I couldn't have. That bastard. That dirty bastard. I came close to killing myself over this.

"After a while, I started to hear all the rest of the stories, you know, from the other firefighters. What I figured was that Easterman must have been below me when I was yelling down for help. He had to have been. No way he wasn't.

"He heard me calling.

"He ignored me, and his arrogance is what killed Bill.

"Now I find out the SOB took credit for *my* save. You can't beat that with a stick, now, can you?"

Thirty-seven

▲

HUMAN SNOWFLAKES

Weeping methodically on the curb, Diane Cooper finished her tale and stared at Mac's boots until he realized he was standing on a dead pigeon, its carcass dried out and flattened by hundreds of car and truck tires.

"This ties up one more loose thread. A firefighter named Ryker claims he heard two firefighters talking inside the fourth floor. They were talking about finding one woman. Everybody took it for granted they were looking for you, but they were looking for the fire victims. They thought there was only one, didn't they?"

"We all thought there was only one."

A battalion chief drove up to the intersection and held an impromptu officers' conference, engine idling, red helmets gathered around his window. Something big was happening. Dabbing at her eyes, Cooper joined them.

The phone beeped in Fontana's pocket. "Laura?"

"They filled our floor up with smoke. We had to go up. We used a fire ax from one of the cabinets to break in. Mac, I didn't think I could make it through that stink. And my head feels like somebody's hammered nails into it."

"From the fumes." The sick feeling Mac had been nursing in his stomach had traveled into his limbs, making him feel almost too weak to stand. "Laura?"

"I think we're okay for a while, Mac. We're two floors up, on the eighteenth. The seventeenth was as bad as ours. There's a lot of people up here. Seventy, maybe. The stairs were so smoky I think I'm going to throw up. I gotta go."

A popping sound came from up the street.

A car backfiring.

Or gunshots.

Fontana walked over to Cooper. "They're flooding the floors with smoke."

"Chief Dondero told us."

"What's going on with the negotiations?"

"Trying to stall them."

"Stall 'em? There's a thousand people upstairs who are going to choke to death."

"As soon as it gets really dark, they're going to try something."

"This is bullshit!"

They stared down the street for a while. Cooper said, "Did you know Chief Freeze used to spend a lot of time at Midcontinental Op where Easterman was murdered? He works on his cars and gets some of his parts there."

"You think he might have killed Easterman?"

"I think Easterman and him were in the alley at the Ratt. One of them might have had incriminating evidence on the other." They thought about it for a while. "You know, Mac, there's an interconnecting passageway between the Belasco and the department store across the alley. When I told them about it, Thurmond told me to get back with my company. The passageway empties out on the bottom floor of the parking garage. With a couple of bars we could get in. If we could get to the fire control room we could pressurize the building. Clear the stairwells."

Another chief came by driving a Dodge, Rudolph Freeze, looking nervous and toothy and strangely bashful, perhaps somewhat intimidated by Fontana's presence.

After the officers conferred with Freeze, a black lieutenant came over to the ten firefighters on the street and said, "I don't even believe this. They want us to walk around to the alley. We're going to break in back there. The others'll create some sort of diversion in front."

"We going to have cops with us?" somebody asked.

"Freeze said no."

They exchanged looks. This was probably the most dangerous task they could have been assigned. They had all been thinking they would follow somebody else in. Put out spot fires. Evacuate citizens. Nobody had asked these troops if they wanted to storm the beach.

Muttering, they assembled directly behind the Belasco in the one-way alley that divided the block in half. Despite what Freeze said, eight police officers were waiting, three with compressed air tanks. Altogether there were ten firefighters, three lieutenants, and Chief Freeze. Eight cops. And Fontana.

Tired and dripping with perspiration from the walk—even with their coats unbuttoned—they sat on the ground, backs against a wall, waiting. It was a typical big-fire operation; hurry up and wait. Freeze left his car at the mouth of the alley in plain sight. The tension in the air was thick enough to float a brick. Their equipment was lined up twenty feet away on the other side of the alley.

Nobody spoke.

One firefighter chewed Skoal, offering a pinch to the other woman lieutenant, who was almost twice as wide through the thighs as she was through the shoulders, and who took the Skoal wordlessly, pouching it inside one ruddy cheek.

It was dark and quiet in the alley, and even though there had been a breeze on the street, here they were sheltered by the Belasco in front, as well as a six-story department store behind. After a few minutes, they heard a whistling sound and a muffled thunk.

"In front," said Cooper. "No. Up there." They gazed up at the windows along the west wall of the Belasco in time to see a huge sheet of glass break loose from the building and begin a pell-mell glide to the ground, fluttering erratically like half of a wet maple seed.

The entire group sprang to their feet.

The sheet of glass planed in a jerky zigzag and banged into the department-store wall a hundred feet to their left. Thousands of shards of broken glass clattered to the alley, silvery particles raining down past a streetlight.

The African-American lieutenant said, "In L.A. the falling windows cut supply lines. They'll cut a man in half."

One firefighter attempted to count up to the floor from which the glass had fallen. Smoke was pouring out of the high window now, curling away from the alley like a giant caterpillar, undulating up the west face of the building.

"Thirty-three stories. Look," said the firefighter who'd counted. They squinted into the darkness and saw an arm come out of the smoke. Then a leg. The individual on the thirty-third floor appeared to be trying to gain a toe-hold on a non-existent window ledge, then, before anybody could say a word, plummeted down the side of the building.

Arms waving.

No shouts.

Just the fall in a perfectly flat, motionless trajectory. They all realized at the same time what the earlier thunk had been, this the second jumper in as many minutes to land on the two-story building across from them.

"Oh, God," said several people in unison. The other female lieutenant averted her face and said a prayer to herself, Skoal dribbling from her mouth.

Hugging his portable radio to his face, Freeze walked sixty feet down the alley as if to gain privacy, his boots shrieking on pieces of glass, while another sheet popped off one of the upper floors. Almost in unison the firefighters pulled down their face shields, tightened the straps on their helmets, and clung to either the north or south wall of the alley while the pane exploded on a roof eighty feet away, a hailstorm of chips and shards splashing Freeze.

"I'll give that a nine-three for distance," said one of the firefighters. Somebody else glanced at Freeze and said, "Could have been a little more accurate." Cooper gave him a dirty look.

A crash came from the front of the building, a sound like a

truck ramming a wall. An ambulance rolled past the east mouth of the alley slowly, red lights winking.

Freeze came back at a trot, slapping a gloved hand at nuggets of glass on the shoulders of his bunking coat. "Okay. That's it. We're going in here. Get your saws. Whatever."

Thirty-eight

▲

WHAT TO DO WHEN YOU GET WEDGED IN A HOLE

Weapons unholstered, several police officers stood guard while one fire crew ripped a hole in the roll-up aluminum-and-steel door at the rear entrance of the parking garage. Smoke had been seeping out around the edges of the huge door, and now a thick jet of it wafted lazily into their faces, the disagreeable tang of burning rubber beginning to permeate their nostrils and clothing.

The arrangement was for the second lieutenant, along with a police escort, to lead her four people into the parking garage and then into the main building. Three of the police officers were already slinging backpacks.

The lieutenant dropped to her hands and knees and wedged herself into the hole in the garage door, her rear and thighs packing the opening, squirming, until Cooper put a boot on her buttocks and gently shoved. Nobody said anything. It took only a minute for the others to disappear into the smoke and darkness behind her.

In the distance, up near the hospitals on First Hill, a helicopter's rotor blades hammered the night. Smoke continued to billow into the alley from the raggedy square hole in the metal door, though a mild breeze was now ushering it east. A second crew stood by with their face pieces loose. Cooper leaned over to the chief, who was in a squat, hugging his knees, and said, "There's a tunnel under this alley, Chief. It'll take us into the D level. Go up three flights and there's the fire control room."

It was as if she hadn't spoken. Freeze pulled out a package of cigarettes and lit one. He was right-handed. Fontana asked for one, ascertained it was a Camel, and tossed it away. The butts in the church behind the Ratt had been Camels. Freeze gave him a funny look and said, "You know, I don't even think you're supposed to be here."

"I was wondering if you saw anything unusual behind the Ratt the night of the fire."

"We got other things to worry over."

"Did you see anything?"

"Like what?"

"Before Easterman died, he told somebody he thought there was something going on that night. Did you see anything to indicate it might have been an arson fire?"

"Say what?"

"Did you see anything that might have indicated it was a set fire?"

"Well . . . why are you askin' this?"

"Because somebody broke into the church behind the Ratt and was sitting up in a window right over you guys. Whoever it was would make a hell of a witness."

"Who?"

"Could have been anybody. Could even have been you, Chief."

Freeze looked at him for a long time before he started laughing, an uncertain, jittery laugh that was so dry his lips got stuck to his front teeth. "I did my job. My radio was acting up, so maybe I missed something. I told them to go to the fifth floor to get that woman. Not the fourth floor like Cooper been trying to make out."

"You said that woman."

"What?"

"That woman. You said that woman. Did you send them up after two women or one?"

"Well, one, I guess. It wasn't until later we found out there were two."

"So when Ladder Three went upstairs they thought they were looking for a single woman?"

"I guess."

Ten minutes into the odyssey, they heard three flat cracking sounds echoing in the garage. Gunshots. A couple of minutes later, one of the police officers exited, tearing his face piece off. At the same time, Freeze spotted a chief's car idling at the east end of the alley and sent a young Asian firefighter out to see about it. One by one, the rest of the crew emerged from the forty-inch hole, drenched, shirts pasted to their bodies under their bunking coats, face pieces spilling sweat.

The cop who had come out first spoke to no one in particular, "God, it was like being blindfolded. This flashlight was about as good as a paperweight. We're lucky we found our way back." Somebody escorted the last firefighter out of the hole and over to a wall, sat him down, and slit his bunking pants to the knee with a Buck knife. "He's been shot!"

"Fuck this shit," said Fontana, picking up an ax from the equipment pile.

He walked down the alley and stopped beside two police officers at a door on the opposite side of the alley next to a sign saying EMPLOYEES ONLY. Swinging the ax heavily, it took him fifteen seconds to destroy the handle and dismantle the lock.

"What are you doing?" asked a cop whose name tag read "Neil."

"Supposed to be a tunnel runs from this store to the Belasco under the alley. We want to get in, right?"

"I'm coming." Diane Cooper glanced up and down the alley. Freeze had disappeared from the far end and so had the chief's van. The other firefighters, except for Cooper's crew, were halfway out of the alley.

Two cops followed Cooper and Fontana into the department store, Neil and a stocky man with a Frankenstein haircut. The two men from Cooper's crew on Engine 40 came also, carrying bars, axes, and their masks. Six of them now.

They followed Cooper into the store, flashlights bobbing, shadows dancing on the walls, a centipede of flashlights tracking through a stockroom, through the children's department, tiny mannequins in winter coats reminding Fontana he needed to buy Brendan a new coat before the cold weather set in. They tramped down an inert escalator and into the budget-clothing department, into another back room, then down some stairs past a boiler room, and down another short flight of dirty concrete steps to a door that was locked.

The crew of Engine 40 began working with pry bars in the confined space.

Obviously it was going to take a while.

Fontana stepped back and dialed Mary in Staircase. Brendan picked up the phone. "Brendan. Dad. I'm going to be later than I thought."

"When are you coming?"

"I don't know. I've run into something."

"You are coming home . . . aren't you? Tonight?"

"I guess you're going to have to bunk on Mary's couch. Be sure and feed Satan. Tell you what I'll do. I'll take you to a movie this weekend to pay you back. Deal?"

"Can I pick it?"

"Ummmm. Yeah. Sure. I love you, Brendan. See you later."

"Yeah, Dad. I love you too."

The door Engine 40's crew was working on broke open, exposing a long, dark tunnel which they entered. It was sixty feet long. The door at the opposite end was identical to the one they'd already pried open. Fontana helped this time, breaking into a heavy sweat as he worked beside the cop with the Frankenstein haircut. It was hot in the tunnel and everybody in the group was slimy with perspiration. Fontana removed his backpack and jacket.

As soon as they got the door out of its frame, the taller firefighter on Cooper's crew said, "We got you this far, but I'm not going in."

"Me neither," said her remaining crew member. "I've got family. I got investments. I don't need this shit."

"You don't think the people up in here have families?" Cooper said, droplets of sweat dappling her tan face, matting the loose strands of hair around her cheeks. Neither man replied, and then, avoiding eye contact, they moved back down the dim corridor.

The cop with the Frankenstein haircut said, "We'll go in, all four of us. Who knows? We may be the only ones able to breach their positions." His head was shaped almost like a block and he had a frightening smile that appeared to rip his face in half, exposing small, gapped teeth.

Fontana introduced himself and Cooper. The cops were named Harry Neil and Howard Tiny. "Get us to that fire control room," Fontana said. "We'll pressurize the stairwells."

They shook hands, all four of them, then slung their masks. Fontana touched a handful of small wooden wedges he kept in his outside coat pocket. It was already uncomfortably humid inside his turnout clothes. The area smelled of smoke, but not enough to justify donning their face pieces. The steel door at the top of the short stairway was unlocked. Outside they found a short corridor, unlit, and, twenty feet away, a main hallway, this one bright under the glare of fluorescent overheads.

"Know where you are?" Fontana asked Cooper.

"Gimme a minute. Yeah, I think."

They headed left down the lighted corridor, alert, listening. Cooper had turned her portable radio off, fearful the terrorists would hear it. They tried doors, finding broom closets, a telephone room, a couple of store rooms, and a room filled with white uniform coats on racks.

One door had a bank of roiling black smoke behind it, though the smoke was not hot, indicating it wasn't close to whatever fire they were maintaining. Fontana felt his way to the other end of the room and opened a door. Bingo. Hot smoke rushed at his face.

He propped that door open, as well as the one leading into the corridor, using the wedges he'd brought, and the stink trailed along, blacking out everything behind them.

They made a left at the end of the corridor, peeking around each corner before committing, the smoke on their heels. Cooper would lead until they got to a door or a corner, then one of the cops would take the point.

They had come into an area with a small elevator. An electrical room, locked. And two doors labeled "A" and "B." Both locked. Through a set of double glass doors they could see into the underground parking garage, which was unlighted and banked down with grayish smoke.

"This area is pressurized," said Fontana. "See how clean air is going out the cracks in the door, rather than bad air coming in. They've got the building fans pumping clean air down here. This thing is just the way they want it. Except for that." He gestured behind them to the door he had propped open.

"There's a utility stairway out here," said Cooper, voice shaky. "It leads up to the next levels."

She led them out the glass doors into the parking garage. She tested a door that went back into the center edifice of the parking well and eventually to the halls above the ones they'd just left. They listened inside the stairwell, heard nothing but their own breathing, then proceeded up a flight, the policemen, guns drawn, leading.

"I think this is the floor," said Cooper. They cracked the door, then stepped into the corridor.

"Nice try, guys!" Behind the door. He had a high tenor voice, an earring in his ear, and an Uzi in his fist. He stood placidly, as if he'd been waiting for them, wearing an open bunking coat and bunking trousers.

Lee Viteri.

The Uzi was pointed at the head of one of the cops. "Drop 'em!"

After a tense moment, two pistols clattered to the tile floor.

Viteri's hair was mussed, eyes bloodshot; he had probably been meandering in and out of the smoke all day. Probably had a headache the size of Kennebunkport. He would be short-tempered, testy, and prone to hasty decisions. Fontana's consolation was that he could see black smoke being pumped out of an air register a hundred feet down the corridor.

Good.

Surprises for the bad guys were good.

Thirty-nine
▲
SLOW KILL

*F*ontana felt the cellular phone in his bunking trousers pocket as it cracked and flattened under the blow from the heavy fiberglass pike pole. A second blow struck him sharply in the solar plexus, this one without a telephone to cushion the impact.

It was an eight-foot pole and Viteri was using it alternately as a spear and a club. The steel point was sharp, but Fontana hoped not quite sharp enough to penetrate turnout clothing, for, though his hands were now tied behind his back, he was still wearing his helmet and full turnouts. The two cops were handcuffed. Cooper's hands were tied.

After handcuffing the officers, Lee Viteri picked up one of the guns off the floor and summarily shot Officer Neil just below the knee, causing him to flop onto one hip and howl in a union of shock and pain.

"That's 'cause I know you're going to try something," Viteri said, displaying a prissy Sunday-school grin. Fontana thought about jumping him then, but the pistol was pointing at his own chest.

"Why did you do that?" Cooper cried.

"Didn't like the way he was looking at me. Anybody tries anything, I'll shoot him again. And then I'll shoot you."

It had made Fontana quietly crazy to let Cooper, under orders from Viteri, tie his hands behind his back with the fabric body loop every Seattle firefighter carried, yet he could think of no way out of it other than rushing Viteri, and that would have been suicide.

What made Fontana's dementia halfway tolerable was the fact that the far end of the corridor was slowly filling with smoke, and Viteri, in his delight at capturing them, had failed to notice.

The floors were gritty with a dirtlike substance Fontana assumed to be ammonium nitrate, their footing slick as if on an icy walkway.

There was a loud noise on his plastic helmet, an impact to his ribs, and suddenly Fontana was sliding down the corridor backward on his hip. Because his hands were tied behind him, his movements were awkward. He managed to roll onto his stomach, scramble to his knees with his face in the grit of the floor, and pull one leg under himself before he felt another spasm in his rib cage.

Sweat poured down Viteri's scalp and into his eyes.

"Come on. You want to die?" Viteri said. "Come on, you want to die?"

He whooped almost in a cowboy yodel, backed to the end of the hallway, stood by the three trussed captives, and said, "Ain't this fun? Who's the big shot now, Chief? Why don't you call your doggie?"

Fontana made it to his feet and looked around in time to see Viteri running toward him. So far, he had managed to deflect most of the blows, taking a few others on his padded shoulders or helmet.

The point of a pike pole was the size of a child's palm, made of flat metal, sharp on the tip with a hook under that, designed to pull down ceilings in fire buildings. Facing the manic glitter in Viteri's pretty hazel eyes, Fontana realized it was only a matter of time before he punctured a lung, put out an eye, or crushed a skull with it.

Because he had braced one foot against the base of the wall, when Fontana leaped sideways he got more distance on the slippery floor than Viteri expected, the pole barely catching a piece of Fontana's coat. Off balance, Viteri tripped and skidded down the corridor on his stomach.

Fontana kicked Viteri when he started to get up, flattening him, but Viteri was young, quick, and agile, scuttling to his feet on his second try in one fluid motion.

Now he was angry. One shot to the lower belly hurt so much Fontana whimpered, the first indication he'd allowed that he was in trouble. Baseball swings were next, to Fontana's torso, three of them, absorbed somewhat by his bulky coat, and then a glancing blow off his helmet. Fontana thought the blow had been glancing. He had tipped his helmet down when he saw it coming.

But he was on his knees.

He had been standing and now he was on his knees. He could hear nothing out of his left ear. Blows began thundering across his shoulders, the top of his helmet.

He could hear the cops yelling, Cooper shrieking, "You're killing him. You're killing him! Stop! Stop, you sonofabitch."

As Fontana rolled into a corner to await the next flurry, a new voice said, "What the hell do you think you're doing? Goddamn you. Where the hell did these people come from? And would you look at that shitty air coming down the hall? Why didn't you tell me you had prisoners?" Viteri was tilted against the opposite wall from Fontana, inhaling and exhaling purposefully, nostrils whistling, exhausted with the work of a slow kill. Benjamin Zellner was standing next to him. "Look at you."

"It's this bastard," said Viteri. "I never did like his looks."

"You idiot. This whole goddamned level is smoked up. What happened? It's even coming upstairs. What you got open?"

"I didn't notice anything."

Fontana had one knee under himself, struggling to his feet. "You?" said Zellner.

Zellner wore a dress shirt and neatly creased trousers, a tie herniating out of his trousers pocket. What was he going to do, collect the ransom money and then ride a limo to the airport? Or was he scheming to mingle with the civilians in the building after he let them loose, make his escape in the pandemonium when it was over? Zellner turned to Viteri. "Been to the barrels?"

"J.C.'s down there."

"You know we gotta circulate people down through or we're going to lose our smoke. One guy can't work in there very long." Fumes were beginning to choke the hallway now, wafting past them to the end of the corridor. In ten minutes the area would be blacked out, uninhabitable. "Where'd they come from?"

"We got an audible on D level. They walked right into my lap."

"Stash 'em in the supply room. I'll call Wayne. Don't let Wayne leave them alone. Understand?"

"You're not really going to let Wayne watch 'em?"

"Move it."

Fluid dribbled down Fontana's face, but it wasn't until he licked at the corner of his mouth that he realized it was a mixture of sweat and blood. His right eye was beginning to swell around the outer edge. He could feel the throbbing. Even though it hadn't lasted long, he'd taken a severe beating. His left elbow was numb, and he was afraid it might be broken, felt it ache in time with his heartbeat.

Zellner was making sheepish eye contact for the first time. The man was responsible for at least five deaths since that morning, but he was diffident.

"How long?" Viteri asked. "How long now?"

"I look like a mind reader? Don't worry. They're too scared not to pay."

"We shoulda been out of here."

"Bennie?" Diane Cooper was on the floor at the end of the hallway, hands tied behind her. "Bennie? Why are you doing this? Let us go. He's shot, and he's all beat up. Just let us go. That way you won't have to worry about anybody guarding us."

"What the hell are you doing here?" Again, the eye contact lasted only a fraction of a second. Zellner could kill you, but he couldn't look you in the eye.

"Trying to save lives. That's my job, isn't it? It was yours, too. And Bill's. How can you do this?"

"Don't talk shit to *me*, girl. This *is* for Bill. That's what it's about."

"Bill wouldn't have wanted you to hurt anybody."

Zellner's attention was attracted to the smoke prowling down the wall behind Cooper and the policemen. "You're a bigger help to me missing than you are out there explaining to Six Avenue Command where we are. And don't tell me about being a firefighter. You don't know anything about being a firefighter, bitch. You got my brother killed trying to be a firefighter. Lee? For godsakes, find out where that smoke is coming from."

Forty

▲

WHEN YOU WISH
UPON A FIREBALL

*I*n the thickening smoke, Viteri and a man named Wayne took them to a room at the end of the corridor, where Viteri told Wayne to stand guard and then left. Wayne wore blue jeans and a firefighter's coat with a fireproof Nomex hood pulled to the back of his head to let out body heat.

They could see the silhouette of a gun in his pocket, but he didn't exhibit it the way Viteri had, acted almost embarrassed about the situation after informing them he had strict orders to fire on them if they gave him a hard time. His face was sooty, and his clothes smelled of heat and smoke and acrid body odor. He appeared to be the perfect young soldier, aggressive, empty-headed, and lacking a moral sensibility.

In obvious agony, Neil lay on his side, hands cuffed behind his back, sweating like a leaky radiator, face pale enough that he might already be dead. Oddly, it was the same basic injury Bill Youngblood had suffered. Viteri's bullet had shattered both bones in his lower leg. Fontana and Cooper offered to splint it, which, they explained, would alleviate a great deal of Neil's agony, but Wayne said, "If you can splint it with your hands tied behind your back, go right on ahead."

While Neil suffered, the others chatted up Wayne, a buck-toothed young man, blue-eyed, vaguely handsome, but gullible-looking, a man who ingenuously let them in on much that his cohorts would have kept to themselves.

That there were eight of them.

That burn barrels were located in a room one level below, near the outside stairway they had used. That the barrels were the only thing in the building on fire. That tons of ammonium nitrate were rigged with a thirty-minute fuse, and that they had failed to establish a way to blow the building from a remote location.

According to Wayne, the deaths had disturbed three of the terrorists, but not any of the others, apparently, including Wayne. One of the group, an ex-con named Alex, a man whose record included kiting checks and stealing pigs, had notched the stock of his rifle with a pen knife after picking a firefighter off the aerial ladder that morning.

Four upper floors had been pumped full of smoke.

Wayne did not know the death count, but he knew it was higher than the news people reported, and when he spoke of it, his eyes dropped and his voice turned raspy. Cooper did most of the prodding, was clever at getting Wayne to unload, though he refused to admit they were doing anything wrong. What was wrong with retiring filthy rich at twenty-two years old? What was wrong with wearing a wristwatch that cost more than the house you grew up in?

Wayne claimed that his commission, assuming they took in what they were asking, would be four million, and he showed them a glossy, dog-eared brochure he had shimmed into his hip pocket that had a photo of an estate in Jamaica he was planning to pay cash for. In Jamaica, Wayne said, you could race motorcars and smoke fine cigars and "bang" all the pretty women you wanted.

Seemingly in need of sympathetic listeners, which Cooper pretended to be, Wayne told them what everybody had guessed, that the operation had been conceived and managed by Bennie Zellner, that Zellner was orchestrating it from the fire control room two floors up, that Wayne was apprehensive about the situation yet intoxicated over the extensive news coverage. "We're gettin' *real* famous. Real damn famous."

On the tile floor were several sets of bunking gear, SFD helmets, a pair of first-aid kits, five green medical oxygen bottles, and a table laden with radios, along with one scanner broadcasting everything the fire department put across the airwaves.

After forty-five minutes, Wayne, sitting in a plastic-backed chair, reached into his coat pocket and pulled out a crackling radio. "Jasper Five, come in."

"Jasper Five, over," said Wayne, glancing at Cooper and raising an eyebrow. "That's me. Bennie's Jasper One. This is Jasper Five, over."

"Got any smoke down there?"

"Not much."

"The hall clear?"

"I didn't look in the hall."

"Look in the hall."

He glanced at Cooper as he stumbled doggedly across the floor and cracked the door, then watched a vertical fold of pitch-black smoke ghost into the room. "Christ!" He stepped back from the door, wheezing, then squeezed the radio tightly. "Hallway is cooking. Goddamnit! It's cooking out there." Cooper and Fontana exchanged looks.

Wedging doors open had been a good move. Fontana's fear now was that Wayne would get orders to shoot them before going to higher ground, something he believed Wayne would do systematically and without thought, the way a hermit would drown an unwanted litter of kittens. "What am I going to do? Christ, there's no masks here. Jasper One?"

The radio hissed. "Hold your breath. You can make it. Follow the wall. Go down to the burn room and pick up your mask."

"Can't you get that smoke outa here?"

No reply.

Fontana was reasonably certain of two things: One, their bottles and masks were down the hallway where they'd left them; two, if they weren't and they made a dash outside to look for them, they would be in serious trouble, for this was toxic, take-a-whiff-and-fall-on-your-face smoke. Burning tires. Wayne took some shallow breaths and rushed into the corridor, leaving the door wide. Fontana rolled to his knees, pushed himself up off his face, and closed the door with his foot. Before the latch could click, it was shoved open again, knocking him into the wall.

Standing in the center of the room coughing, Wayne gripped his revolver in one hand and knuckled his watery eyes with the other. Fontana butted the door closed and slid down the wall into a sitting position to dodge smoke swirling around in the room.

"Just hold your breath. You can make it," Cooper said, mocking.

"What?" Wayne walked to her and pointed his gun carelessly at her head. "What did you say?"

"Why should we help you?" Fontana asked. "You won't help us."

"What do you mean, help me?"

"You been in that smoke all day? Your bloodstream's screwed up. It's not going to take too many gulps of bad air before you're gone. Zellner just scratched your name off the payroll."

"Bullshit."

Wayne squatted and pulled out his radio. "Jasper One. Come in, Jasper One." No answer. He tried several more times. "Damn!"

"He thinks you're out in the smoke dying," said Fontana. "Let me loose, I'll get you a mask."

"Lee said not to let you guys loose. No how."

"Did Lee tell you to die here with us?"

Wayne mulled that over, and from the look on his face was considering every possibility, working through every alternate stratagem. "I die, I die."

"Brilliant," said Fontana.

"But there's no fucking way I'm letting you bastards loose."

"There is one way," said Fontana. "That oxygen bottle over there. Turn on the regulator full, button up your coat, and put it underneath." Cooper gasped, but Wayne paid her no heed. "Put your nose down your coat and you'll be breathing pure oxygen. It won't be as clean as the compressed air you'd get from the nice tight seal on a mask, but it'll get you there." It took Wayne a minute to set it up and then he was out the door and gone.

After kicking the door closed behind him one more time, Fontana managed to get the Buck knife out of his turnout pocket, fumble the blade open, and saw his hands free. His left elbow functioned, but just barely. His ribs ached when he breathed. His knees were sore and raw, and one eye was swollen enough to distort his vision.

"That was a nasty trick," Cooper said as Fontana cut the cord on her hands.

The Frankenstein-haircut cop said, "What?"

"He gets in that burn room, hot as it's likely to be, he could turn into a fireball. All that oxygen he's going to have in his clothing. That's one reason our breathing apparatuses have compressed air instead of oxygen. Oxygen would turn half the firefighters in the country into fireballs."

One of the cops had a hideout key for the handcuffs, and after they were freed, Tiny and Cooper found a first-aid kit among the stored supplies in the room and scissored the pant leg off Neil. "It's going to require two people to get your buddy out of here," Fontana said to Tiny. "And you're going to need air. I'm going up the hall for our masks."

"I'll come with you," Cooper said.

"You'll do a lot more good here."

Inhaling small amounts of smoke, it took Fontana two minutes to feel his way to their masks and don one of them. When he got back to the room with the three extras, Diane Cooper, sans bunking coat, was wrapping the bloody splint on the cop's leg with Kling stretch bandages. She gave Fontana a ragged look and said dismally, "You really fixed him."

"I didn't realize what you were doing, actually," said Tiny, "or I would have stopped you. There had to be a better way to get him out of here."

"What are you talking about?"

"We heard Wayne on the radio. He got downstairs just as you left."

"He didn't do so well," said Tiny.

Fontana dragged the three masks inside and closed the door, peeled his face piece off, took one of the radios, and said, "Listen. We've got to get him out of here. Now, before they come back."

"I guess we screwed up good," Tiny said. They were finished

splinting and bandaging Neil's leg, and already some of the color had returned to his face.

"I think I can find the fire control room and put a stop to this," said Fontana.

"*I'm* going," said Tiny.

"It's going to take two of you to get him out."

Officer Tiny got an offended look on his face, ran a hand over his crewcut, and sputtered, "Well, hey, if anybody should go out there to confront the bad guys, I think it should be me. I'm a trained police officer."

"You've seen the hallway. What do you think your chances are?"

"What are yours?"

Fontana looked at Cooper, who said, "Experience in the smoke makes a lot of difference."

"Okay, but I'm not happy with this."

Cooper said, "It was on the radio. Jasper Five is down. You know what the other guy said? He said he hit Wayne with an extinguisher but Wayne wouldn't go out. Gave a real nice *glow-by-glow* account. You know what the kicker was?" Her words were milky with emotion.

"What was the kicker, Diane?"

"Every time he keyed the mike we could hear Wayne in the background screaming. It was almost like he was in the room here with us."

Fontana looked at the three of them. "He would have shot you in a minute."

Tiny and Fontana took two radios from the table, turned them to the same frequency, and ran a test. A minute later Tiny and Cooper cradled the wounded officer between them in a shoulder-carry and went out into the corridor. Everybody was wearing a mask now.

Before he left, Fontana exchanged his white chief's helmet for one of the yellow SFD helmets so that he would be indistinguishable from any Seattle firefighter—also from Zellner's crew, seven of them now. He strapped on a service ax and picked up a pike pole from the supplies on the floor.

Forty-one

▲

ALL THE DEAD PEOPLE
YOU KNOW

*F*ontana fumbled his way to the stairs, wedged the door to give the smoke more reign, went up a flight, and discovered a hallway relatively free of fumes. These were subfloors, labeled alphabetically instead of numerically, and he was on B. Once again, he wedged open a stairway door, then went down two flights to the level at which they had entered the building. Cooper and the others were nowhere in evidence.

He was perspiring heavily. The mask he was wearing weighed thirty-four pounds, the clothing twenty. Add the four-pound ax, pike pole, portable radio. He had read somewhere that a knight's armor weighed approximately fifty-five pounds, yet he was carrying ten pounds more than that.

On D level the stairway led out into the garage, where the smoke was stale and gray and he could see six or eight feet. He tamped a wedge under the stairwell door, then went around the corner through the main portion of the parking garage to the glass doors that led back into the island of storerooms, machinery, and corridors. The burn room should be nearby.

Between the double doors he found a clump of smoldering rags.

He stooped to examine them before realizing it was a body, their buck-toothed former jailer, Wayne, facedown, scorched, helmetless, hairless, almost certainly deceased, though the torso was rising and lowering. He prayed these were post-mortem agonal respirations and not the heavings of a man wrestling with the Grim Reaper.

It wasn't a pretty sight, but Fontana told himself he hadn't had any choice but to dupe the little sociopath. Curiously un-scathed by flame, the brochure about Jamaica protruded from Wayne's rear jeans pocket.

Dragging the lax body into a corner by one booted foot, Fontana ran into torrents of black smoke in the main hallway, the heat blasting and immediately drying the sweat on his exposed neck, everything blacked out to knee level. Clearly no one had found the doors he'd wedged earlier.

He ran his bare palm along the walls, feeling for heat, stum-bling along in the sooty blackness, noting with disgruntlement that his arms remained quivery, his legs rubbery. Twice he had seen men burned to death, and the memories came to him vividly right now. One was in a car fire and one in a kinky suicide, so his imagination was just a tad overworked thinking about it, perhaps more overworked than it would have been had he witnessed Wayne's demise, for then there would have been only *one* version. The way it stood, he would be dealing with an infinite number of versions.

The burn room was behind the second door inside a small alcove. He could feel the heat through the door. At least one man would be inside stoking the barrels.

In the corridor he leveled the pike pole in front of himself and proceeded slowly down the hallway in the dense smoke. He could not see the end of the pole. He could not see his hand on the pole. Anybody waiting in ambush would be very near, for to stray in this murky environment would be to risk losing your quarry or yourself. When he stopped breathing for half a minute, he could hear no other regulators making their dragon-nostril sounds in the corridor.

On each of these subbasement levels there were the stairs

he had used twice, and, at the other end of the corridor, the bottom few flights of one of the building's two primary stairways. At each doorway he put his flashlight against the door, yet he could barely see the light, much less a designator on the door. The hallway was gray-black now, and he could see only if he held a flashlight in his fist and pulled it close to his face.

Down a side corridor he struck his shin hard against something metal. It hurt so badly he wanted to sit down and cry, but when he knelt to touch what he'd run into, he couldn't figure out what it was: a steel rack of some sort. The process of finding a door to the other set of stairs took six minutes.

The stairs were smoky and much darker than the corridor. Fontana listened carefully for another working mask, but all he heard was something moving perhaps ten or fifteen stories higher, footsteps or shuffling.

He headed up. One flight. Two.

Three.

He tried the door on the fourth level, which he figured was level A.

This was where he hoped to find the fire control room with switches to control the air flow to any floor in the building.

The door was locked.

It was standard procedure in a building such as this to keep all the stairwell doors locked from the inside when the building was in fire mode, so that panicky people exiting into the stairways were forced all the way down to the safety of the street, which was where they belonged.

Removing his helmet, Fontana pressed his ear up against the door, heard nothing but the buckles of his face mask scratching the door. In the blackness it took only seconds to knock the doorknob off with the ax he was carrying, and, when the knob's guts spilled out, he was able to ease the door open.

The smoke on this level was light enough for him to read a maroon sign on the wall. He shook his head in disbelief, for, disoriented by the smoke and his exertions, he had counted wrong, had reached the wrong floor, was on level B.

The four of them had avoided these stairs on their way into the building, fearful that they were either monitored or booby-trapped, so when Fontana stumbled against a bundle on his way up the next flight, his heart pushed out a couple of extra beats. It was blacker than the inside of a parson's sock. The bundle was a body in a sitting position on the stairs, slumped backward.

It was one of the terrorists, probably still alive, though his respirations were down to almost nothing, face piece off, AK-47 beside him. In this kind of smoke, it didn't take long. Fontana removed his own gloves, ascertained the rifle was empty, yet was unable to find any ammunition. The man had run out of air and failed to make his way to sanctuary, had probably gotten turned around in the smoke and roamed around in circles until his lungs were filled with soot. This wasn't a place for amateurs.

Eight terrorists. Two down. Wayne and this Dugan.

Several steps above the man, Fontana found a woman lying on her side with a baby one step below. They were both stiff, had been gone a couple of hours. When he took off his gloves to be certain, the heavy-bellied baby felt like a plastic doll, smelling of milk and the almost-sweet ammonia smell of an unchanged diaper. The mother's hair was coarse and wiry. When he touched her face her glasses clattered to the floor. Any remorse he felt over Wayne faded as he gently fitted the stiff baby back into his mother's arms. It was an eerie feeling, bumbling along in the smoke, unable to see, unsure of whether or not he was about to stumble into another corpse, a man with a gun, or even Laura, dead.

Up one flight he heard voices through the door, shouts, the clanking of equipment. This door was locked also.

He climbed ten steps, grabbed the handrail, turned, and sat, arranging his pike pole alongside in case a situation were to come up in which he needed a weapon. He was still wearing the ax in the scabbard. In his pocket was a folding Buck knife with a razor-sharp blade. He made sure the radio was off.

It was good to sit. To rest. Even though the longer he sat and thought about things, the angrier he became.

Fontana sat on the stairs with the corpses feeling a pulse in his temple thump against his slick face piece. He didn't know what time it was, but at that moment Brendan could very well be watching the Belasco on the news at Mary's. Christ, if the building blew now and his son saw it . . . He was playing terrorist lotto and first prize was another few minutes of life, yet he didn't have to continue. He could climb three, four, ten stories, break into the main building, and wait it out with the hostages.

After a bit, the door opened and he saw some dim light before somebody muttered through a mask, "Shit! I can't see shit! It's just as bad in here."

Fontana quit breathing and gripped the pike pole. His only hope was that they were going down. A staccato series of semiautomatic gunshots rattled him. Another series. They were clearing the stairwell in front of themselves, peppering the stairs with bullets. Two rifles firing simultaneously, shooting down the stairs, not toward him.

These Dugans were paranoid, firing at everything. Transfused with fear, they were working in an environment over which they were no longer the authorities.

Fontana pulled himself up and, before the door shut, inserted the pike pole in the doorway. "Quiet! What's that?" Both men stopped on the stairs. Now nobody in the stairwell was breathing. Fontana had not been ready for this, would probably be capable of holding his breath only a few seconds. If they held theirs longer, he was dead, for they had not rounded the corner yet, had a direct line of fire in his direction.

He began a slow count to himself, got to eighteen, head spinning, lungs burning, when the men on the stairs let out another burst of gunfire—the other direction—and rounded the corner. They had put bullets into the dead mother and child and, if he hadn't been on his way already, had sent their comrade with the AK-47 to hell. But then, Fontana thought, that's what this was all about, wasn't it?

Sending people to hell.

Forty-two

▲

BRINGING IN FAT LADIES TO HELP

*T*he A level was almost as dark as it had been downstairs. Fontana knew two things: that the fire control room was probably within fifty feet of where he stood, and that there were men on this floor, Bennie Zellner and at least one other, for he had heard their detached voices.

Before proceeding twenty paces, a figure bumped into him in the smoke, the impact jarring Fontana's teeth and knocking his helmet half off. The figure he had collided with stuck a flashlight in his face and then a revolver.

Batting the pistol away, Fontana hurriedly stepped back and windmilled both ends of the pike pole through the smoke, then heard the pistol clatter to the tile floor. Listening to a second exhalation valve, Fontana stepped forward. For three or four seconds they stared through the sooty atmosphere into each other's bubble face pieces. Somewhere in the background a television ran a news program about the situation in Seattle.

Throwing his entire weight into the labor, Fontana rammed the steel point of his pike pole into the man's solar plexus and walked him until the man's back and bottle clanked up against the opposite wall. When movement at the other end of the pike pole had stopped, he pulled it back and listened to the body, bottle, and helmet strike the floor. Kneeling, he found his opponent unmoving, air blistering out around the edges of his dislodged face piece. Even with his flashlight on his face, he didn't recognize the man. The bottle would drain itself shortly. Fontana groped around for the pistol.

"George? Where the hell are you?" It was Lee Viteri, and he was not wearing a mask, nor was his voice distressed by the smoke, which meant he was in a room that was clear, probably standing in the doorway. The sound had come from Fontana's left, which proved a conundrum, since he figured the direction he had to be moving in now was to the right. It was so simple to get turned around.

Lacking a more obvious target and having given up on the pistol, Fontana stumbled toward the voice, pole leveled. If he touched anything soft, he was going to stab quick and hard.

After two steps he glanced off a wall.

Running his glove along the polished wall until he reached a doorway, he tried the knob, startled at the amount of light punching him in the face. It took a fraction of a second for his eyes to adjust, turbulent black smoke cruising into the room from behind.

It was a strobe-light camera shot. Two men. Bennie Zellner climbing into full turnouts, a mask at his feet, a cigarette between the fingers of his right hand, and Lee Viteri, face piece dangling at his waist, an Uzi semiautomatic pistol nearby on a small wooden table. A television was running on a small stand.

This was the fire control room. The red control panels were built into the wall, doors open. From here everything could be manipulated: alarms, door locks, stairway telephones, elevators, intercoms, and, in this case, explosives.

The strobe-light truce lasted only seconds. Viteri calmly picked up the Uzi and started to bring it around. Fontana stepped back. The door closed on its automatic closer as half a dozen bullet holes ripped through the metal backing.

Except for the pencils of light angling out through the bullet holes, Fontana was in complete blackness again. From behind the door, Zellner shouted, "Kill him. There he is. Kill him."

A moment later Viteri burst into the hallway in a tornado of whirling smoke and refracted light, firing in the wrong direction, toward the stairs, toward the fallen man. Viteri stitched the darkness with deliberately calculated rounds.

Fearing they would hear his regulator over the echoing gunshots and tinkling brass on the tile floor, Fontana stood tightly against the wall and slowed his breathing.

The muzzle sound grew louder as Viteri turned and, for insurance, began to punctuate Fontana's end of the corridor with bullets. Like a man playing a punch board, he took his time. In this direction, he was not nearly as thorough. A bullet here. One over there.

"You got him?" shouted Zellner through a mask face piece. Another glimmer of light as the door opened, then total darkness.

"Shush! I think I heard his regulator. I think he's up this way."

"He went *that* way."

"I heard something up here."

"George should be around. George! Damn it to blazes. Maybe you got George. Maybe that's what you heard."

Viteri coughed. "George should be able to take care of himself. It's that fuckin' fire chief my girlfriend's been banging." Viteri coughed again. "I know it is. That screwball transmission from the burn room about Wayne flaming up. I knew I should have gone down there. Next time I'll listen to you, man."

"Big Frank and Little Frank'll take care of that. You just put your mask on. This stuff'll turn you light-headed before you can spit."

Now there was no noise anywhere in the hallway except for a tinkling on the floor—empty bullet casings kicked by Viteri. He was five feet closer, coughing. Another cartridge spun tinnily along the corridor, whizzing to a stop under the toe of Fontana's boot. Despite the fact that he was farther away than Zellner, Viteri's voice came clear and calm and surprisingly close, perhaps because Viteri still had not donned his face piece.

"I've got fresh air coming in through the lobby now," said Zellner. "We should be able to see in a minute."

More Uzi fire. Then a large-caliber pistol booming close by. Zellner was maybe six feet away and had fired downward, directly over Fontana's helmet, the bullet nicking the plastic of the brim. Fontana felt his head jerk. "You even know which way he went?" Zellner asked.

"What?"

"I said are you sure which way he went?"

"What? I can't understand you through your mask." Viteri coughed and his Uzi went off once in reaction.

Then Zellner spoke clearly, without the face piece obstructing his words, and Fontana knew he was using a trick of veteran firefighters, clamping his low-pressure hose so air wouldn't escape, then lifting the lower portion of his face piece. "I said, are you sure which way he went?"

"I hope he's dead."

Fontana squinted into the blackness, knowing the smoke was the only thing keeping him alive. If Zellner was right about getting fresh air onto this floor, it was time to move.

Fontana plunged upward with the pike pole. They made contact, the big man closer than Fontana estimated. He was afraid from the metallic sound that he'd whacked the back of Zellner's air bottle and helmet. Zellner didn't go down but fumbled with his mask, which he'd been holding aloft from his face, losing air in a rush and firing his pistol backward past Fontana's head. The close muzzle blast was deafening in the smoke, and, if it hadn't been for the protection of his face piece, the blast residues might have blinded him.

Viteri yelled, "You got him? Is he down?"

Without breathing, Fontana moved as far to the right as he could, then charged the blackness where he thought Zellner stood. Wielding the pike pole as a lance, he made contact briefly, heard another pistol shot, danced to the right again, then stabbed at where Zellner should have been, catching nothing but smoke this time.

Viteri fired toward them, which meant he was shooting in Zellner's direction as well as Fontana's.

Another pistol shot, but not toward Fontana. The two of them were shooting at each other, Viteri out of carelessness, and Zellner out of what could only be rage or self-defense. Fontana heard Viteri's body drop, his gun clunk on the tiled floor.

"You fuckin' idiot," Zellner screamed into his mask. He

pulled the trigger again, but the hammer clicked on an expended cartridge. Viteri moaned.

Listening patiently for the inhalations and exhalations of Zellner's mask, which Zellner apparently didn't have the ability to control, Fontana advanced, stabbing at the darkness. He was trying to work it so that when they made contact, Zellner wouldn't get a grip on the pike pole. A hand-to-hand fight with a man as large as Bennie would be a mistake.

More guttural moaning from Viteri, as if he were strangling on his own juice.

The air was beginning to clear, so that as he got closer Fontana could see Viteri's crumpled form in the center of the hallway, a pool of dark liquid fanning out from around his head. Judging by the location of the pool, the bullet or bullets had hit him in the throat. Fontana skated unexpectedly in the slippery blood, almost went down.

Now he could see the pinprick of a flashlight twenty feet away, Zellner's flashlight, moving, weaving.

When Fontana walked closer he saw that Zellner had armed himself from a stockpile evidently kept somewhere in the open hallway. He was whipping a pike pole through the smoke.

"Come on, Bennie. Enough is enough. I think you've made your point. Wayne's all burned to hell. George is over here. You just shot Lee yourself. I saw two people outside jump to their deaths. There's a dead woman and a baby on the stairs. Don't you think you've done enough?"

"You sonofabitch. I stop, I'll get the rope for this and you know it."

"Maybe not if you give yourself up."

"Don't be a moron." Zellner moved forward, pike pole at waist level. "Any judge and jury lets me off with less than hanging, there'll be hell to pay."

Fontana knew there was one more loose pistol on the floor, the one that had belonged to the man he'd speared, and as Zellner advanced he backed away, scuffing the floor with his boots, searching. Zellner was eighty pounds heavier, and, if they started monkeying around with these poles, it could get ugly.

"Sure. Okay. Take a head start. Give me the fire control room. That's all I want. Bennie. For godsakes, people are dying.

They're going to give you the money. They've got it ready.''

"First you want me to surrender, and then you say I've won. Make up your mind. As far as people dying, if they'd paid me off when I asked for it, I wouldn't have had to sacrifice any units.''

"Bennie, your career was saving lives, not taking them.''

"Yeah, and the fine city I was serving decided I had a bad attitude and could no longer do the job. Well, *they* made this happen, not me. It's this damn liberal-ass Commie city killed them. This all was going to happen sooner or later. I'm just making it sooner. Afterwards, they'll change their fire department. Don't you get it?''

"Yeah, I think I do. The city is run by morons and you madmen are here to straighten them out. Is that it?''

"Who but a moron would put a woman in a fire suit and call her a fireman?''

"You smoke cigarettes. Camels. Unfiltered, I bet. Just like your dad.''

"What the hell are you babbling about now?''

"About the thirty cigarette butts in the church behind the Ratt on the morning after the fire. About the fact that they were unfiltered Camels, just like your old man smokes and you probably smoke. About the size-thirteen boots somebody used to kick the doors in. You were there, Bennie. Viteri wasn't because he was in Tacoma establishing an alibi, harassing an ex-girlfriend. He went under the name of Shaddock, didn't he? You set fire to the Ratt.''

"You're crazy.''

"Viteri had a gripe against the management and you two decided to run a little test, see what you could get away with.''

"That's bullshit.''

"What you did was, you ended up killing your own brother.''

"You fucking liar!''

"We've got fingerprints from that church. They just didn't have anybody to match them to, Bennie, but they'll match yours. And it won't be hard to prove Viteri rented a place at the Ratt under an assumed name, Shaddock, and got thrown out two days before the fire. I knew it when he was attacking me downstairs. He kept saying, 'Come on, you want to die?'

That's what the tenant said at the Ratt two days before the fire when they kicked him out. I'm willing to bet he drives a red Mustang too. He was hounding me, trying to frighten me off the case.

"You got your brother killed, and you went next door to watch from the church. I'm not saying you knew he was going to get killed, but you set the fire. Pat Easterman saw you in the church. In the window maybe. That's why you killed him."

"Now, how the hell did you know that?"

"He must have called you after I spoke to him. That's why you guys attacked me that day down here in the basement. You were going to put me down for the count, weren't you? Easterman was nervous because I was asking too many questions. He thought I was going to find out you started the fire and he was probably trying to protect a fellow firefighter? An old friend? He probably knew you would get charged with your brother's murder. And you knew he was the only thing linking you to the fire, so you killed him and left a bomb in the building, then sent a message to my fire station in Staircase asking me to meet him. A nice little double murder. You were working your way up to this."

"You know Fontana, I've had so many so-called fire-department 'experts' tell me you couldn't take a building hostage, I almost had to do it."

"I can understand that. It was your duty."

"Want to play this like firemen? Is that it, Chief? Okay, let's see who's the best firefighter. Just you and me. Or did you bring some of the fat ladies to help you out?"

"I don't need help."

Forty-three

▲

JOUSTING

*Z*ellner bunched up his shoulders and began to trot forward, jabbing and sticking, feet planted crablike one in front of the other. Fontana countered and got a piece of Zellner's arm, then backstepped quickly into the thinning smoke. His pike pole was longer than Zellner's, but Zellner had a reach that almost made up for it.

Zellner lunged and missed. Lunged again, moving like a fencer. Fontana parried and knocked Zellner's pole down at an angle, but even using both hands he couldn't hold it there, Zellner lifting violently and throwing it into his face where it smacked the rim of his helmet. Zellner stepped close, shouldered him, then whacked him across the side of the head.

Fontana had hardly recovered from the first bump when a second one caught him full on the ear and knocked him to the floor.

On the floor he squirmed and stabbed his own pike pole at the intersection of Zellner's legs, not a clean shot, but enough to make Zellner momentarily forget his purpose in life. Fontana scrambled to his feet and stepped back into the smoke.

Confused, Zellner bellowed into his mask, brought his pole around, but Fontana was already at the other end of the corridor hiding in the smoke, where he stopped a moment and listened to his opponent inhale and exhale like an engine short on fuel. Fontana's pike pole had gone flying in the exchange. His arm hurt like hell, and his back was numb, but he tightened the strap on his helmet, lowered the visor, slipped both gloves back on, and removed his service ax from its scabbard.

Half a minute later, Zellner lumbered into view, clearly hurting, for, after he spotted Fontana, he leaned over and took several deep breaths, hands on knees. In his right fist was a heavy-duty ax, two pounds heavier than the smaller one Fontana carried. Where the hell had he picked that up?

Fontana rushed forward and swung at his head. Tired and sluggish now, Zellner was still quicker than he had any right to be. He blocked the blow with the haft, one-handed. Fontana swung again and again. Not hard blows, but quick ones, trying to keep the big man on the defensive, trying to wear him down, moving around him as the axes shuddered. Attack, parry. Attack, parry.

The big man stepped forward and butted Fontana in the face with the blunt end of the blade. The plastic face piece of the air mask absorbed most of the shock as it splintered. Air rushed across Fontana's cheeks. He'd seen Zellner moving but hadn't been able to counteract it.

Zellner raised his ax high over his head, but Fontana stepped back and he buried the pick of the ax in the tile floor.

Before he could lever it out, Fontana stepped in and struck him hard across the top of the shoulder. Zellner dropped to one knee, and Fontana clipped him across the top of the head, popping his helmet off. It skittered down the corridor. Then Fontana felt a sharp pain in his right knee. He gave a short, sharp move and butted Zellner's forehead with the end of his ax. The big man roared and swung his ax wildly three times, tried to rise up off his knees, tried another feeble baseball swing, then toppled, face piece askew, cheek pressed against the floor.

Fontana dropped the ax, looked around at the carnage, and breathed hard. He backhanded the sweat out of his eyes. He wanted nothing more than to lie on his face beside the huffing Zellner and take a nap.

"Did you kill him?" Diane Cooper came through the stairwell door, stopping to stare at the bodies, at Fontana. She gave him an uneasy look that reflected the horror of three downed men in this corridor and another three bodies in the stairwell she'd just left. "He's looking for a contact lens."

"No, come on."

"He's not gonna die. Tie his hands behind his back." Cooper bequeathed a pistol to Fontana. He could barely raise his arm to accept it. Then she pulled out a pair of handcuffs, wrestled Zellner's thick arms behind his back, and shackled his wrists together under his backpack.

"We're not going to need this," Mac said, looking down at the gun. "Thanks for the thought."

"Tiny arrested three of them downstairs. Two had rifles, and the other one wasn't even wearing a mask, just wandering around in the smoke half dead. I thought you might be in trouble, so I came up. There's a lot of radio traffic outside. I think they're about to try some sort of assault."

"Thanks for coming back, Diane."

"Did you think I wouldn't?"

Fontana limped toward the fire control room, but when he got there he found the control panels foreign to anything he could remember. Cooper walked in behind, flipped some switches, and said, "That should do it."

Forty-four

▲

KISSING TWENTY-SIX STRANGE WOMEN

While Cooper spoke on a portable radio to the forces outside, Fontana staggered out to the lobby, grabbed the elevator keys out of one of the key boxes, and rode the elevator to the nineteenth floor, where a band of bedraggled men and women stood dumbfounded.

"It's okay, I'm one of the good guys," Fontana said, glancing at two men hefting scraps of broken furniture like cudgels. He unslung his mask, popped his helmet off, and scanned the throng for Laura. It was terribly warm on this floor, somewhat smoky, and everybody's hair was matted, armpits sticky, eyes bloodshot and runny. It smelled like an elementary-school gymnasium on a rainy Friday afternoon.

As a buzz of puzzled conversation swept the area, Laura came running from another room, pushed her way through the group, ran into Fontana's arms, and gave him a slobbery kiss full on the mouth. Catching her weight made him realize he probably had some broken ribs.

"You all right?" he asked. Her face buried in the dirty chamois shoulder of his bunking coat, she nodded.

261

People were clustering around now, fifty, sixty people in disheveled business suits or rumpled dresses, looking wrung out and relieved and half-drugged with the easing of tension. A silver-haired man with manicured fingernails and a hearing aid said, "Are we really out of here?" He was the only male on the floor who had neither removed nor loosened his tie.

Fontana smiled and nodded.

A pretty young woman with long brown hair stepped quickly past Laura and cradled the back of Fontana's head in her hands, pulled him down, and kissed him hard on the mouth. When she released him, a heavy-set African-American woman in her forties with bright mauve lipstick plunged into her wake and gave her own heartfelt kiss. Fontana peered beyond her shoulder and saw all the women in the room queuing up to fulfill what they apparently viewed as some sort of unorthodox patriotic obligation, Laura having given them all their cue. A twinkle of amusement in her bloodshot eyes, a washed-out blue-gray now without her tinted contacts, Laura stood to one side.

In all, twenty-six women kissed Fontana, each with her own brand of fervor or hesitancy, or combination of same, and it quickly became an experience quite unlike any he had undergone, like the liberation of France, as if he were the agent in some preposterous social engineering project.

As it turned out, Wayne Dorhofer survived the night only to pass away in the burn ward two days later. He had been twenty-two, still living with a mother who spent about half her time in mental institutions, Wayne in and out of the juvenile justice system since he was ten. Nobody knew anything about his father, for Eunice Dorhofer had never been married, never had any truck with men, and refused to speak of the father.

The Dugan Fontana had found on the staircase with the empty AK-47 had been christened Addison Love, though for the past few months he had been living as Alex Silver. His history included rape, selling stolen auto parts, and thirteen years in the army before being discharged for drug use and selling exotic cats with false pedigrees.

The man Fontana had encountered on A level before Viteri

and Zellner and who had shoved his pistol in Fontana's face was a former welder at Todd shipyard with no recent criminal history, though as a juvenile George Trowbridge had lived near the Lighthouse for the Blind in south Seattle and had been convicted of robbing the blind on their way to and from work. George was dead when the medics got to him. An autopsy two days later revealed a ruptured aorta. George had been a deacon in his church in Redmond, and left behind two children and a wife, who admitted to the *Seattle Post Intelligencer* that they had been going through some dire financial setbacks.

Lee Viteri died at Harborview Hospital on the operating table. Had he lived, he would have been a quadriplegic, for his spinal cord had been severed by a single gunshot wound to the neck. Viteri was only twenty-four, but journalists located two former girlfriends who had previously fled the state to avoid him. Viteri had served short sentences in three local jurisdictions for assault and battery, malicious mischief, and property damage, all of it involving love affairs gone sour.

Over the course of the ensuing weeks, Benjamin Zellner underwent four lengthy operations to repair damage done to his brain during the scuffle. According to reports Fontana received from acquaintances in the King County Police, one of the operations had left him mentally impaired, and while he sometimes recognized his mother, he recalled nothing of the Belasco, nor could he speak coherently about anything else. People had been calling him an idiot for years; now it was official.

Ten hostages had died during the siege, five of them jumpers. Three, including the woman and baby Fontana had found, died trapped in one smoky stairwell or the other. Two telephone repairmen expired from smoke inhalation inside an elevator car.

One firefighter died of bullet wounds received climbing an aerial early in the ordeal. A second firefighter recovered from bullet wounds but retired from the department four months later.

Exactly three trimesters later, twelve babies were born to women who had been cooped up in the building, prompting a statistician at the University of Washington to pen an article in which he claimed, given the exact number of how many hostages had been female and of childbearing age, et cetera, that the rate was four times normal. Orgy jokes circulated for weeks.

Experts from every major fire department in the country took junkets to Seattle to study Zellner's setup and to postulate measures to prevent a similar debacle in their own cities. Chief Thurmond gave tours personally, relishing his newfound status as expert strategist and deftly inflating his part in the event.

Laura Sanderson went away for six weeks to complete her book while dashing off several feature stories on the Seattle situation, one of which was titled "The Belasco Fiasco." She phoned Fontana one evening to say she was arriving at Sea-Tac for a layover on her way to Japan, and could he spend an hour with her in the airport lounge. Brendan came along to ride the underground train and marvel at planes taking off and landing.

"I'm going to be rich," she said, indigo contacts glittering. She wore a short, black skirt, and looked both lethargic and strangely pretty.

"How are you planning that?"

"I'm writing the definitive book on that crap in Seattle. With what you'll tell me and what I experienced, and the people I'm already interviewing, I'll be on the best-seller list next fall. Other books are being written, but I'll get all the talk shows because I was there. The secret is getting booked on the shows. I've got a huge contract."

"If you're going to write a book that hinges on information from me, you should ask me first."

"Well, yeah, I suppose. But I assumed you wouldn't have anything against my becoming successful, Mac."

"I'm sorry, but I haven't spoken to anybody about what went on in there and I'm not going to. When people die I tend to get personal about it. It's not something I *can* talk about."

"You realize I could make liberal use of my imagination on this. I wouldn't want to have to do that."

"Neither would my lawyer. Want you to have to do that."

Laura was sullen and stumped at his attitude. "Well, what am I going to do? After all, the public has a right to know."

"Do anything you want, as long as it doesn't include me."

"All you have to do is tell exactly what happened in there."

"I haven't told anyone exactly what happened in there, and I'm not likely to start with someone whose avowed purpose is to sell as many copies as possible."

As the weeks passed in the Seattle department, things began to settle down for Diane Cooper. The rumors slowed and then ceased completely. A few of the men who had worked with her began sticking up for her, and after a while it had happened often enough that sticking up for her became trendy.

In January, to general fanfare and public acclaim, Chief Thurmond and three others in the administration announced their retirements. In the resulting flurry of appointments, Rudolph Freeze failed to receive a promotion, publicly blaming racism for the transgression, while at home griping that his "politics" were not suitable. In February of that year, he went to a small attic fire in the University District, where a piece of tile from the roof fell forty feet and broke his shoulder. He was on disability five months and claimed privately that he thought the tile had been purposely dislodged by a firefighter who knew he was below.

The first day after the Belasco, Fontana ran Brendan to school and spent the remainder of the morning in bed. Around noon at the doctor's office he sat under the X-ray machine and learned he had a broken rib in addition to a dozen bruises and cuts and a chipped bone in his elbow, along with what the doctor called a mild concussion. He typed part of his written report of the King Street fire, then napped on his bunk in the station house. He couldn't recall ever being quite so wrung out.

A week later, still not recovered, he took Brendan on an overnight hiking trip to Annette Lake near Snoqualmie Pass, where they stayed two nights, fished, spotted a bear, played crazy eights around the clock, snapped pictures, and lazed about in the sunny autumn afternoons. Mac had been promising Brendan an overnight camping trip since they'd moved to Staircase, yet this was the first they'd been on.

After promoting Kingsley Pierpont to lieutenant, Fontana hired two full-time firefighters for Staircase. One had previous experience in a county fire department and the other was a twenty-six-year-old woman from the Staircase volunteers. She hadn't passed the highest on the physical-agility portion of their entrance test, but she was bright, enthusiastic, and, of all the applicants, Fontana judged her the most eager and industrious. Thus the Staircase Fire Department gained their first affirmative-action employee. Mo insisted their next hire would be a person of Spanish-American descent.

Fontana went to Mo Costigan's office one day and said, "I came for my raise. I want to make ten percent more than the mayor."

"But the mayor . . . "

"Is not a full-time job. Fire chief is."

"The raises for this fiscal year have already been allocated, Mac. I don't believe the fire chief is on the list. We've got enough trouble hiring these new people. And we haven't got our beaner yet."

Fontana stepped out of the room and came back with a yard sign, fire-engine red with white lettering. It said FONTANA FOR MAYOR. Mo was speechless, but returned to her natural state soon enough. The raise showed up on his next check. Six weeks later, Mo had put the incident far enough behind that they danced together at the Bedouin, and, once more, Mac marveled at how such a cantankerous woman could be such a beguiling dance partner. Mo said, "You dance okay for a sonofabitch." He could feel her cheeks tense up as she smirked in the dark.

Next door to the station the Fricks woke up at two A.M. to set all their clocks back from daylight savings time and turned them the wrong way. Their drapes remained shut.

Kingsley grew more comfortable in his role as lieutenant. Duck-calling classes began in the Bedouin on Saturday mornings. Mo read a book on chastity in the modern age and went temporarily chaste.

Satan knitted up.

Diane Cooper showed up at Staircase's fire station one rainy afternoon in sandals, jeans, and a red blouse spattered with droplets of rain. She had read all of Youngblood's diaries.

"You know," she said, "Bill and I would have gotten married if I hadn't taken that test. Is that a hell of a deal? I remember this funny look in his eyes, just for a second, when I said I was thinking about studying for it. I sometimes wonder if it's good to want things as bad as he wanted lieutenant." She and

Fontana had lunch together, sole survivors talking over probability and fate and the vagaries of being human.

Before he finished the King Street investigation, Fontana located a witness who placed Chief Freeze in the basement of the building next door for several long periods during the blaze, which meant Freeze hadn't been watching his post, nor had he been inside in the smoke urging his firefighters on, as claimed.

One of the rescued women was able to identify Cooper in turnouts and a helmet, said she was certain Cooper had been their rescuer, not Pat Easterman. It became clear, although there was no way to prove it, that Pat Easterman had heard Cooper's cries for help from the fire escape yet had ignored them, whether out of pique, malice, bullheadedness, or just plain stupidity, nobody would ever know. There was little doubt he could have gotten another crew upstairs in time to save Ladder 3.

In the end, Youngblood died because his partner became hysterical; add to that Pat Easterman refusing to acknowledge Cooper's cries for help, Freeze standing in a warm basement next door, and Youngblood's leg fracture. Hazards of the profession.

The ugly irony of the Ratt was Bill Youngblood rejecting a woman and a black as partners and choosing a white male, the one person on that particular crew who couldn't do the job, for the real hazard in firefighting was having a partner you could not trust. Youngblood's freshly minted intolerance had blueprinted the scenario for his own death.

In the end, Reba Vine sued the city and collected a disappointingly small amount, while Ginnie Buchanan sued and garnered enough to quit her job and buy a new house, largely through the city's fears that she had a better case—her husband's death (getting trapped in a room) having been reversible with prompt attention, Clinton's (falling into the elevator shaft) having been termed a classic hazard of the profession—the irony being that Clinton had behaved heroically, while Buchanan had not. Reba believed the difference in amounts was due to the fact that Clinton was black.

When Brendan's papers came home at the end of the first semester Mac found a letter printed in pencil.

Dear Mommy,

I miss you. A litle after you died, Sprinkel did to. Dad sad cats and peple go to the same place, so you might see Sprinkel. We got a dog. Mac says he's ugly. His name is Satan. Last summer he saved my life. We went fishing and I cauhgt 4 trout. I still love you, XXXXXOOOOOOO, Brendan.

P.S. Do you remember me?

Over the next few months Mac had ammonium-nitrate nightmares. Ax-fight nightmares. And every once in a while, just to break the monotony, he dreamed he was being kissed by twenty-six strange women, one after the other.